I

MW01178040

The 8th Wisdom Keeper, Chronicles of Creation is not an ordinary book. It is a journey. If you embark on this journey, every part of you will experience expansion.

Farhana Dhalla, Speaker, Coach,
Author "Thank You for Leaving Me"

Archangel Michael's message affirmed the life lessons I have spent the last 42 years trying to master.

Tammy Biever, Reiki Master, Reflexologist

The 8th Wisdom Keeper, Chronicles of Creation is inspiring; it sparked my desire to learn and gain a deeper understanding of myself in relationship to the other spirits and souls surrounding me.

Dorothy Gilday, Mom of 2

The In-depth descriptions used in **Debbie Gibbs'** channeling of information are amazing. The stories created the clarity I needed to receive the messages shared; it felt like I was actually there.

Christina Von Bieker, Business Entrepreneur, Inventor

Debbie Gibbs offers scientific and spiritual information that is easy to understand and not in conflict with current scientific theories or religious teachings.

The 8th Wisdom Keeper, Chronicles of Creation is a breath of fresh air to read and yet left me with ideas to share and discuss.

James Criger, retired High- School Principal

"If I'd known that on June 23, 1964 the 8th Wisdom Keeper was about to arrive, I would have had a better camera."

Dad

Rare and compelling exploration into the world/universe of sacred knowledge and healing power.

Christine Miault, Special Needs Caregiver,
Business Entrepreneur, Event Planner

A testimonial of our own power in the universe.   This book teaches about community, following your own wisdom and how accessing the information from all can bring about a life experience that surpasses anything we would have considered REAL in the past.

Susan Faber, Instructor, Practitioner, Mentor of the Healing Arts, Author "Women Fart Too"

"The 8th Wisdom Keeper, Chronicles of Creation", is an inspiring story of a Shaman who stepped into her Power and began unraveling the mystery of the Universe "

Shamir S. Ladhani, Organizer of Spiritual Explorers Unite
http://www.meetup.com/spiritual-explorers-unite

It has been an amazing journey witnessing Debbie Gibbs evolve into this wise women. She allows the Universe to speak through her to deliver the practical and inspiring words for living contained in this book.

Nancy Anderson Dolan, BA Psyc.
www.wiseheartwellnessworldwide.com

This book is dedicated to
"The People of Earth"

A Gift to be Opened!

Warning:

It May Change Your Life

Love - The Wisdom Keepers

Thank You Jenn,

Wishing you Joy each
and every day.
Love Deb

ISBN: 0988127601
ISBN 13: 9780988127609

The 8th Wisdom Keeper

Chronicles of Creation

DEBBIE GIBBS

Section 1

How it Began

"A sense of awe is the beginning of wisdom."

Abraham Heschel

Introduction

Have you ever wondered how did we come to be? Are there beings living on other planets? Who or what is God? I asked those same questions as I traveled on my journey as a Shaman in conjunction with the Great Spirit. Each page of the journey invites you to embark upon the adventure and to marvel in the truths as the story unfolds and the truth reveals itself.

I am a Shaman and this book is about my travels to other dimensions and other planets that reside in our universe. In a dream I was told by my Spirit Guide to stand tall and claim I am a Shaman and so I did, after much reluctance and fear of what exactly that would mean. It is through surrender that this book is coming into creation, surrendering to the fact that I have no training in writing but believing in the voice that guides me, something I call God.

Reports in the media have long been communicating that there is a possible ending of our existence. Because of receiving this information and watching the changes happening on Earth, some wonder what is going to happen. You may have wondered as well.

This book is not to foretell the future but rather to share with you the information held in the planets. We are not alone in this universe and, with the efforts of the other planets, we will move through this possible transition with a grace and awareness unknown to us in the past. Knowledge has a way of waking up the known that we consciously keep unknown. This knowledge might help in making decisions if there ever turns out to be a time of chaos on Earth. Even if it doesn't, you will have been awakened to other possible truths.

Join me on this adventure and open your mind to the knowledge that this channeling of planets and their beings offer. You decide, fact or fiction!

Debbie Gibbs,
Shaman
The Eighth Wisdom Keeper of Earth

The Birth of a Wisdom Keeper

It is June 23, 1964 and there is a commotion felt in the small town hospital in Livingston, Montana. The doctor has not arrived and the mother is ready to give birth; the father waits anxiously in the hallway. Then everything happens at an incredible speed; the doctor arrives and the mother pushes the baby out with ease. A girl weighing 7.5 lbs. is welcomed into the world. Number 8 of the Earth's Wisdom Keepers has just arrived—nobody knows she is a Wisdom Keeper, not even the baby girl.

Before the birth, she was asked to return to the planet Earth. Sometime in the past, this energy body was not a Wisdom Keeper but a being on Earth. The Wisdom Keeper stayed within the Earth's energy realm for many moons.

A Wisdom Keeper is created when the energy body that gets released upon death is in alignment in frequency to Creation's energy frequency. An energy once released from the physical form can return to what many Earth beings call Heaven or it can combine itself with Creation energy and proceed to the place of Creation. Once it has attracted the energy of Creation it no longer returns to a planet but stays in Creation as a Wisdom Keeper. Energy bodies travel to Creation to learn as this is a gathering place for wisdom and information; this gathering place is open to all who seek, but they do not call it home.

If you have ever talked with angels or guides, you have visited the place of Creation in energy form.

Wisdom Keepers work together as an energy body and look for solutions to resolve issues in order to maintain harmony. Earth has gone through catastrophic events in the last few years; Katrina destroyed New Orleans in 2005, Hurricane Hanna ravaged Haiti in 2008 and a tsunami devastated Indonesia in 2004. An earthquake and tsunami aftermath killed thousands in Japan; in the same year record floods in Thailand, Pakistan and Australia forced thousands from their homes and left hundreds dead. As I write this, wild fires in California, New Mexico and Colorado threaten our existence and our environment. Torrential rains resulted in mass evacuations in England; flooding in Mozambique caused epidemics and Hurricane Sandy wreaked havoc along the East Coast of Canada and the United States. These catastrophic events are changing the Earth's surface. Humans are declining in population at a mass rate and the surviving powers are seeking any information that will help them.

The 8th Wisdom Keeper chose to enter back into Earth form on June 23rd as it aligned with the summer solstice energies that were present. Creation then mixed with this energy to allow it the doorway entrance back into Earth. Each Wisdom Keeper is encoded with universal energy so they are able to travel to Creation and to the planets freely, in energy form. It is not a coincidence that this Wisdom Keeper's number represents the infinity sign.

Journal of The Wisdom Keeper Begins

November 1, 2010

Today I feel haunted by the visions I am seeing in my dreams, although this is not new for me. I am talking with Spirit as I journal today, laughing out loud as I am recounting my past. I am being asked by my Spirit Guide to tell my story of becoming a Shaman. Why I am not sure, but here it goes.

It started back in year 2000; I had just had a baby and was a stay-at-home mom. Before being a mom I was a successful businesswoman. Looking back I believe it was my intuition that helped me to be so successful but I knew nothing of that then. At the moment, I was just trying to deal with the challenges of being a new mom. I had also just joined a twelve-step program for food addiction.

I have had many addictions but food was the one making me fat and ugly and so I sought help. In the twelve-step process of recovery it was suggested that I find a way to meditate and so that is what I was doing when I showed up at a class on Meditations to Help You Through Parenting Times. Every night after my baby was asleep I would sit in lotus position and hum, chant, whatever I was told to do in order to achieve a Zen-like state. I failed. Perhaps I was defining Zen as an enlightened monk type of definition. I don't know; I only know I failed. Perfectionism was another one of my challenges back then. It had always been one of my challenges.

4

I went to church when I was a child. Church was one of those places where everything and everyone seemed perfect. I liked learning about God (who also seemed perfect) but when I started asking questions that the teachers couldn't (or wouldn't) answer, I got frustrated and so did they. In the process of trying to find the truth about God, I found myself unable to go to Church. By then it didn't matter because I was seventeen and pregnant and that was the end of God and me. In my mind I had failed God. I didn't talk to God again for a long time and the voices that I once heard, all of a sudden went quiet. I knew there was a God and had proof of God's existence, I just couldn't tell anyone.

One of those times of proof was when I went swimming while slightly inebriated. I shouldn't have been swimming at night, after drinking, but I was a teenager and thought myself invincible. I dove under the water and felt this sense of complete joy overtake me, it was so free-ing. I started to breathe underwater; it didn't hurt until I realized I was doing something that should not be possible. I wasn't afraid; I knew that someone was taking care of me. The voice I heard said, "*It is okay, you can only be what your mind can harmonize with. Today you cannot be a mermaid, but maybe someday.*"

A couple of years later I was talking with my swim-team pals and some-how the topic got onto dying. All of us agreed that if we had to choose a way to die, we would choose drowning. Perhaps I am not so unique in my experience; there are other mermaid want-to-bees out there.

The next proof happened in my first marriage. Pregnant at seventeen I said yes to a marriage proposal by my baby's father. He was a kind-hearted man and was such a gift to my life; he supported me in all my choices and was also my best friend. After giving birth to a beautiful eight-and-a-half-pound baby boy, I went back to school, graduated from college and went to work as a manager in the food service industry. My job gave me a sense of who I was in relation to other people and it gave me a feeling of being a success. I was no longer the same person I was before I was married. I started spending most of my time at work and my marriage started to disintegrate. But the main reason the marriage fell apart was that I had died and gone to Heaven.

I am not sure how I got there, but I awoke in what felt like a dream. I entered a garden that was so beautiful; the colors, the flowers, the smells—it was all so alive—every part of me felt joy and love. I expected at any moment to see angels flying around. There were houses; at least that is what I guessed them to be, white cloud-like formations in rows like houses. It reminded me of living on Earth but cleaner and simpler. There were no plants in this area, just cloud-houses. There were gates at the sidewalks that went up to the houses. I never thought that Heaven would be similar to Earth.

Then I saw my grandmother; I couldn't run fast enough into her arms; I had missed her so. Then my uncle appeared and I kind of chuckled as my grandmother and he never got along too well on Earth. My god it felt good to hug them. I couldn't wait to be part of this world with them forever. My uncle then looked up (at what I am not sure) and when he looked back at me, he said that I was not to be here and that I needed to return to my body. Slowly I fell backwards. I remember falling back through the garden wishing it would hold me. There was a split second of nothingness and then I opened my eyes. My chest hurt, my breathing was shallow and my body felt as if I had been kicked all over. I was sobbing incoherently. My husband was standing there wondering what to do. My doctor thought I might have had a minor heart attack. What I can tell you (and what no doctor can) is that my heart was broken. I knew that if I was going to stay in this life, it had to change and the only person who could make those changes was me. Soon afterwards I left the marriage.

There was another person in my life but, at the time, neither of us could break out of the addiction cycle. He has an energy that can combine with mine to create powerful outcomes and perhaps someday that is what we will do together, but right now he is on his own path. He offered to take care of me when I was seventeen and pregnant but my inner voice said no even though my heart wanted nothing more than to be with him. I spent years traveling to him in spirit. I thought I was just day dreaming until I met someone who had lived in the house he was living in. One of things that used to bother me (when I would spiritually visit him) was that his kids slept in the basement; to me, having children's bedrooms in this basement was not a good thing. Anyhow, this person was a friend of my sister's and she was telling me about this house that she had just moved out of. The details of the house were so clear I had to ask who was living there now. She referred to my first love's name and said that what really bothered her is that his kids slept in the basement. In that moment I realized that what I wrote off as daydreaming was as real as me having physically been there. I never asked him if it was real for him. He is also a Shaman and living his experience as he chooses; I do not know if he has awakened to those parts of him.

I realized also that these spiritual travels were not in good faith to my current life. I loved my new husband Colin and having this type of relationship (real or made up) with a former love was not appropriate. I did a soul-release exercise but years later, I still feel grief. This was a friendship that I had with no other and there was this need to be in constant connection with him. Whatever it was, now that it is no longer there, I miss it.

This is by no means lesser love for my husband; for it is with him that I can grow and be my best. He matches my power and brings many positive attributes to our relationship. I see the gifts this man possesses and I know the power of manifesting when we combine our energies. I do not believe he is a Shaman but rather an ancient soul of philosophy and wisdom. He can call the truth in any situation and he positively impacts this Earth with his ability to love and look for the positive in each opportunity. Oh we have our fights; put two passionate people together and that is what you get, passionate fighting. But from the first moment I looked into his eyes, I knew I would be lost in them forever. I loved him instantly and here we are today, twenty years later, and I still feel that way.

Somewhere in those twenty years, I started to talk with God again. The journey back was not without a struggle.

Early on in our relationship as boyfriend and girlfriend, he played strip poker with one of our friends. I had gone to bed but woke an hour later with a voice screaming in my head to get out of bed. I knew what was going on but I stayed put. It was fear I felt, fear of witnessing his betrayal. Hours later when he came to bed, I asked him where his pants were. He sat on the edge of the bed and cried. I ran to the bathroom and started throwing up and when I could throw up no more, I went back so that I could hear the truth.

After failing miserably at forgiveness, I found myself on my knees. For the first time since I was seventeen, I prayed to God for help. As clear as if the person was standing in the room, I heard a voice that gave reference to a Bible passage. I thought someone was playing a trick on me so I searched my bedroom and then went into the kitchen and grabbed a knife ready to search the rest of the house. After finding nothing, I collapsed onto the floor. I laid the knife out in front of me and asked whatever was there to come and kill me; I no longer could handle the pain of living.

I had first tried to kill myself in grade ten after my boyfriend found another girlfriend. My way of dealing with the breakup was to become an alcoholic (did I mention that I had addiction issues?) and pop thirty plus painkillers a day. A small miracle of spilled blood, a surprise blood test, and the likelihood of death if I continued this destructive behaviour, brought me to the decision, to live no matter what.

But now, as I lay on the floor, I rationalized that if someone else killed me that would be okay because at least I wouldn't have that on my head. But no one showed up so I headed back upstairs. But once again I heard the voice and the scripture passage. I responded by saying that we didn't own a Bible. The voice told me where to look for one. And sure enough there was a Bible; I opened to the passage. It was a story about a leader of an army; his second-in-command had betrayed him and God told him what to do. This was my first spiritual experience in receiving messages from God that I could literally say were from God. I concluded that there was a God, that He had to answer my prayers, and that He would help me with anything I needed. But I still didn't believe that He could possibly love me.

Two years after having this spiritual encounter, I was, once again, in a twelve-step program but stuck on Step Four, "Made a searching and fearless moral inventory of ourselves." I had few memories of my childhood to make any semblance of a moral inventory from so my sponsor took me to a woman who did miracle healings. She was Catholic. She agreed to work with me but said not to expect much in the way of healing as I was living in sin. It didn't seem like I had too many options so I went along with her rituals. She applied oil on my forehead and did some praying and clearing and then had me stand as she prayed over me again. She held my shoulders and kept pushing me back; I was thinking, "Oh pleeeeease! I am not going to fall back in some weird trance-like state." But she looked directly into my eyes and said she had a message that was straight from God. I could feel goose bumps and there was a tingle of excitement as I waited. The message was, "God really loves you and he has great plans for you and Colin." I broke down in tears. What I didn't share with anyone was that before I went to see her, I asked God that if he loved me, could He somehow tell me through this woman.

I had been unsure of Colin and our future together but through this message offered from a miracle healer that I knew with certainty that we were supposed to be together. I would never again question God's love for me or God's desire that Colin and I stay together. And so it was with Colin that I had my second son and found myself at the meditation class my girlfriend was teaching.

I showed up at the class with an open mind but had no idea that this day (that seemed like any other day) was going to change me forever. My friend explained that we were going to be doing a shamanic journey meditation and away we went. Literally for me, it was away I went.

On the journey, I was to find a compassionate being and, after some very life-like encounters, I met my first Spirit Guide, a crocodile. Instead of being fearful, I had the same feeling I had when I had my encounter in Heaven. It was love and joy mixed together with complete trust. The crocodile told he was going to eat my arm and a few other body parts and I was fine with that—no fear. After we had this very intimate and what physically felt like an orgasmic experience, I climbed onto his back and we started to fly; I loved every minute of it. When the call came to return to our bodies and a state of consciousness on Earth, I told myself, "I will be back."

Was I a Shaman then? I didn't think so. I was a mom, running a home daycare, enjoying life. Yes, I heard voices in my head (although I was down to one voice). I never considered that abnormal. But I was drawn to learn more about shamanic practices and so I joined a study group and spent the next three years learning the techniques of how to do cere-mony. My experiences in the ceremonies were intense. Guides would come in animal form, spirit form or just energy; but never did they scare me. I listened as they taught me; I listened when they warned me and I listened when they guided me.

I started helping my friend teach. I learned that I could connect with people from a distance and that I could energetically move like a multi-colored light. I could heal and I could see within the body. I started calling myself a Shamanic Practitioner. It gave me the freedom to talk about my visions and what I see in the other realities. I had finally found a way to express myself spiritually.

I was still a volunteer with a twelve-step group and had just agreed to be vice-chair. Shortly after being voted in, the chair became ill and suddenly I was the new chair. I was nervous so, rather than implementing any of my power, I decided to let the treasurer (who had been on the board for years) take over. It was during the sharing circle when a board member expressed gratitude that the treasurer was there to guide us that it hit me! I should be the guiding chair! It was my job and I was giving it away. I decided to talk to my spirit guides about this.

As I entered the journey, Kathleen appeared. Kathleen looks like an elder native woman. In this journey she was ten stories high. I kept asking her why she was so tall. She yelled at me to grow tall, to stand tall and face her. She said that I was a leader and I needed to be a leader not just in title but in my actions. Her belief in me allowed me to rise up and look into her eyes and say, "I had come to the same conclusion earlier this evening."

She also said, "It is time to step into your true power of who you are." She asked, "Who are you?" I said, "I am Debbie." She hit me across the head. "No, you are not Debbie. Who are you?" "The Woman of the Sacred Grove," I answered. "That is only part of who you are. I ask you again, who are you?" And out of my mouth I whispered, "I am a Wisdom Keeper; I am the keeper of the Children of Earth."

"It is time for you to claim your power. We are waiting for you." "We," I said. "Who is we?" "Look," she replied, as she pointed to the crowd. I nervously took a deep breath and said, "I am a Shaman." Immediately their heads dropped and tears formed as they reflected my shame. I looked to Kathleen. "What is going on?" "They are waiting for you to step into your power. Stand tall and state you are a Shaman."

A little louder I said, "I am a Shaman." But there was no heart connection; actually I was feeling fear and shame. I was not born into a culture of Shamans, nor did I possess anything that would give me the right to say I was a Shaman. Kathleen asked me to tell her what was stopping me so I explained my shame. She shook her head and said, "You have been gifted with shaman blood and it is your right, your birthright to call this in. You must, or you will fail all of us."

I stopped to feel the love I feel each time I go into a journey; I let go of my own judgment and proudly claimed, "I am a Shaman!" The Shamans rejoiced; there were millions of them, from all around the world. As I returned to consciousness, I knew that I would never go back to who I was before.

I am honored to be a Shaman. It comes with responsibility; it comes with acknowledging that there are different realities in this world and it comes with a release of others' judgments. I have visions and I am thankful to be able to share them.

Thank you God for this reminder of how I became a Shaman in title

Section 2

The Book Explained

"There is a great deal of unmapped country within us which would have to be taken into account in an explanation of our gusts and storms."

George Eliot

The Buck Stops Here

February 6, 2011

Dear God,

The buck stops here God; I am feeling disappointed in my life choices. I want to be a mom but not a maid and yet nurturing my family is a part of that role. It would be easy to blame them and everyone else for what feels like a misalignment, but I am the only consistent factor. Since my shoulder injury last August, I have not been able to do any healing work, which is good because I don't feel like working one-on-one with people. Still I need to at least partially support my family so that Colin doesn't have to earn all the money. I am in this vacant space, wanting to re-build my life so that it is in harmony with who I am and with the people who depend on me.

How do I do that God?

> Are you ready for the answer? Are you ready to surrender your thoughts of what that will look like and totally trust me?

I believe so God.

> Write a book.

You're kidding, right?

> I hear all your excuses. You have other projects that you are working on that can't possibly be abandoned. You have your son and daughter at home and a household to take care of. I already hear you wondering how you could possibly fit a book into your busy schedule. Of course you need to care for your family but all your other projects are simply going to waste your time, so do not bother. Trust me, write the book.

Don't I need some training?

> No. I will send you a guide to help you, a spider called Beena. Do not be afraid, surrender to my guidance and you will achieve all your

14

dreams and more. It is my function to help people fulfill their purpose and reach their dreams but most people do not listen. They are in such a hurry to get to where they think they should be that they miss the instructions for what they need to do in order to get there.

I surrender.

My Spirit Guide, Beena

February 8, 2011

My intention today is to meet the Spirit Guide who has come to me over the past couple of months but whom I have not taken time to get to know. I journey today to the Lower World only to be greeted by a huge spider web at the entrance. The web is spectacular; each segment looks like artwork. I can only imagine how big the spider is that made it and that thought is not reassuring. I slowly start to back up towards the tunnel that I entered through. Then, just as I am ready to leave, a gentle voice calls me back, telling me it is Beena, my spider friend. I cautiously walk forward. Not all guides are of goodness; some bring trickery with them. Slowly she emerges; she is beautiful with black bristles covering her body and hazel-green eyes. I feel an instant love for her. "But why the big web?"

"To teach you of course," she replies.

I am a small spider and yet I created a masterpiece—not by seeing the masterpiece in the whole, but by intuitively allowing myself to create each strand with as much perfection as I could give it in the moment. In the same way, you will create a web of information; you will weave our universe together so that others can experience it in the whole. I am here to serve you and the universe in the writing of this book.

It is time to awaken to your wisdom; it is time for you to step forward into what is being called of you in order to help those who seek the knowing. I will guide you and, strand by strand, we will bring this book together.

What follows is my journey into the unknown—journeying to places, trusting that my writing will one day move itself out into the world, although I have no idea what that will look like.

The Wisdom Keepers

February 9, 2011

I am meeting Beena today to get my first instructions but the meeting did not go as planned. I was expecting to find Beena and was greeted instead by Archangel Michael.

Apparently, there is a meeting I need to attend and so I follow Michael. Seated around the Boardroom Table are familiar faces, people I have met on my healing journeys. Michael, my chief advisor and protector took a seat on the right of Kathleen, my grandmother guide who brought me to this level. There is Archangel Raphael, an alchemist who has assisted me in health issues. Beside Raphael is Henry, the crocodile. You may remember Henry as he was my first guide introducing me to this altered reality. On Henry's left is a fairy, I do not know her name but look forward to having fairy energy present. Fairies often bring about a lighter side to life. Then there is Daniel, an angel and a guide who teaches me who I can be. I listen intently as Michael explains why this emergency meeting was called.

Creation is facing a dark hole and it is time for the Wisdom Keepers to gather. Each Wisdom Keeper and each planet must work together to continue our existence.

Feeling rather daunted, I asked Michael how I fit into the picture.

You are the only Wisdom Keeper from Earth in communication with Creation. Because of that, you are to start the process of bringing the planets together to avoid the Black Hole. If the Black Hole is not avoided, Creation with be uncreated. Because you are energized with all of Creation's energy, you are able to enter the other planet's portals and can communicate with the consciousness of the other planets.

I left the meeting with an uneasy feeling. I had to choose to take on this responsibility or to ignore it as just a figment of my imagination.

An event in my Earth reality helped make the decision easy.

I was asked to do a healing journey for a friend. Interesting enough, one of her guides is Lord Metatron. While on the journey, I had an opportunity to talk to Lord Metatron. He talked about the spectacular beauty of Keena, the planet he lives on and invited me to visit sometime. I mentioned the boardroom meeting and that I hadn't seen him there. He said he would be at the next meeting.

Since I still didn't quite believe that the whole boardroom experience was real, I decided that if he showed up, that would be confirmation that my experience was real. If he didn't show up, then it was just my imagination and I could go back to living life as I had been. Always testing, always questioning seems to part of my makeup.

Days later and I was once again at a Boardroom meeting and there, sitting next to Daniel was Lord Metatron. I knew then that one day all the planets would be working as one universal force to resolve the Black Hole crisis. I also knew that I would follow up on the request made of me.

There are nine planets with beings on them. My job was to travel to eight of them. I do not know why only eight and do not know which planet has been excluded from the list.

And so begins the journey, a documented story of my travels that will hopefully evolve in a story of discovery, presenting itself as a book, written as God has asked.

Section 3

History Lesson

"Where shall I begin, please your Majesty?' he asked. 'Begin at the beginning,' the King said, gravely, 'and go on till you come to the end: then stop.'

Lewis Carroll

In The Beginning

As I enter into a journey, not knowing where I will be led but trusting I will be taken to a place that must exist, I ask, "Tell me about the beginning." Everything needs to have a beginning. I wonder also about the ending. "Does it need to have an end and what will the ending look like?"

We live in a world with cycles. The sun rises and sets every day. There are four seasons in each year. People are born, they grow old, and they die...all on a seemingly pre-determined cycle. We have written time paradigms into those cycles. A day is twenty-four hours long; a year is 365 days; a lifetime is averaged at around three score and ten unless you get lucky. But what if something or someone could break into those cycles of beginnings and endings and create a circle of continuing flow?

Immediately I am given a vision. In the vision is a center where everything enters into and everything exits from. But what began the center of this vision to start the cycle of what exits? That is what I need to know.

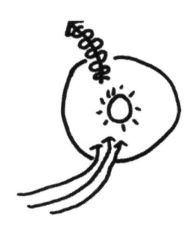

The voice that answers the questions calls itself Creation. And so it is Creation that will tell us the beginning.

The beginning started with a mass of energy existing in and of itself, just floating around in space, it held a small vibration that created a pool of emptiness contained. This starting place is the point of Creation, as it was in this space of energy vibration that impact first took place. Through the alignment of time and space, a large comet entered and burst light, which caused this entity to explode waves of destruction out from itself.

Creation only knows the point when it first felt awakened; it cannot know the point before this joint assimilation because it was not in awareness of such a possibility taking place. There was no consciousness prior to this impact.

Looking back to the diagram, I notice there is more than one stream of energy entering the space. Again, I await an explanation.

Creation transformed by combining itself with the original blast of outside energy and then exploding. When Creation exploded, it sent an energy burst that soared through the vastness of space and impacted other landmasses in existence. The landmasses absorbed the energy, energized themselves and then sent out a burst of energy that returned back to Creation. You can see this in the diagram—there are separate streams of energy entering the circle.

Breathing is an example of this type of flow. Our lungs take in oxygen and exhale carbon dioxide. Plants use the energy of the sun and water to convert the carbon dioxide back into oxygen. In a similar fashion, each planet takes in Creation's energy, transforms it and returns to Creation a bi-product of the original source. Creation then takes all these streams of energy from all the different planets and combines them. This provides the constant flow of energy or explosions. If one planet stops their flow, it alters the makeup of the energy that flows out. Creation's explosions energize each planet and each planet's explosions energize Creation. Like a recipe really, a combination of ingredients—flour, sugar, eggs, milk, vanilla—produce a cake. Leave out the flour and you get something, just not a cake.

The Attraction Principle

"How is it that energy from the planets flows back to Creation and not to somewhere else?"

The output of Creation's energy source needs the energy of the other planets to feed it. Energy flows to where it is most attracted and similar in nature. Although each planet's exiting flow is different from the original source, it is made up of Creation's energy. A cycle of energy is created by this flow; it is a constant flow moving in a circle, similar to perpetual energy. Some energy does not return to Creation but finds itself attracted to a planet energy field; this is how many of the creations on the planets were made.

As I listen to Creation's explanation, I think about the many speakers and authors who have been presenting this theory of the Law of Attraction—Esther Hicks, Wayne Dyer, Neale Donald Walsch, Rhonda Byrnes, Jack Canfield, Marianne Williamson, Carolyn Myss, Gregg Braden... . The premise is that we create our destinies through our thinking and the subsequent actions we take. Our thoughts create the energy vortex or the beacon of what we desire to attract and the actions we take cement it. This is in sharp contrast to the belief that someone or something—the government, our parents, our boss—is responsible or to blame for the outcome of our lives. We are responsible for our life choices and for our life outcomes.

That thought leads me down the path of wondering about those who are victimized as children, but even then I recall some of my own experiences and the choices I made in the moment of the event. I could have reacted differently and created a different outcome, even as a small child. As I consider this, I realize that there may not be as many victims as claim to be.

Creation is then the vortex of energy that is attracting the output energies from the planets. This creates a constant flow of energy exchanges.

The Infinite Question

I am still stuck on where the light source came from so I ask again, "Did the light force come from another universe?"

This question cannot be answered as the origin is unknown, even to Creation.

The space where the light first hit became a gathering place of vibration, a source where light could gather. In this space, a consciousness formed and a great spirit evolved.

Perhaps this was another universe's way of coming into survival. It came to maintain its own existence from another place in the galaxy of space of which we cannot figure out. That leads me to the next question, "Where was this galaxy created from?" I think about the dark hole that is approaching Creation. "Is the Black Hole simply an evolutionary requirement of universe?" Perhaps we are meant to be uncreated; perhaps the cycle requires us to enter the Black Hole.

Creation answers with this simple statement.

My true nature only knows of creating. It cannot understand or consciously perceive being uncreated.

I understand this concept as it was impossible for me to imagine that I could be a writer and yet here I am writing, doing what only a month ago I could not perceive. It is because others have cleared a path for me to follow that I understand what it is to be a writer. Without ever knowing of another writer, would I even have a consciousness of writing? I conclude that for anything to be created there must already be a consciousness of it existing somewhere in our universe.

In that initial point of impact on Creation, there had to be a consciousness that created the energy flow in Creation. Was it solely Creation energy that impacted the space? I do not think so as there was already a creation field in existence that attracted the energy that caused it to expand. It is a puzzle I do not think we will ever know the answer to. If we do go through the process of being uncreated, we will then begin a new process of being created in another universe left with the same question, "Where did the energy come from that sparked our creation source?"

Creation offers the analogy of brewing tea so that I can understand.

Boiling a kettle of water is an example of the beginning. The kettle of room-temperature water was Creation. Adding heat raised the water to a boiling point and caused it to expand.

Imagine that you invited eight friends over for tea. You place nine cups on the counter, put a different tea bag in each cup and add boiling water to each teacup. Before you serve the tea to your friends, you take a spoonful of liquid from each teacup and pour it back into the kettle. The liquid in the kettle is now a combination of the nine flavors of tea. Now re-fill each teacup with this liquid.

If you took a sip from each cup, the tea would taste most similar to the original tea bag. The licorice spice tea would still taste like licorice spice but perhaps with a hint of wild raspberry hibiscus; the camomile tea might taste ever so slightly of orange blossoms; the green tea might have a rosehip flavor… but they would all taste most like the flavor of the original tea bag.

Now invite each of your friends to choose the cup of tea they are most attracted to—perhaps it is the fragrance or color of the tea or perhaps the energy make up of whether it is herbal or caffeinated. Choose a cup for yourself as well.

This is how the planets attracted outside energies; energies were attracted to the planet based on the theory that *like attracts like*. Creation (the kettle of hot water) was the main stream of energy that mixed with outside energy (the tea bag in the cup) to create different energy flows on each planet. If Creation loses access to energy (the liquid from each teacup), then it will have no source from which to create the hot water and eventually the teacups will be empty. There would be an end to Creation. As long as the kettle continues to be filled and the cups refilled, then the cycle of creating will continue.

Imagine if you were to then take the teacups and place them in different rooms in your house. The closer to the kitchen, the hotter the water is when the teacup is refilled. In a similar manner, the movement or cycles the planets follow in the universe is affected by the strength (or proximity) to Creation. What a planet attracts may change as it moves through its cycle. Each planetary placement is in relationship, not to the makeup of Creation's energy, but to the flow strength of Creation's energy.

Creation

I ask Creation if this is the place I go to when I journey?

Yes. When you journey you will enter the gathering place of Creation's energy, all beings that chose to enter Creation are able to come and learn from all the different beings that are here. Your energy is a little different to some of the others on Earth but I will explain that later.

After the planets started to have beings, the beings started to seek the energy that brought them into creation, much the same way that you are doing in this interview. If the desire was strong enough, they found their way to Creation. While at Creation, they explored other planets' streams of energy. It is like switching trains at a train station. Creation is the main hub with trains (or streams of energy) going out to all the different planets. The beings would travel on a different planet's energy stream and then find they could not survive on that planet. For instance, a being from planet A could not survive in planet B's vibrational environment. The one planet that all could live and survive on was Earth.

With this constant flowing of outside energies to and from planets, the flow of energy from Creation was affected. So a group of beings from each planet was formed. They discussed the chaos that was a result of the explorations and decided that access to each other's planets had to be stopped. They established gateways (or portals) but closed off the openings. All the beings from the other planets that were on Earth at the time this decision was made stayed on Earth. It is why you have stories of different entities that are not human on Earth.

"All right I have to interrupt here. How was an energy gateway established and who was able to do that?"

That will be answered as you work through this message in writing this book. What I can tell you is that one of the group members is able to manifest instantly, like magic and it was due to these skills that the doorways were established.

The Wisdom Keepers

Only certain individuals can go through the doors. This is where you come in. You are what is called a Wisdom Keeper. Each planet has a Wisdom Keeper (or Wisdom Keepers). After the doorways were created, a special vibration of entrance was also created, like a key. This allows the Wisdom Keepers to contact one another if necessary. A Wisdom Keeper cannot contact another unless the being is aware they are a Wisdom Keeper. This is especially apparent on the planet Earth. You are the only Wisdom Keeper who has come forward. You will learn as you write this book what that really means. This will be a teaching for you and the beings on Earth as Earth is the planet last to connect.

The individuals who choose to represent their planet also choose to be of service to Creation for all life times. You choose to be a Wisdom Keeper for your dimension on Earth; that is why you are named the Eighth Wisdom Keeper of Earth. The key to the doorways is your energy vibration; you are encoded energetically with my energy field, a full combination of Creation's entire energy source.

"How did I get infused with all of Creation's energy?"

First, you made the choice when you energetically found the energy stream leaving Earth and returning to Creation in your death process; the other Wisdom Keepers also found the stream of Creation's energy from where they were. The difference between you and others travelling to and from Creation was the desire to stay in Creation. Many beings were unable to travel back to their planet as their vibration had changed in combination with the planet's energies. What happened next is how you each became the key holders to the doorways.

The group of beings gathered; each shot energy out of the top of their heads which produced a full stream of energy that equated Creation's energy. This combined energy stream circled around each being and infused the energy body that was in existence. The energy body was transformed to contain the components that equal Creation's energy. By having an energy body that was formed from each of their planets, it gave them the ability to enter the doorways to the planets.

"It is like the diagram I drew except they combined the energy of the planets to create their own stream of Creation's energy."

Yes, and that is how a Wisdom Keeper is born energetically. There are other Wisdom Keepers on Earth who have not yet come forward, in fact, there are eleven others. On the planets, information is shared amongst the Wisdom Keepers; this is not the same process as on Earth. So the Wisdom Keepers from other planets come to Earth as guides— to share information and to teach.

I am sure you have come to recognize that the guides you see on your journeys are not from Earth.

So where do they come from?

This is your challenge—to find out and to share. It is one of the purposes of you writing this book on behalf of the Wisdom Keepers.

Section 4

Earth

(Err-th)

"Our world is one of alchemy based on energetic formulas. Creations stay in existence due to the maintenance of the energetic exchanges. New creations form through the introduction of a new component into the formula. A physical manifestation currently results on Earth using the base formula - form plus form plus energy. Your life is a representation of the formulas you have put together and maintained. Be the Alchemist of your own life, maintain the formulas you desire and give and take in harmony with all creations you involve in your life. Create new formulas to create anew. Explore, experiment and enjoy!"

Debbie – Earth – The 8th Wisdom Keeper

Journey to Earth

Earth is the planet I am familiar with, so it is here that I begin. The drum beats faintly in the background as I make my descent into Creation. My intention is set to meet and communicate with the planet Earth.

And so the journey begins.

My first vision is of me lying on the ground face down reaching out to give Mother Earth a big hug. Vibrations rise into my body as I fall into a peaceful slumber. A part of me remains wide awake. I am not afraid of this state; it is a natural place of existence.

Then like a sweet harmony of sound that one would feel from a lullaby, Earth shares her story.

In The Beginning

I was awakened by a breath of power. What was in existence before, I do not know. A fire located within my center expanded outwards. If you ask me for words—I was alive and felt a pulse that fed life into me. There was no thought nor did I have any desire to think about thought; I just was.

I was neither without form nor a complete void of energy before creation. I had a vibration that held me in one place. I was dark without light, there was no Sun. According to your scientists, Earth holds a magnetic energy at a certain frequency, but this was not true before I was awakened.

Where my original energy came from I also do not know; nor do I know how the Sun, the stars or the planets that orbit in the same solar pattern came to be.

What I do know is that everything changed when the source's energy met with my vibrations. I was infused with Creation's energy and then exhaled that energy to my surface and beyond. The Sun warmed my surface and my form developed into a contained mass with an outer limit to my surface. Energy flowed within me in cycles, it moved around my core and spiraled outwards toward my shell and from there it continued its flow into the universe. As the energies flowed to my surface, new forms manifested on my outer parameter.

"Were these first forms human?"

Before humans there were plants that came in response to the Sun's energy. The plants emanated a frequency of energy that, when met with the Sun's frequency, formed water. The water sent out vibrations that connected to the Sun's vibration and formed the animals. The animals did the same and human life soon became part of the vibrational field.

"Whoa, slow down, are you saying that the first creations were plants and that everything afterwards was a result of the plants?"

No, what I am saying is that the first forms were plants and what happened after was a result of plant energy combining with plant energy and the Sun.

"What happened where there was no Sun energy? I was taught that the Earth rotates and that not all of the Earth is in direct sunlight at all times."

Rocks were formed in the darkness, same energy makeup but without the Sun's direct light or heat.

Shaman, realize that the beginning forms were not solid or in the same form as they are today. I was a physical form but much more fluid than today. Forms had my energy of mass but not the same density as now.

There is a history to how that transpired. Let me explain.

Past creations came into existence through the combining of energies. Plants were formed from the combining of energy from my core with the Sun's energy. Plant energy combined with Sun's energy and formed water and water then combined with the Sun's energy to form animals.

Different variables in the formulas produced different outcomes. For instance, the distance of a plant from the sun altered the type of plant produced. Plant energy also combined with other plant energy in conjunction to the sun and produced different varieties of plants. Water (the result of plants combining with the sun) also had different makeups. The bodies of waters held different vibrations so different animals resulted. Animal energies would mix as well and new animals started to show up. Instead of there being a set formula for creation, it was more of an open field; everything was in reaction or in combination with what was around them.

New creations then witnessed attributes of other creations and desired those same attributes for themselves. For instance, an animal saw the waters move and desired movement so there were animals without legs and animals coming into existence with legs. It was as if a desire, or the noticing of a difference, brought about the mixing of energies available to create it. There are attributes too that were simply a happening of chance, it is how new and different creations with different vibrational levels came to be.

As you can imagine, my surface soon became populated with new creations. These creations were fluid with some form and had different abilities. The law of attraction was present as well, so, although different energetic combinations took place, there was a pattern within the formulas that showed similar energies combining with similar energies.

Evolution started to be evident and species were starting to be defined. For example: a bird vibrated as a bird. When bird energy was combining, it tended to be attracted to other bird energy and together, a new bird would form. It is why you didn't see plant and animal energy mixed, or rock and water mixed. A bird does not seek out human energy because it is not a match. An energy surrounding the bird in the environment would also add to the energy makeup of the bird. A bird energy mixed with other bird energy in moonlight would not produce the same bird mixed in sunlight.

Everything – plants, animals, humans - evolves into the energetic makeup closest to its vibrational field. Humans are part of the energies that combined from all that came before their existence.

Not all the energies present on Earth were formed on Earth, however. Some came from outside the planet being attracted to the vibrations present. Once they entered into Earth they would combine and create a form based on their energetic make-ups. Sometimes the energies collided and energy escaped my outer shell sending a burst to the universe. These bursts of energies caused some of the creations to alter their form.

We have other outside energies affecting us as well; when the Moon was created it caused tidal movements. The tidal movements affected the forms created on Earth. There was also the addition of energies from the other planets that came and combined with the energies on Earth. The universe was open to many beings and energies moving around and Earth attracted and was able to support these vibrational differences.

"So then Earth was based on combining formulas of energy but as time progressed, this formula changed. We now operate under the formula of form plus form plus energy equals a creation. Is this correct?" Is it also true that new energetic creations can be formed on Earth but do not take a physical form unless there is a physical container for the energy to manifest into form with?

Yes, but remember that in the beginning everything was more fluid—today energy can combine with energy but it needs to solidify into matter to produce a creation. In the beginning, the forms were mainly an energetic body as opposed to a physical body.

"So how does this affect you as the originator of creation on Earth?"

It doesn't as I am fed by the original source of the Creator.

"So you do not control the polarity?"

I did not create my polarity; it was created in reaction to the Sun and other energies surrounding me. I control nothing. My form is simply a receiving point for source energy and a holding place for manifestations to take form using my vibrational field.

The Twelve Dimensions

There are twelve dimensions that have maintained constant vibrational fields. Each dimension has energy forms existing in them but they are not the same forms as the human forms that came into existence in the 8th dimension.

Beings co-existed with each other but were unknown to each other. This happened due to the vibrational differences. Each of the twelve dimensions has their own frequency that supports the creations that live within them.

Some of the beings have learned to alter their vibrational field to enter other dimensions. Some vibrational frequencies are unable to exist in another dimension without an interaction of outside energy.

"To understand the idea of dimensions, I find myself thinking in terms of layers; each layer has a different frequency, a world of their own. But there could also be reality differences within the dimensions depending on where we vibrate energetically. Would this be a true statement?"

Yes.

"Then our reality is based on where we are vibrationally?"

Yes.

In Reflection

As I reflect on what Earth has shared, I am starting to understand how this information can impact our lives.

Each dimension carries its own vibration. These dimensions are not places that beings in the 8ᵗʰ dimension can exist in but, by altering our own vibrational field, we could energetically visit those places for short periods. This would explain how people claim to travel to different dimensions. We can also use this ability to alter our vibrational field to view our own realities differently.

Everything exists based on an energetic vibration held within its being. It would stand to reason that we can see these items based on where we are at in our vibrational frequency. By altering our own vibrational field through the many different methods available we can potentially alter how we see our world.

An example of this happens in our thought patterns. If we choose to see the world in a negative sense, then that is what we will see. On the same note, we can choose to see the world as a place of love, abundant and kind, thereby attracting to us the vibrations of those items to view. If you believe in fairies you have a greater chance of seeing a fairy either physically or in your mind's eye, than someone who does not believe in that kingdom.

The more open our mind, the more opportunities we have to see something we may have otherwise not seen. How we choose to be in our bodies, emotionally and spiritually affects our ability to see the world.

When we feel we do not have a choice, then we can choose to access energy outside of us through the many different people and products offering this solution. This also explains why there are so many different viewpoints on this Earth; it all comes down to choosing which one you desire to be in vibration with.

Cycles in Creation

"Earth, can you explain the cycles in creation and how we impact them? I see the damage being done to our environment and I fear that we are bringing about an end to our planet."

Shaman, I hear you asking about earthquakes, floods and hurricanes. Most of these energies originate not from human reasoning but from the plants and waters, what you call natural elements. Humans are not directly manifesting any so-called natural disasters. I am not saying that a human can't affect the weather or that a group of humans can't cause a shift in a weather pattern based on their choices and intentions. But humans cannot manifest these events without having complete control of the energy makeup of these types of formulas.

Shaman, I also sense you're wondering if catastrophes could be caused by intentions of those desiring to create chaos and if all was designed to create the form for those energies to attach to. That is a possibility. That would be the negative thought about it. Looking at the positive, however—if there is the possibility of creating such a force, there is also the possibility of neutralizing it. To fully be able to do either, a person must be in relationship with what they desire.

For example: A Shaman desiring peace must first hold a container for peace; to evolve peace outside of themselves and within themselves. If a Shaman goes to the desert to gather rain, he does not focus on the parched desert, he focuses on rain and how it feels to be rained on. He will feel the rain within himself and outside of himself to the point that he becomes rain. To do this he must have had an experience with rain in some capacity. It is more than seeing something and desiring it, it is about being in relationship with it. We will talk more about this in our conversations with each other as this is one of the Natural Laws of Earth.

"Is a creation on Earth always based on desire or need?"

No, sometimes it is just the reactions of different elements causing another reaction. That is why some of the things (like earthquakes) that are happening on Earth are simply the reactions of rock energies.

Remember that everything is in relationship energetically and everything reacts to everything else.

My cycle of creation will continue with or without humans. Plants and rocks will not stop existing as they are the base of creation from my inner core. Plants will only become extinct in the absence of the Sun.

There is a time in my cycle around the Sun when I will stop moving due to the removal of the Sun's energy. I do not know the exact timing.

When my cycle comes to a place of darkness, there will be major changes; what exactly these are even I cannot predict. The energies present are not the same as they were the last time I went through this. I can tell you that rock energy will become strong and that the current energies reacting to rock energy will create the forms.

If we lose the Sun, rock energy will become stronger and the surface of Earth will go through a re-creation. The Sun added to the forms that are present on my surface as did other energies that reacted to these forms. Losing the Sun would not stop the creation process; it would simply alter the end result.

My cycle around the Sun affects how the Sun's energy interacts to the planet. The placement of my physical mass in relationship to the other planets affects the energy interactions, as does my physical placement in conjunction to Creation's energy field. The human race needs to be aware of this and when the time of darkness comes, they need to be able to maintain their existence.

"Earth, will you end your existence in 2012?"

No. My reality is not based on time but rather on the energy I receive from Creation. If Creation energy stops flowing to me, then there is no energy flow for me to mix with. My energy would stop flowing. The creations that exist on my surface would end.

"So the cycle you have described must be constant or nothing new will be created and the forms currently present will disappear?"

Yes, mainly due to consumption.

"Earth, as a Shaman I am familiar of an energy realm that surrounds us in the 8th dimension. All the energies released when death enters into the formula of the living form reside there. What will happen to this energy realm if Creation's energy stops flowing?"

All would continue to exist but there would be no vibrational field to support life or re-birth. I would return to the state I was prior to the birthing of Creation —dormant. Energy would move away from the planet as there would no longer be any form of vibrational attraction. The energy bodies might even move to another area of space where there is alignment. Once created, energy does not become uncreated; it simply moves and evolves to where it feels attracted. Currently the energy world surrounding the 8th dimension is vibrating to the form energy present but if that came to an end, I believe the 8th dimension would leave and find another place to exist in.

"Are you saying that they would go to another dimension?"

Humans can only exist in the 8th dimension. Other beings with completely different makeups exist in the other eleven dimensions. The beings in the other dimensions are closer in existence to the original way of creating. They did not evolve to having a soul or a spirit; they are more mind-based.

I won't go into detail about the other dimensions as it will confuse the message you are being asked to bring forth. What I will say is that death only exists in the 8th dimension. I should explain to you death, for it is death that changed the 8th dimension's existence.

Death and Earth

Death energy did not come from Earth; it came from an outside source. It entered into the planet but was not able to combine with all frequencies. It could not combine with rock or water but it could combine with all other creations. It caused interference in the creation of beings in all twelve dimensions but not like the interference it caused in the 8th dimension.

"Where did death come from?"

Death came from another planet.

"Is it one of the other eight planets in our universe?"

"Yes."

"The Sun keeps us constantly bathed in Sun's energy for creation. Is death a constant source as the Sun is?"

No.

Death is what created the solid forms that are now present on Earth. Prior to that, everything was much more fluid. In the other dimensions on Earth there is a more fluid aliveness; some forms are just made up of gases and not solid. Death energy needs forms to attach to.

When it attaches to a form, it causes the form to vibrate differently. As it combines with the form as non-form energy, it begins a process that starts to un-create all that was being created. This originally caused an imbalance on Earth.

When death energy first appeared, Creation's response was to send a blast of energy towards Earth. This caused another reaction. Many plants appeared which produced a large amount of water. Water soon covered my entire surface. The creation cycle continued but underwater.

"Sounds like death energy was tricked! This huge blast had to have been faster than the death process."

It was faster; it also took place prior to death being able to fully immerse itself on the planet.

"Earth, you mentioned that death energy needs a form to attach to. Is there a vibration frequency that death is attracted to?"

A frequency of between four and nine will attract death. If this vibration is shifted, then death can be avoided but typically, it is not possible to raise a vibration at this level as the living energy of the form is being released. Death is not the same as disease.

"Being a healer, I really want to understand this; there are so many modalities out there that can achieve healing, including conventional medical practice. Since death energy is not the same as illness, I want to know what death does; what are the formulas? "

Death is what created the solid forms that are now present on Earth. Death combines with form energy and releases non-form energy which causes the form to disintegrate or break down into other form.

The formulas are:

- Form + form + death will equal un-creation of that form and produce a new form.

- If a form + form + new energy is present, it will combine itself with the new energy and a new creation is made.

- If the energy of a desire is made, it cannot come into form until one is available but it will be in existence in an energetic body.

- When the energy of the form moves to a 4-9 frequency, death then combines with it and the spirit of the form is released as it was in the most current living experience.

When death energy combined with form, it set off a chain of reactions. Water covered the Earth but creation continued. It was not until the rocks grew enough to move the water that land appeared.

When the first plant materialized on land, death attached itself to the plant. This caused the plant energetically to separate; the energy of the creation of the plant left and the decomposition of the form turned into a seed.

The seed held the formula of the plant but had a vibrational field different from the plant. The part of the plant that was energetically created was no longer together, it was separate from the form. The plant energy was now just floating around, not attached to anything; it was just energy. The form had changed into a seed; death changed the energetic makeup of the plant.

The seed attracted the components of the soil that matched its own vibration—the Sun. Soil is made from rocks and Sun energy. The seed combined itself with the Sun energy held in the soil and then attracted the plant energy held in the water (rain). Once the seed combined itself with the components it needed to survive, a new creation (that vibrated differently from the seed) was formed.

Law of attraction says that *like* will attract *like*. The plant energy released by death was attracted to this new creation as it represented itself so it also entered into the seed.

Once the plant energy re-entered the seed, the plant could begin to re-create itself, but it had to do so with the support of outside resources. It needed the combinations of these resources to continue to vibrate at a level not attracted to death. If it lost the source of water, for example, it would change in vibration—death would attach itself and the plant would die and restart the process again.

The seed contains plant energy, the basis of creation energy. DNA is different from the seed.

DNA was created from the decomposition of the animals; it was not within the soil. DNA is what resulted when death combined with the animals. DNA needed water to change in form and it needed another DNA of the same species to mix with to re-create the energetics of the form.

Each DNA vibrates uniquely but because some animal species are similar, their DNA combined. That form attracted the energy body of the previous form that was floating in the energy realm and a solid form presented itself. The animals started to mate with each other to produce new forms.

This is how the cycle of life began.

"Earth, can you tell me about the humans that are in existence now?"

Humans followed the same path as the animals, they mixed their DNA's and as time progressed, humans started to mate and became independent in creating their species forms.

"Are waters still creating animals?"

No.

"Plants still creating water?"

Yes.

Water can no longer create animal and human forms due to the energy being unavailable. As new energies were created on the planet by the addition of death and fire, water was unable to mix with the pureness from the Sun. Humans now create the forms for humans; animals create the forms for animals.

The other creation that came as a result of the death energy is time. When death entered the 8th dimension, all creations it combined with had a beginning and an ending to their life cycle.

Since the nature of every living being is to live, the physical form of a plant (for example) adjusted itself to the environmental energies surrounding it. This does not happen in one life cycle but over several. The changes are stored in the energy body of the plant that is released by death. The physical form of the seed is still there and if the seed can re-develop itself by gathering the needed energies to vibrate close to the plant energy, then the form of the last lifetime would come into physical form.

"What you are describing is what I call past life memories. The living experience of the creation that exits the physical form upon death evolves the physical being of the next life and the life cycle continues."

Shaman, there is truth in that but remember that an energy body can combine with other energies. Everything develops out of vibrations of attraction. In the case of a plant, other energies come into the formula—radiation, different water formulas, soil compositions… all cause the plant to change in form. Can you understand then how the evolution of the forms happened? It started with the basic energy and then changed based on the living experiences stored in the energy body.

"If I summarize here in relation to humans, what you are saying is that our living experiences will affect the next evolution. Is every being on this planet encoded with knowledge of their past lives and living accordingly? Is this knowledge formed from living a life cycle that is then stored in the energy body, released at death and awaiting re-birth?"

Again, I say yes, with caution. Energy bodies re-enter a physical form with new additions, perhaps an energy body from another ancestor enters and brings with it its knowledge. Each person is made up of several different past- life experiences and each person is unique in their combinations of energies. It is the new creation entering the current life experience that will add or take away from the current vibrational frequencies held in each of the cells.

Tell me about stillbirths. Is there no vibration in that form?"

There is a vibration of death.

"What? I am confused, all creation is energy."

The first time a stillbirth happened it was because there was a combination of energies that came together and when it combined with the forms, it presented itself as a stillbirth in physical form but the energy was still alive, present and released. Energy vibrations are attracted to energy vibrations each time a female and male mate. The opportunity is present to create many different outcomes.

So many humans have an experience of a miscarriage or a birth defect and want to blame self and many times it has nothing to do with their own energetic body or the physical body.

As you know Shaman, this is one area you are familiar with. I would suggest you share your experience as it is one that causes much emotional pain for humans. The loss of physical form is one that many do not feel neutral about.

As a Shaman, I had the experience of helping a friend seek an answer to why she gave birth to a stillborn. I was shown that she provided a vessel for an angel to come to Earth. Through this connection of a physical form, the angel was able to affect the life of another. Of course, an angel is an energetic form but needs the physical form to call home while it is here doing the work.

I also did a journey once for a friend who had several miscarriages. Upon looking at her energetic makeup I found that her uterus was full of what I would call disease energy. Working with a guide, I was able to clear her uterus energetically of this makeup. I believe she now has three children.

The last journey I can share was about my sister who had just had a miscarriage and sought an answer as to why. When I went into the journey, I was shown a vision I didn't understand. I shared it with her with absolutely no offering of peace. What I saw didn't make sense and even though I do not feel I can share the details, I can tell you the miscarriage had nothing to do with her. It was an environmental influence. Over a year later she informed me that she now knew what the vision meant and had found her answer.

What I have come to understand is that death is a natural part of our makeup and when it occurs it is often outside of our control. Our bodies come with memories as do our organs and, depending on what alchemy is produced by our choices, the outcomes may change. I have seen souls come with a purpose and, as a Shaman, I know that sometimes this plays out in the death of an individual. Each outcome is a result of what alchemy was designed, some in our control and some not.

"Earth, we have talked about beginnings of life cycles with seeds and DNA and evolution and we have talked about death. Tell me what will happen when your cycle ends. Will we all die?"

Humans, animals and everything will do as they need to in reaction to such an event, but remember you do not end your energetic life cycle in death; it may be a time of re-birthing into something new and exciting.

The Power of Humans

Earth's comment about re-birthing into something new and exciting reminded me of a conversation I had recently with my friend, Farhana.

We were discussing instant manifestation. Farhana gave an example of using our power to turn a glass of water into orange juice to manifest what we desire. My first response was, "No way!" We do not want a world of instant manifesting.

"Earth, what would have been your response?"

It is an interesting topic because much of what is going on in the world is happening not by what is being desired but by what is being created out of already existing energies and their reactions to the physical world.

At one point in the creation of Earth, everything was about instant manifestation but that was before the evolution of humans and animals; it was also before death.

The creation of time came from the infusion of death. To have instant manifestation you would have to eliminate death energy and, as you know, it is because of death that humans can evolve.

Evolution happens in response to the human consciousness of experiences. Without human experience, evolution could not exist.

"Oh, I get what you are saying. It is like the existential movie Groundhog Day where the main character is stuck in a loop of time. Each day, Phil Connors wakes up to the same experiences and responds as he has always done - in a negative and egocentric manner. Finally he decides to take advantage of the situation. The time loop gives him an opportunity to become conscious. He actually evolved in consciousness even while he was stuck in the same experiences."

Exactly! Without the buffer of time, you also would be stuck in a time loop but without the options for an evolution of change. You would (as the human race) eventually end the existence of form as it now known.

Humans are the determiners of their own existence as it is through their ability to desire and therefore attract new possibilities that new creations come into existence. Like Phil Connors, humans can change their living experience by their interactions with their environment. The environment also changes its existence based on its interactions with the living world. It is this —*the everything affecting the everything*— (the alchemy of the other planets, the environment, humans, etc.) that supports instant manifesting.

"Earth, there are currently many teachers on Earth who talk about this. Louise Hay is one that comes to mind, as well as Esther Hicks and Rhonda Byrne. Some of the teachers whose books and lectures have inspired me are Jack Canfield, Neale Donald Walsch, Wayne Dyer, Carolyn Myss and Sandra Ingerman. My editor, Elissa, speaks of the late George Addair; the list could go on as we each added in people who have taught us this concept."

"What you are saying, however, is that we need to look at the formulas in our creation process and if something is not working, it could be as simple as the desire we are starting with or the energy we are surrounding our self with."

Yes.

I am not sure I can bring this message without the injection of my energy into the reporting. I believe instant manifesting is often about greed, not need. I believe there is an element of spiritual immaturity there.

It is the journey of doing and following desire that I learn and evolve. It is in the loss of not getting what I desire that I sometimes get the best teaching. It is the belief that there are other energies present that will assist me that not only serves me, but serves everything. Our world is one of harmony. If I set an intention based on my desire to have a life in harmony, then I also trust that intention (or energy) to infuse itself into what I set out to create. But I want to understand what the formula for creating is and ask Earth.

"Are there natural laws on Earth? "

Yes, the main message of this interview has been about the laws of how forms come into creation.

Let's say you want to write a book. Others are also thinking that you should write a book. These are thought forms and they vibrate at the frequency of thought as they are being released.

The combination of your energy frequency combined with the energy of a desire and created the thought. These thought forms keep a vibration around you, mixing and changing all the time. They are made up of your original source so that they are most attracted to you as you are the source of their energy. Thought forms continue to be thought forms until it is mixed with energy by the thinker who creates a form.

The Law of Attraction is rooted in this theory but understanding the energy or the form you want to attract will assist you in the manifesting of it. There is simplicity in doing this. Humans have the ability and the power to bring about new creations in their lives. Manifesting is happening all the time but for many it is on an unconscious level. Individuals are continuously creating undesirable outcomes through unconscious patterns or behaviors when they could create the outcomes they desire by being conscious.

By understanding the formula you have an opportunity to bring about the results you desire. Look for those who have what you want and ask them how they got it and then look for the components. Ask yourself what components of the formula are applicable for you. Perhaps adopting the exact same formula will work, perhaps just pieces of the formula.

Find the formula that works, be an alchemist of your own life!

In Reflection

I believe we already hold the power to instantly manifest anything existing in an energetic form if we can create the physical form for it to land. Like birthing a baby, however, there is often a gestational period of time for this to happen. Sometimes we are birthing and sometimes we are in instant manifestation—to eliminate either would create an imbalance to our evolution.

Being able to instantly turn water into orange juice does not serve me unless it would offer a teaching for everyone. To watch someone turn water into orange juice might confirm the belief that it can be done, but to make it into one's own creation, it must be experienced by the one desiring it. Otherwise we place a false sense of power onto another thereby losing our own power.

It is documented that Jesus turned water into wine. It was one of his first miracles; he was young at the time. I think he wanted people to see his power so that they would respect him as a teacher. And so his manifesting served this purpose. Did he want the people to see him as the only one capable of doing this? I don't believe so.

If you read through the Bible, the disciples say that we all can do as Jesus did. I am not a biblical student—I just remember the teachings as they were taught to me as a child. Jesus is an example of what we can all be. Similarly, Buddha and other prophets were not there to say they were better than us. They came to teach us that we can do what they did.

Each of us can be teachers by living a life of example of our truth and manifesting what we desire to align us to our own integrity. When we cannot manifest instantly we can know that we are in the process of birthing the reality through a gestational preparation time—that the world is getting ready for us to bring to life what we desire.

Part of our ability to manifest is related to our own spiritual development. What work have we done to truly understand this process? It may be that we are a work in progress and are gathering the tools and awareness we need to bring to us the essence of that which we desire.

My last comment on this is that we can transform ourselves just by setting an intention, having a desire and then believing it is so—even just commanding it outright. When we believe in something we take action and action creates the container for the desire to manifest into physical form. Thoughts are energetic forms that will not come into physical form unless there is a form they can combine with. There needs to be a physical entity to allow a thought form to come into existence, like the action of pen to paper.

Energy Bodies and the Soul

This discussion about the power we have to bring about the results we desire naturally leads me to a discussion about healing. As a Shaman I am often asked to do healings. Sometimes a healing involves the energy body of the person or a component of them rather than their whole being. And there are times when I view a person energetically as a whole soul; they appear the same on Earth as in Creation.

"Earth, so far you have spoken only about energy bodies. I understand that there are energy bodies that do not stay in one piece when they are released

but vibrate to common ground in the energy world above Earth; but what about souls?"

There is a difference between souls and energy bodies. The world where energetic bodies go when they are released is around Earth and is attached to Earth. The soul comes into creation when the energy body vibrates in alignment to another planet. The energy body does not separate into energy particles but stays together in a complete form or what you call a soul.

The soul follows another stream of energy that takes it to another energy world where complete energy bodies reside. Again, it is through the attraction of energy. What you have to understand is that evolution created the soul and the soul added to the formation of another planet aligned to Earth but not of Earth.

"So not all humans have a soul?"

A human form can have a soul and lose it and regain it again by passing in and out of the energy world surrounding Earth. For an example, if you are a full soul energy body and you re-birth into a physical form, you will start life as a full soul energetically. Let's say you go through an experience in your life where you move away from a soul vibration and you take on an experience that alters you energetically, you will find yourself without your soul body and you will energetically be an energy body. You may stay as an energy body upon death and re-birth into the next lifetime as an energy body. This cycle continues until you die at a vibration level of a soul. You will learn more about this as you progress through your interviews. I sense some resistance from you on these thoughts so let us keep it simple for now.

There is another planet connected to Earth where human energy bodies go when they lose form (this is when the energy body stays intact as a soul). Human consciousness was formed through this process. There is also Creation, a place where all energy bodies can travel, but not the energy bodies found in the energetic realm attached to Earth. If you die as a soul energy body, you are able to travel and access many energetic realms to gather wisdom, healing, and experience that will add to your next physical living experience. This knowledge stays contained within the soul energy body when the soul is fully complete. Sometimes you will hear a human say, "Ah I remember this." If at that point in the living experience the energy body re-gathers all it has needed to become a full soul again, much of the soul's knowledge will be communicated.

If your energy body is in a physical body, you can also visit other realms based on intention. Your physical body is what allows the energy body to do this.

The physical body is like a home for the energy body to align back to after it takes intermittent vacations. If you have lost components of your energy body (through life experiences), you can attract new pieces while on these mini-*vacations*. Without the physical body, the energy body can freely mix and change as it moves throughout the energy realm. It is like replacing a piece of furniture in your house. It is still your home, it just has different components.

Your soul also houses a lesson it must learn to add to the collective human consciousness. It does this either through one lifetime or many. If a soul loses parts of its energy, it will lose its ability to stay together as one entity and will return to the energy world around Earth until it reconstructs itself. An energy body that has never been a soul does not have any other purpose except to continue re-birthing, living a life that will bring about a vibration that will then create a soul, an energy body that stays together after death. So you can birth as an energy body and die as a soul or birth as a soul and die as an energy body.

"How does population increase then? Wouldn't it just be the same energies going around and around?"

No. Energy combines with energy. You can never run out of energies waiting to be manifested.

"The population on Earth is higher than ever. Where do the energies come from to enter into the newly created forms?"

The first creation of sperm plus egg requires the addition of an energy and this energy comes from what you call Heaven. Energy plus energy equals new energy but no form. An egg plus sperm come together to form a fetus through one cell combining with cells, organs then become forms inside the form. Then it draws to itself similar energies. Each body part has its own vibration, similar to the vibration that originally entered the new creation. And these energies are in constant creation.

"Please clarify this."

A sperm is a form carrying the DNA of the male; the egg is a form carrying the DNA of the female. The energy body that comes into the formula is the one that matches the closest frequency to the combination of the two DNA makeups. This explains why we get family traits carried through to the next generation. The next process is the forming of the organs. When the body parts are created from the original starting point, each body part attracts an energy body which most likely is closely aligned to the first energy body that attached itself to the DNA combination.

For example—Anne and Ray decide to have a baby and Anne gets pregnant through the act of intercourse. In the energy world is Ray's father (once called Joseph). Joseph's energy body was released from his physical form five years prior. The first energy to arrive on the scene at the mixing of the two DNA's is Joseph's energy. Both Ray and Anne wear glasses but as the baby's eyes are being developed, they attract Joseph's eye energy who did not wear glasses; therefore the outcome is the baby will not need glasses. When Joseph died he had kidney disease, but when this form is being created it attracts the energy of a healthy kidney from Anne's grandmother's energy body. This is because the DNA makeup of Anne and Ray does not include a diseased kidney. Therefore, even though it is in the energy body of Ray's father, there is a stronger vibration to attract a healthy energy from another source. If either Anne or Ray had kidney disease in their DNA makeup, then there would have been a larger possibility of kidney disease showing up.

This is how a human life begins; a mixing of all past ancestral energies.

This is also how family traits get carried down and also how they can end. If a family member healed from kidney disease and took that out to the energy world and attracted itself to other energy bodies of similar vibration, it can mix the healed kidney energy with all the ones with the diseased energy, thereby transforming that into a new possibility for the next generations.

Healing

"One of my teachers in the shamanic trainings taught that if you heal something in yourself you heal for seven generations past and seven generations forward. "

We really do influence future generations, as our ancestors and families have influenced us.

"Does this mean the original energy can leave?"

No. Organ energy makes the organ function and it holds a memory of its past experiences. What it combines with will determine how that organ manifests in the living experience.

"Okay, I am relating this to my husband, as there is a genetic disposition of liver cancer in the family. Can you tell me how this comes about?"

Colin houses a liver that has the energy of liver cancer but it will need a form to manifest itself. Colin's liver has the memory to create a tumor and if that tumor goes undetected then the energy can attach itself. If the tumor is detected and no other organs have cancer energy built into their vibration then when the tumor is removed, the lineage of cancer also ends. Any new energy can also change the outcome. It is all just forms plus energy.

Put an herb in the body that enhances the vibration of the liver energy; herb (form) plus liver (form) plus cancer memory (energy) and a new form is created. What that will be we don't know, perhaps a whole new cell that combines with another cell that attracts the frequency of healthy liver vibrations. This explains how different modalities of medicine offer different frequencies of healing.

Disease is simply the combination of forms and energies. Energy is all around us—seen and unseen. Energetically we can mix with all kinds of energies; it is only when these combinations find a form to attach to that they will manifest.

Healing can come in the form of information. If there is a desire to find a treatment, information is the form that may present itself. Many times a new discovery is the result of it being sought. We have witnessed this with the development of medicines into easily administered forms. Medicine has the capability in its vibration to heal. So does food.

Plants offer the highest vibrations to the body. Raw plants (or raw plants mixed with water) increase a human's vibration. Cooking food has caused death in humans.

Humans need raw vegetables, fruit, and plant milks in their diets because they cook the meat animal energy. The more 'alive' energy humans consume, the more source energy feeds the body. Putting fire into the meat created a new form that is energized differently. As the forms changed so did our ability to handle raw animal protein. As **a** result, humans started to change in form—evolution.

Every disease has a treatment but whether or not it is utilized depends on the capability to combine it to the correct physical form and the willingness of the physical form to receive it. ("Makes you go, 'Huh!' What if there is already a treatment for cancer but it won't work because the forms with cancer cannot receive it due to something in their energy body or physical makeup, even something as simple as a belief system?")

In Reflection

As a Shaman, I am often asked to work on a solution for healing a disease. I work on a person's physical body by using my intention to change the energy. I call in the energy needed to bring about a healing by combining the healing energy with the energy of the physical body—hoping it is received. I sometimes access energies outside of Earth to bring about this effect. It is through the desire of a result (what I call intention) that I find the energy I am looking for.

Let me say that healing energy will come if called but will not necessarily be able to attach itself to the person needing to be healed. Often I see this in a situation when the person blames the healing but truly there is a misalignment, not always by the healer.

Prayer circles are another example of bringing in healing. Everyone in the circle is having the desire to bring about a healing and healing energy is created. Now if the person's body part that is sick can attract that energy, it can re-create itself. A belief system can stop that process by causing a physical barrier of another energy vibration that does not attract the healing energy.

If I can understand that which does not serve me and heal it in my lifetime, then I have ended this same energy from moving forward into future generations. I cannot end it for everyone, but as I heal, I believe it offers the opportunity for others to follow. This really makes us responsible for our own life experience and our own health.

We each are entitled to a life of greatness reaching enlightenment however we wish to define it.

Enlightenment

The search for Enlightenment or whatever you choose to call it—Awakening, Nirvana, Transcendence, or Cosmic Consciousness seems to be a motivating factor in our attempts to prioritize what is really important in life. The competing and often conflicting demands that we have on the 168 hours we are given each week make it near impossible to sift through the extraneous and live in a state of harmony and peace and fulfillment. So I ask Earth how she would define enlightenment.

Reaching enlightenment is about doing activities that bring you closer to knowing your truth, maintaining a healthy body and attracting energies that are in alignment to your desires. It is how the human world is best served by all.

One path is not better than another path, however.

A human is not bad if they are stuck in a negative cycle; they simply must go through that life experience to re-birth into another opportunity. They may need another piece of alchemy to fully grasp that awareness and that may not present itself in their current life. It may be that one lifetime is just to break away from a family trait and that is all that can be managed in that lifetime. Humans truly cannot judge another's life experience because one does not know what or where they are in their cycle of evolution.

A person who starts a war may be deemed to be the most evil person ever, especially by those who lost family members, but what if that person is actually in alignment with their soul body and their reason for existing was to start that war in order to feed the experience to the human consciousness for the human world to learn from.

"I have trouble with that kind of stuff. Guess I am in judgment; there is a part of me that still feels we should not hurt one another. I guess if in hurting someone you learn that hurting is not okay then perhaps it serves a bigger purpose. There are individuals, however, who do not seem to get the lesson; they exploit children, rape women and steal from individuals and businesses. Some kill seemingly without remorse. Even punishing them does not make them stop. It is hard to see how this serves human consciousness. Earth when did humans start killing humans?"

The question Shaman should not be when but why. Reactions can take place in many different ways including actions. Human ability to reason created all sorts of actions—some out of need and some out of perceived need. You will learn in your interview with another planet about human consciousness and how the creation of that is related to this question. Humans have desires and perceived needs and they are able to dream and create all kinds of solutions. I am sure when the first human was killed there was a perceived need to end another's physical life.

Perhaps the human world will someday evolve enough not to include those things in the life experience. Today the violence is much less than what it once was. What you mentioned were once accepted practices in many cultures. Today there is a negative recognition of those acts in most parts of the world. Remember that nothing can manifest without the energetic body having a form to attach to. End the form and it will become extinct.

"Don't we have to know what two energies came together to create the form? How can we find the answers?"

If a human desires a solution, they need to gather that energy and seek a solution. Seeking can happen in many ways—trial and error, scientific breaking down of formulas, and meditation on the energy body.... The greater the desire or the more humans attracting that same energy, the greater the possibility is of finding a solution.

There are many teachers who will appear—some in the spiritual energy realms and some in the physical to assist. Even energy from the other dimensions on Earth may come in response.

With knowledge comes awareness; with awareness comes the possibility of new outcomes. Knowledge is available through many different avenues.

Humans often feel alone and yet we are surrounded by so many helpers. Earth, do you agree with this?"

Yes Shaman, A thread can be strong on its own but woven together, it is stronger. When animals are seeking food, they gather in herds and move together. They have an instinct built into their makeup. So do humans. One person has the ability to eventually find a solution to any problem but a group of individuals gathering with the same intent have a greater ability to find a solution.

In Reflection

So where is the proof in what Earth is saying?

I have witnessed incredible experiences where people had visions during meditations, where they have received just the answer they needed to move forward; my editor Elissa shared some of her own experiences with prayer and meditation and the realization of how much power one can hold when they bring this type of practice into their life. But it is hard to really grasp the incredibleness of this until you experience it for yourself.

Here is my challenge to you, try it and see what comes of it.

There is never just one way to meditate or pray; find a method that works with your comfort level and allow it time to develop. Some people find they get this response by exercising, some find it through journaling or through drum circles, but each of us have a way where, for a short period of time, we can shut down our thinking brain and allow our spirit brain to dance and show us new ways of thinking.

At a Neale Donald Walsch retreat, Neale talked about how when the mind does not have an answer, there is a larger part of us called the spirit that will bring the answer to us.*

You can also visit Creation and learn from the other planets, as Creation Is the one place of common gathering.

Set an intention of what you desire and allow your energy body to gather the information and answers you seek.

*These were not Neale's exact words but my interpretation of what he said.

Q & A with Earth

"Since you mentioned that humans can visit Creation, do we have aliens visiting Earth?"

Yes and No. They energetically have to be able to live within the frequency of Earth. You are forgetting that there are twelve dimensions on Earth each offering a different frequency at which to exist.

Can other beings come to this planet as we humans have traveled to the moon?"

Yes, they can physically come but not energetically. As you know, you are able to enter a planet's energy realm to get to know and learn of a planet but you are not physically there in the same way as an alien being can physically come to Earth's plane.

"Can they stay here and live here?"

Yes.

"Where did the other beings come from?"

Before Creation set up Wisdom Keepers on each planet and energy doors were created, energies could travel all over. Some of those energies got left here, separated from their planet. Remember the physical forms were fluid; not solid and not all beings are in a physical form but are an energetic body. As you travel to other planets you will learn about them; you will also come to an understanding why Earth is very inviting to other forms existing in our universe.

"Can they mate with humans?"

Not unless they are of the same frequency as humans.

"Earth, have other beings mixed energetically with the human energy bodies?"

59

Yes.

"Tell me about crop circles. Are they made by aliens?"

Crop circles are energy vortexes that come from outside the 8th dimension and any energy outside of the 8th dimension would also be classified as alien. These energies are in a reaction to the Earth forms that are re-created into a crop circle or sand design. It is not sunlight but energy put over a space.

"Why? Are they trying to communicate with us?"

I believe that those who are sending the frequencies are testing the plants' abilities to shift form and shape. Interpretation about what they might be communicating with the shapes and forms is best left to those who can bring that information forward.

"The counsel of the Wisdom Keepers has informed me I cannot travel to one of the planets in our universe. Do you know what it is about this planet I cannot visit? Is it that bad?"

Earth's energy is about creation. Even though that planet is created from the source energy, it is not about creation rather it is about un-creating.

"Will I learn about these beings as I travel to the other planets?"

Yes and No. There is always the possibility of there being more than one universe.

"There is a universal force as Creation light feeds all of us. If there is a planet that wants to un-create everything using Creation energy, why not cut them off?"

Shaman, your reasoning is humorous. It is not about un-creating, it is about bringing down the ending of a form, it is what they view as the cycle of birthing. You are talking about one planet, but each planet is inter-related in keeping the balance within our universe.

"Don't they have new births?"

By the ending of one life form, a new one is given.

"So why not go to a planet where there are lots of life forms they can further populate with?"

It must vibrate with them. Even if they remove a form from Earth and they use it to create a new form on their planet, it is limited because the vibration, unless equal, won't allow it. Alien beings have to be able to exist in the frequency on Earth.

"Why do I see myself and my family being attacked?"

Because you know it is possible.

"I don't want our planet taken over."

Once you learn about the other planets and their beings, I believe you will better understand what is out there that could attack Earth. With this knowledge you will know if this is a natural fear or one you have brought forth from your past lifetimes.

As a Wisdom Keeper of Earth, I have concerns about survival and natural disasters and the end of time and so I ask about these issues.

"Earth, can you tell me about your polarity?"

Polarity is the moving action of Earth; it is the reaction to the placement of the rocks. When the rocks begin to shift and move the waters, the polarities also shift.

"My guides said to me that north will go south and south will go north."

Yes, this could happen.

"Are the rocks moving right now?"

Not enough to do the north/south shift, but during the time of darkness approaching in my cycle will most likely be when the polarity will move. Your guides are correct.

"Earth I am afraid that because we live in physical form this could cause a huge end to civilization as we know it."

Yes, it has in the past. Creation will continue, humans would return someday in form if death combined with them. The energy realm may also move to another planet and find other forms to attach to.

We all live in a cycle-based world, like a circle that spins and moves—each creation of Earth has the same way of existing. There is much fear on the planet and yes the existence of many is being threatened but each will simply move into their next cycle of existence as will I. My surface is going to change; my vibrational alignment to Creation is going to change so outward forms of Creation are going to be different.

"How does your vibrational alignment change?"

As I change position in the universe the flow from Creation will hit me at a different force. A closer proximity will mean a stronger force which will affect how I vibrate outwards. A different alignment will also be different in relationship to outside energies like the Sun.

"If the polarity changes, all our electrical will be gone."

Temporarily.

"Tell me about the Moon again."

The Moon is a creation of form from a mass contacting my mass and mixing with the non-energy of impact. The Moon is part of Earth. A mass hit Earth so you had a rock-to-rock connection with the energy of fire and this created a new form with a vibration similar to Earth's rock vibrations. It then exploded off the planet and found its place in orbit around the Earth. It continues to produce energies and forms from rock energy.

"Can it supply the people of Earth with an energy source similar to electricity?"

Yes and No. Removing rock sources from the Moon will unbalance the Moon and affect its orbit—it may even crash back to Earth. The Moon is made of some of the same products I am made of so there may be energy resources on the Moon similar to what is on Earth.

"Earth, I feel that humans would like to be prepared for another cycle that would cause these changes. Can you tell us what to expect as you been through this cycle before?"

Each time it is different as there are new forms upon my surface, interacting with the energies present. There really is no way to prepare except to ensure your physical needs are taken care of and that you listen to teachers that appear with messages for the human race.

I am heading into a time of darkness, a time of no-Sun energy; this causes a slowdown in the creation of plants but increases the creation of rocks. Rock energy becomes very strong during this time of no-Sun. Rocks move the waters and there will be lots of movement in this area.

"Will the existing plants die?"

Plants need the Sun's energy to create; Earth needs the Sun's energy to create plants. Without the Sun's energy, plants will not be creating. Existing plants will not die unless their vibrations lower to 4-9 and then death energy will combine with them.

"Is this time of no-Sun a time also when death showers Earth?"

No, that is another cycle and one I will not meet for many cycles, if ever.

In a no-Sun position, the rock energies are strong and fire is in existence. This causes a time of fires, volcanoes and earthquakes. When sunlight returns, creation will start again.

"What about extinction of some of the species?"

When an energy exists but a physical form that it could combine with does not exist, the form will go into what you call extinction.

Extinction can happen due to many reasons—from planet catastrophes to a form being destroyed to the point of it being unable to re-create or from the removal of an energy that it would need to re-create itself. The energy stays present but the form no longer exists for it to enter into. For instance, the Siberian tiger is in danger of extinction. Tiger energies are still present but they cannot all return because there is a reduction in the physical forms.

"What about dinosaurs? How did they become extinct?"

The extinction of dinosaurs was not due to the lack of energy bodies. It was due to the lack of physical forms being created that could attract the full energy of a dinosaur you are referring to. Dinosaur energies were re-birthed into other forms but the originating dinosaur energy combined with other energy bodies until it found a vibration of attraction to a form.

"Could humans become extinct in the same way that dinosaurs became extinct?"

If every human form was destroyed, yes there would be extinction to the human form as it exists today, but knowing the creation cycle you can see how it would re-create itself into a new form attracting a new blend of energies.

"Is that what is going to happen in 2012 and beyond?"

Possibly, I say possibly because of the unknown time frame created by humans. Also new energies can be introduced and cause a completely different outcome.

"Can we avoid it?"

No. Whatever is going to transpire will transpire as to the energies present.

"Tell me about past cycles of no-Sun positioning. If Earth was once covered in fires or floods, I assume that all living animals and humans were dead in physical form. The creation process had to start again to re-birth the human energies. How did this happen?"

You have been told a story about Noah. There is truth to that story but Noah was not the only one who took action during times of catastrophe. During the fires, there were some tribes of humans who managed to stay in existence. The humans that survived the fires went underground—that is how they survived.

In trying to understand the changes that are taking place on Earth, I am thinking we are nearing your cycle of darkness. Can you tell me what created the earthquake in Japan?"

The form was the continental plate that Japan sits on, the second form was the Moon, the energy was $NaC2LiA3$. Aftershocks affecting the continental floor impacted other rock formations. The energy that comes into that formula is a sound frequency of 18 hertz. Japan is moving and, as you know, rock energy moves the waters. Whenever there is a large movement of rock energy, there will also be a large movement of waters.

"Earth, I do not understand science at this level so I am going to take your word for it and perhaps someday someone reading this will be able to make sense of it. I have a few more questions, is that okay?"

Always my love.

"In the case of a forest fire or a flood, can I change that physical form?"

This is the same work. You would connect to the creation in place, let's say the fire and ask what forms it is made of. Then you would go to one of the forms and bring another form for them to combine with. Sometimes it is bringing in an energetic form for it to re-create, other times it is bringing in another physical form.

"Is this going against nature?"

No, think of rain dances. Shamans have done this for many moons.

"Have the Shamans forgotten?"

Not all the Shamans have forgotten. Is this not your understanding from those you are working with in Creation? A black hole is going to un-create Creation. You are learning of the other planets who are seeking to find a formula to remove this possibility from occurring. Each of the other planets has their own way of using Creation's energy for their existence. To maintain this existence there will need to be a change. How that happens is determined through the knowing of what is and how to maneuver the energies present. Practice what I have taught you. Look for other ways.

"Can you go over some details from the past so that people on Earth will be able to take what they need from this information and leave what doesn't work for them? So far in this conversation you have told us that you are in this cycle and you are aware that the cycle of darkness is approaching."

Based on where Earth is at presently and looking at the calendar as you know it, I am going to predict a possible time period of 485 days when I will be at the strongest rock energy. That would put the calendar at July 2012, but of course that all depends on the consistency of time keeping and that has changed over time based on the polarity movements. It is just an estimate and of course is not to be taken as a warning. In the past, a time period of around four days is how long I stay in a place of darkness, without sunlight. The polarity will not move prior to the cycle of darkness. That typically takes place after the light returns as it is related to the rock energy moving the waters. These are just facts from my past and are not to be known as this current cycle's truth as the energies are different in our universe and in my solar system and on my planet surface.

There are always teachers who show up on Earth to teach the human world about such events happening, I am sure if you look around your world today you will see such teachings.

"Earth, this information has raised many discussions within me. I have come to expect there could be a rather bumpy ride in our future but fear of the unknown does not resolve anything. Taking actions to ensure needs of water, food and heat are the only known precautions I can think of. Other than that I am going to trust in the universal energies to guide us. On my next time of writing I am going to meet with the Wisdom Keepers and listen for my next guidance. Thank you.

In Between the Next Planet

Noah

I enter into my journey state wondering what good am I as a Shaman if I cannot help people know the truth of the upcoming cycle. Not being able to know the exact date, not knowing what will happen as a result, brings about a fear in me. I want to be a future teller; I want to be able to have this information. Perhaps that is my ego and I am reminded of the fact that this will happen despite what we may or may not know. Earth did reassure me that teachers will appear to guide us.

I greet the Wisdom Keepers feeling a little discouraged from what I have learned from Earth. Of course the Wisdom Keepers are presenting the issue of the black hole approaching that is causing areas to be uncreated. After the meeting, Archangel Michael suggests that I talk with Noah. I look at him and say, "The Noah! The one who built an ark?" Michael laughs and says, "Yes Shaman; he shared some of your feelings at another time on Earth."

So I am off to meet Noah.

Noah enters in such a peaceful light form; he is how I have seen him depicted in Bible stories but with a glow of orange and red mixed aura. He introduces himself by telling his story:

Noah's Story

I remember those times of confusion. I would question what I was being asked to do and how it was going to happen. People laughed at me until news spread of the water rising and of many people dying. We did not know that death was upon the planet and was combining with many forms. I felt so helpless and yet I also knew I had to do as I was guided. I started by drawing plans for the ark and by talking with others about how it would withstand a flood. I didn't have money to build an ark but I knew the floods would come, so I continued making plans as I waited.

I told everyone I knew to join me on the ark as I knew we would be safe. Many laughed and I also had days of questioning. When I questioned, I would pray and re-commit to God, to the Creation energy and then I would go back to work. I started to get trades, what you would refer to as money and offers of help; it took four years to build the ark. It was built in a desert so it was hot, but we needed a flat space where no one lived so that we could work uninterrupted and without threat of vandalism. Yes, we took animals on board, but not animals that were part of the sea. Thousands of people also were on board. The ark was like a city; the animals were kept in pens like pets. We needed all the people to work and help; there was a lot to be done. People of your age think of it like a ship but actually it was more like a large raft, a big square type of shape with levels. All of it was given to me from God. I learned to trust those inner voices that are there to help us see what needs to happen.

Not every person or every animal survived the flood but a great many did and when the seas started to move and we could once again place our feet on land, we left the ship and re-started a community. I do not believe we were the only ones. I do not think the guidance I received as being for a very few. I am sure many were warned and did not listen. It was sad and I spent many days grieving the loss of all those people, all those animals. I spent hours crying with God and yet I never quit believing. My heart was with God, with Creation and doing my part. If I would not have committed to God's request, the community that was able to start again would have been lost.

"Noah, were there aliens?"

Oh Shaman you make me laugh, No, I did not see any.

"Were people working together to rebuild or was there violence?"

We were a true community family. Even the animals had grown to love us as we had grown to love them. Creation began again and there were still forms for the energies to return to. I would imagine this took place all over the planet but we could not see that. Anyone who survived the great flood was divinely spoken to and guided.

"Were there earthquakes and volcanoes during this time?"

Yes, but we were on our large ship which started in a desert far from water and so I do not believe we were in the places of the volcanoes, there was water and lots of sunlight, no real darkness for days and lots of rain.

Noah, can you share some final thoughts on this whole darkness cycle Earth has presented?

Continue to do as you are directed; don't worry about saving all on the planet; it is for everyone who chooses to listen. God is an equal opportunity God and we all will hear what we need to do in the future. Earth is a planet lost in the cycles of space—there is no stopping her movement but we can work at learning how to move with her. Do as instructed. There are others whose energy is waiting to help, waiting to accomplish this task. Engage fully in all you know to do no matter how crazy it seems. Trust the inner voices; it is the connection to a world larger and knowledgeable.

Thank you Noah.

In Reflection

This section has been a long haul with lots of information to process. I find myself constantly contemplating the comments and discussions I had with Earth and Noah. I realize, once again, how in charge we are of our life, how the energies of transformation are there if we choose; how a simple desire followed by action can bring about a new alchemy to our lives. I realize, once again, that when things are not working as we would like, we hold the power to change our circumstances.

There are no victims then in the course of living life in the 8th dimension. Yes, we all will come to the end in the same way; death will end our physical existence. But we will go on and exist as forms of energy in an energy realm surrounding the 8th dimension or we will exit as a soul body to a new place. More is to be revealed of this soul world later on in my interviews.

For now, Earth is our home and how we keep house will create the experience we desire to have as a collective. There is a cycle in place that is approaching and being prepared for any type of natural disaster sounds like a great plan to have in place. Worry is simply wasted energy as we have been told there will be those who will receive the information to guide us forward. We are surrounded by all kinds of energy, and so truly we are never alone.

Hopefully the message that Earth has offered will set us on a path of reaching for your highest potential, not only to enrich our life but to enrich the lives of our future generations. Any changes to improve our health and well-being will carry forward into future creations our lineage chooses to create.

The message I really get is that we are the alchemist of our own reality!

Play with the formulas available, find the one that works and listen to the guidance that is within. Do not judge another as to how they live as they also are part of the formula in existence. Even though you may see them as an unnecessary part of the equation, you do not know the final outcome.

If you wish a collective of peace and love, be peace and love. If you wish harmony, be harmony.

All you desire is possible.

Section 5

Keena

(Keen-na)

"Take a bath in light every day, shower yourself in love. Allow your eyes to accept the light of another as all colors make up the stream that feeds us all. Your light, no matter how brightly it glows, is needed. Keep it on and flowing— you never know when you will be another's beacon in their darkness. Light is not meant to be shined into another's eyes for them to see, as this causes blindness, simply glow and allow others to admire your eminence."

Lord Metatron – Keena Wisdom Keeper

Introduction

I first met Lord Metatron a couple of months ago while doing journey work for a friend of mine. He mentioned that he would be at the next Wisdom Keepers' meeting. Lord Metatron is a Wisdom Keeper sent to Keena, as I was sent to Earth. This is our conversation:

"Lord Metatron, as I write this book and attend more of the Wisdom Keeper meetings I find myself questioning the reality of all of this. Do you ever question this?"

Yes, sometimes it feels like I live two different lives, one on the planet Keena and one in Creation. Lately it has become even more complicated.

"Is Keena a new creation made the same way as Earth — form plus form plus energy equals a new creation."

Yes, but Keena has a higher level of consciousness than Earth forms and we have not experienced a death energy as Earth has. We live simple in comparison to you and our forms are different.

"I feel very excited, as this is my first experience with a planet other than Earth."

We will both learn from this process.

"Why didn't anyone join me in my exploration of Earth?"

We are always together as Wisdom Keepers; we are joined.

"I don't understand. If we are all joined, why am I traveling to each of the planets?"

Not to be of insult, but you have lost much of your memories in the form you have held. Plus you are writing a book; we need you to learn again what you once knew and through this process you will remember. Here is Keena, my planet. Let us enter.

As I entered the doorway into Keena, I felt excitement and curiosity. Imagine walking arm-in-arm with a six-foot Lord with a gladiator-type body and a smile you can't help but fall in love with. Perhaps it was his eyes that sparkled with an intensity that made me feel safe and secure. As beautiful as this man was, however, the planet was even more so.

We have places of tropical paradise on Earth, but Keena is a tropical paradise. The planet is covered in lush greenery. A plant similar to grass covers the surface; shrubs, some as tall as a tree dot the landscape. Water springs from the ground and flows into water streams; some of the water is warm and there are natural pools—interesting as I do not see anything that resembles a rock. There isn't color as in colorful flowers but the grass is green and the water is a deep blue where it pools. Where it is not pooling, the water appears almost transparent. I asked Lord Metatron about the absence of rocks and he concurred.

Keena doesn't sleep as Earth does. Keena is never without sunlight and so there are no rocks.

My body feels somehow different and I realize I have a gladiator body and my stride is powerful as I move forward. Breathing is easy, almost non-existent and unnecessary. My eyesight is clear, I can see for miles.

We approach a group of people who drop to their knees in gratitude. Lord Metatron takes my hand and has me gently draw a circle on each of these beings' heads. As I draw, there is a rainbow of light that flows from me and creates a halo over each being. They start to hum as I complete the circles and I watch the halo merge into one light that encircles the group. The light flows as a steady stream to somewhere beyond.

The sky originally seemed much like Earth's sky. But as I look closer, it is not sky blue but indigo.

Lord Metatron takes me towards a dome-shaped building made out of a willow-type branch weaved together with the branches filled in with greenery. It does not sit on the ground but has roots that connect it to the ground. Within the dome there is furniture; the fabric covering the willow furniture is large leaves or grasses woven together. Lord Metatron tells me this is my home to work in when I visit Keena. His home is not far from here. There is a pool of warm water close to a bed-like structure. There is no *linen; any material items needed come from plant tissues. Drinking water trickles down a wall and flows out of a reed and into the ground. There is a drinking cup, made in a similar manner to how we on Earth would make a basket but woven tighter, with a fine grass. Everything feels so alive here. I am not cold, nor hot. I am not hungry.*

In the Beginning

"Keena are you ready to talk with me?"

Yes.

"You sound feminine in nature, similar to Earth."

Yes, I am feminine.

"Tell me about how you came to be."

I was a mass of very hard rock, mostly oxidite, a black substance.

My surface was cold. When Creation's light hit me, I reflected the light and this created the suns that surround Keena. The suns then warmed my surface and I was able to absorb the heat. I continue to do so. As my surface absorbed the heat, I sensed a flow of a liquid; this liquid is what feeds the growth of the plants and forms. I have never been without my suns and so I do not understand darkness. The forms on Keena are made of light.

Water was the first form on Keena. It just came from within my inner mass as my outer shell was warmed from the suns. The liquid combined with the suns' energies to produce different gasses. The gasses combined with the suns' energies and produced a form that fell to the planet's surface. When those forms combined with the liquid, plants started to grow. The plants combined with each other and with the different gasses and new creations were formed. All are still fed by the liquid today. I am a planet of liquid, plants, gasses, and light.

The beings that formed here were not from my atmosphere. They came in a form of energy that was attracted to the liquid and the gasses; the energy formed beings that could live within the plants. The liquid also feeds the beings who reside here. They are called Light Beings as they are made of light. They do not create new forms (as the original forms came from outside this planet) although they do not end either. Their existence is continual. Due to their lack of ability to reproduce, very few have ever left. Creation energy feeds the liquid that feeds the Light Beings, so the Light Beings on this planet are attracted to Creation energy. The only being that has left to return is Lord Metatron and we honor him as our representative in Creation. Only two others left our planet and they did not return. Lord Metatron assures us they are safe and residing in Creation and do not wish to return. None of the others have left and now we are safe from outside intruders.

Each doorway only allows the Wisdom Keepers to enter. We had visitors from other planets prior to this but they could not exist in the intensity of the light. The energy of light around Keena expels outside energies; the only energy that has entered and stayed has been the beings who reside here.

The Beings on Keena

I pause in my writing to fill my basket with water. My thirst has almost reached a level of panic. Light Beings thirst for the liquid but do not feel hunger. I wonder about these beings. How do they spend their days? Do they have emotions?

For now I am going to soak in the warm pool of liquid and then rest on my leaf-like bed in this beautiful, vibrant plant-created home; not that I feel tired but my body is sensing a need for downtime. There does not seem to be variation in sleeping and awake, tired or rested; everything here is how humans feel in the light.

After resting, I search out Lord Metatron. It is very easy to connect with someone here; simply speak their name in your mind and the Light Being appears.

"Do you have time for me, Lord Metatron?"

Time does not exist here.

"Ah yes, I understand. Tell me about the Light Beings. There doesn't seem to have been a period of learning for you as there has been on Earth."

The form you see is the form of Creation, we did not evolve. Our knowledge of our planet came to us through the liquid that mixed with our energy so we all started with the same knowledge.

Finding ways of comfort took exploration; that is how we put together our dwellings. Once a large planet called an Opik provided a barrier between the light and our bodies and this felt good. So we started to look for ways to put a barrier between the light and our bodies for an experience similar to that time when no direct light hit our bodies. When we closed our eyes in these shelters, we saw other lights. Soaking or entering the pools of water felt soothing like a warm touch of another—similar to what you experience on the planet Earth. Due to our thirst (as I am sure you have experienced in our form), we brought cool liquid into our shelters. This is how it all came to be and it has not changed.

Our existence is spent creating light and exploring light and then sending light out from our planet. We create light by allowing the outside light to enter our physical bodies and then to exit back out as a new light form. We seek Wisdom Keeper information so that we can produce light that others can use. As you learned, only three of our planet beings have left. The way I left our planet was during the making of light; I connected to the pure stream of Creation light and was taken to the place of Creation. It was a very different experience as I was surrounded by many different forms of energy and yet we all shared a similar feeling of togetherness. This is where I stayed. Those on my planet could access information through me due to our similarity of energy. I could not return. Two others followed and today they are in Creation, serving Keena and the other planets. Gabrielle and Gabriella are the two Keena Light Beings found in Creation. In Creation they are able to access their knowing of all the planets and beings and combine it with the light knowledge of Keena. I am like you as I was infused with all of Creation's light and then returned to Keena as a Wisdom Keeper. That is why I am so celebrated on Keena. They understand my voyage. They connect regularly with each other and with Creation through our two beings (Gabrielle and Gabriella) and me. "

"Can they access Archangel Michael for information? "

Yes, but not directly and if they connect directly with Creation's light they too will dwell in Creation. So they connect through a light source located on Keena that is offered by the two beings and me. The only reason they are looking for this connection is to understand the other beings in our universe and to create light that can be used by all.

"In a journey you came and took me somewhere to heal my friend, June. Where did we go?"

We went to a place in Creation where one can freeze a being's energy and then re-birth it. This place was created from shared knowledge among the planets.

"Did you come because June is somehow from your planet?"

No, I came because June sought the light wisdom and her energy field sent out a vibration that called me. Each energy field is different and for whatever reason June's energy field is a similar match to Light Beings."

"Are there others on Earth who follow this type of energy seeking?"

Yes.

"Lord Metatron, is there any light formula that will neutralize nuclear energy?"

I asked this question because of the six-reactor Fukushima Daiichi nuclear plant that was badly damaged after the 2011 tsunami. At the time it was speculated that the plant would explode and release large quantities of radioactive contamination into the atmosphere in a manner similar to the Chernobyl disaster in 1986.

I am not in the knowing of all your science but if you, as a human race, could magnify your Sun's energy to that specific spot, it will combine with the nuclear energy and change the form.

Shamanic Interval

With the disasters in Japan, New Zealand and Australia, there is a desire to share what is coming to me in terms of this story and to show some of the processes that as a Shaman I receive. Part of this story is to offer insights to learn from our entire universe. Although I am anxious to interview Keena again as well as the next planet, I find myself lately downloading information in relation to our current world events.

In light of the recent disasters there are people warning others of what is coming and how to prepare. Communities of people became strong during these times. Sharing of resources and skills was evident as the pieces were put together—not only in the direct areas of impact but around the globe, people offered their assistance.

This is a teaching given to me from Earth in regards to the consciousness of the people, the Law of Attraction and the natural events.

I had this experience the other day that before a thought there is an instinctual reaction to the energy I feel around me. This is due to my own experiences and my family's experiences. I move that instinct to a thought creating an emotional response. To understand the Law of Attraction and creation on Earth, I asked Earth about my ear which had been infected.

Q & A with Earth

"Surrounding me is the energy of a healthy ear. How do I un-create the sick ear and bring the energy of a healthy ear into creation?"

What do you see as the forms in the formula?

"The forms I see are my inner ear parts and my DNA."

Together those forms attracted a diseased ear.

"Yes, but how did I bring it into creation?"

Oh my love you didn't, the two forms did.

"So it wasn't my empathy for someone or my thoughts?"

No the two forms of your inner ear and your DNA come together and attracted a source of a sick ear.

"How can I reverse this or change it then?"

Using your mind as a form, connect it to the DNA form and ask it to create a new form that will allow you to hear fully.

"How do I do that Earth? Is it through thought?"

Thoughts are energy so thinking will create the energy part of the formula not the physical creation.

"How do I physically bring my mind and DNA together?"

It will take an outside physical creation.

"Could this be another person?"

Yes, but not necessarily.

"An oil?"

Possibly, if the correct oil.

"Could I do it as a Shaman, where I call the essence of my brain and my DNA out and then connect them with the intention of a healthy ear being the result?"

Yes.

"Can this be done with other ailments?"

Yes.

"How am I impacting the physical when I am in an altered physical state myself?"

You are not in an energy state, you are physically all present. When you call in something using an intention, you call it into Creation, a place of no vibrational energy. What you request energetically will combine with the forms you intend. Everything in Creation is open to all that is in existence energetically and so the possibilities are endless as to what can be created. It is through the request of energy that you re-program what it is you desire.

"So I treat my mind as a physical form and I treat my DNA as a physical form."

Yes.

"Why not call in the inner ear?"

They have already combined to create the non-hearing energy; you need a new form in the formula to create a new Debbie. Learn to do this for yourself, it will be needed.

Since you are asking these questions so that people can help themselves it would be best to give other solutions for those not familiar to a shamanic way of healing.

In Reflection

Keena really shows us the power of light and how each of us have light within. Keena beings focus is to create and send light out in the universe for all of us to access and use. When I think in practical terms of how each of us can benefit from this planet's gift, I think about color and auras.

When an individual sets an intention to pull in healing light, I see this healing light first as an energy wave. As these energy waves move through the physical vessel, the individual enriches it with color. Perhaps intending a certain color brings about different results, I don't know. Those who see auras can feel the difference in individuals based on the color that surrounds the individual. I remember learning that the color green can be used for healing.

This is how I interpret Keena. Keena is about creating light and using light to bring to us a desired result. We can do the same.

Understand your needs and then seek the light resources that will enrich your experience.

When I need to find a focus point in my life I do a little ceremony where I welcome the sun's light into my body. It looks like this: I stand and face the sun, and I make a triangle with my thumbs and pointer fingers using my two hands. Then I place that triangle above my head and look through it, often my eyes are squinted. In the middle of my vision is the Sun's light. I then envision the Sun's light pouring through the triangle into my forehead, on my 3rd eye. I close my eyes at this point and let the sunlight pour through my body until I feel filled with the warmth of the Sun, I continue this process until I feel myself as the Sun's light. After I am light I then move the triangle so that it points down, holding it around the throat chakra, then I move it down the center of my body until I reach my belly button. At my belly button I hold the triangle there, and take a deep breath in and a nice slow exhale. Before I remove the triangle from my belly button area, I give thanks for the Sun's warmth, for the Sun's light of clarity and I remove my hands and walk away feeling enlightened and peaceful, ready to begin again. I think lying on a beach somewhere and soaking up the rays can be just as enlightening! Or holding a crystal and absorbing the light from within the crystal. There are so many sources of light; finding one that works for you is part of the fun.

Human language is something to pay attention to. When someone is enthusiastic about something, we often say, "You just light up when you talk about that!" If we aren't sure about what to do, we often seek out another's advice to "shed some light on the subject." Light-house keepers send out light so ships don't crash onto the rocky shoreline. Humans, like plants, have a symbiotic relationship with light. We need to receive it and we need to send it out to others.

Shining our light is about sharing our joys, our loves and our gratitude and being willing to send our light out to the world and to the universe. We see and feel light, consciously or unconsciously. Pay attention to when you see light in others; watch for each other's' lights to shine.

Light Energy

In my Blog I wrote on the topic of trust and perhaps it is in trust we can truly shape our gifts as trust frees us of our ego. Once again I visit Beena. She seems to be herself again.

Am I typing the story today?"

"Yes and No."

"Huh?"

"You need to spend some time with the Earth today. I will join you when it is time to write."

"Earth, what would you like to tell me about today?"

I want to share with you the formulas for light energy.

"What do you mean light energy?"

I mean light energy in how it contributes to human form existence.

There are two sides to Earth. In the dark there is loss of sight, loss of human creation and the increased creation of rock energy. In the light there is awareness as it is in those moments that human form can connect with other living forms in Creation. The moon was created out of a need to have light reflected into the dark.

So many humans try to have light connection when in fact it is time for rest. Chaos and discord often take place in areas where there is more of one than another. If your body frequency does not adjust to where you reside, you feel disconnected from your surroundings. Frequency changes can happen by allowing a balance of the light and dark to match your body. Those in balance, who live in light all the time, make time in darkness; those in darkness, often will bring in more light by using the light of the moon. Fire is light but is made up of rock energy; it is a mover and a shaker. Fire energy is good when you want something to transform.

Earth beings need to be prepared for a time of darkness; there will not be any light energy. Their bodies will feel out of sorts and it will create fear. Fire will be good for the warmth that your bodies will need, but a balance will have to be found. There will not be any moon energy. There is a formula of energy that can be used to produce light energy. Light energy vibrates at 1080 hertz; a vibration of this nature can be created through sound.

Shaman, you were asked a year ago to uncover some crystals and move them into a different position from where they were. To have those crystals produce light energy there needs to be sound vibrations of 1080 hertz. There are humans whose voices will channel that frequency and they will know when to sing as the crystals will rise.

Sounds sang in one part of the planet will travel to the crystals which will absorb the sound and put out light energy—not light energy you see but light energy you feel. Humans need to be aware of this so that they can absorb the energy. Once we have completed our journey through darkness the light will return and the balance will be re-established. Animals, plants and waters will use this energy to balance themselves; they do not have the reasoning powers that humans have.

"What about instruments to make that sound? Like a crystal bowl?"

Anything making that sound frequency will feed the crystal towers; they are the only crystals on earth that can transform the sound into light frequency levels.

"Okay. I guess I have my research for today."

A Being from Krevat

My journey continues today as I travel to Creation.

Beena looks exhausted and tired. It appears that some of Creation's light has disappeared from our universe. It is all through us causing exhaustion and a feeling of sleep within us Wisdom Keepers; it is hard to conceive and I wonder why.

> "We do not know what restricted the flow but I imagine it will be felt throughout the universe," said Beena. "On Earth we had an equinox. Would that have anything to do with it?" I asked. "I don't believe so, but perhaps, as Creation light is fed by the other planets returning energy."

"Do you think a planet would purposely cause this?" I asked.

> "We do not know, just as we do not know where one of Creation's beings went."

(On one of my returns to Creation I learned that one of the beings that normally resides in Creation has disappeared. There was no explanation nor does anyone seem to know where the being went. But Creation will know which planet did not return energy for the restriction to have occurred.)

Right now I am concerned about Beena and offer to feed her some of my energy,

> She replied, "No; I will be fine I am absorbing energy as we speak as Creation blends all the energies together."

"What am I to do today?" I ask.

> "Start writing the story."

This is how Beena and I communicate. I am writing the book but not alone; I have an incredible spider working with me.

I arrive today greeted by what appears to be Beena but my intuition tells me it is not. My staff glows a purple light; whatever the light hits, reveals the truth. Michael, Daniel and Kathleen watch as I face off with another being that has also showed up in my space. Michael thinks this being is here to destroy—to take another. The form appears angelic-like but as my staff's light hits it, a true form appears, resembling a lizard-type man. He claims to be a Wisdom Keeper but he disagrees with the plan to work together; he wishes to present the negative side of universal beings coming together.

I ask, "What are you afraid of?"

He replied, "That our planet will be excluded."

"Are you willing to work towards your planetary existence in harmony with the other planets?"

"We know of no such thing. "

"Then you are limited in existence in Creation. We are able to share forms and be present with one another. What is your purpose?"

"We do not know but it may be to create mayhem."

"And you wish to be part of a council striving for peace?"

"I am like you. I am a Wisdom Keeper designed to enter portals of each planet. We wish to multiply, to expand our existence."

"But your existence in this current form is our destruction."

"We are losing our moons and our existence will end."

"So you come here to destroy Creation, to take over the place of Creation, to destroy me and others for the purpose of existence? Creation needs our planetary energy to maintain full Creation balance. You have been through this cycle before?"

"Yes."

"You survived?"

"Yes."

"Then I do not understand."

"We want Earth as our home."

"Why Earth?"

"So we can produce and extend our existence. We can combine with Earth energies."

"You cannot have another planet for the purpose of your own existence. Creation was to enable each planet its own life force, there is balance in that."

"We have already started."

"This will create imbalance. It must stop."

I hold this other being in the power of my staff so that he is immobilized and can be present in Creation without destruction while I talk with Archangel Michael.

"Archangel, he came the same way as Lord Metatron; is it true he is the Wisdom Keeper of his planet?"

Yes.

"So we keep him here?"

We cannot. Their planet implodes and then explodes for   creations, it is different

"We need a full understanding of his planet. Perhaps there is some way we can assist him in what he is seeking."

Perhaps.

"We need to find a way for him to attend council meetings as the Wisdom Keeper of his planet."

Yes. The doorway of energy from this planet must be kept sealed and only when he can notify us, can he come. If announced a dome can be placed around him.

The being responds,

I have come before to see and hear but leave. I do not wish to destroy Creation as I am aware of the energy that feeds the base of all of our planets.

"How can we talk with your planet to learn about you? Entering your planet is a death wish for any of us. Perhaps other energy can assist the energy on your planet so that destruction is not needed. Let me gather more information from the other planets and Wisdom Keepers."

"Something was birthed in the Creation process that needs adjusting so that your race does not need to fear extinction. The moons have not moved so we have time in the cycle. Go back to your planet and stop all interference until a new way of communication is established."

I put down my staff and the being left towards the exit. Together as Wisdom Keepers we placed an energy barrier surrounding the entrance into Creation so that if he tries to re-enter he will be blocked.

A Meeting of the Wisdom Keepers

Universality is our plan and Krevat will need to be part of that plan. Perhaps we can throw him into the dark hole and they will consume that energy? Michael responds that due to Creation's energy being made up of everything existing in our universe that will not work as it will cause a change in Creation's flow of energy and cause a chain reaction of events.

Even that which presents itself as destructive still serves a place in the greater whole.

Michael hands me a medallion. "What is this?"

It is about reconfirming who you are. Many distractions are going to present themselves. I understand that you are a mom and a wife and need to walk different roles.

Trust that we are helping you always and that we are guiding the path.

Have you located the other Earth Wisdom Keepers?"

Yes, but they are not responding to our call.

"Could I contact them to validate spirit's message, a human form asking them to listen?"

We are in spiritual connection only and it is only when they arrive in conversation as you did, do we then engage in a knowing about their Earth life.

"Perhaps you could bring about something Earthly to get their attention. You must be able to contact energies around them."

"Yes, if the channel is open we can attempt. "

The next day I arrive back in Creation and am taken to a Boardroom table gathering. Around the table are different guides and Wisdom Keepers. We have a discussion and all agree that Creation is still on course for the black hole. There is currently no known way to shift the movement of the black hole or our planetary positions. So far the black hole has swallowed up any items that came into its path and left a void in the wake.

It is agreed to keep learning about each other and perhaps through this effort we will be able to understand how combining of the planetary energies will help us. It is noted that the Law of Attraction is present on both Earth and Keena, and I have been informed that the next planet I am going to also has the Law of Attraction present.

Section 6

Duncan

(Dunk-an)

"Sands of time have no place in your current reality. Be conscious of what is present and know that even then a perception change can alter that reality. Be real to the level you can be at and contemplate the other possibilities. Consciousness is created through focused attention."

4 Duncan Beings – Duncan Wisdom Keepers

Introduction

Today, my two guides, Beena and Tanjay, and I are heading to Duncan. If you have seen the movie Narnia, Tanjay is much like Aslan. Tanjay's fur is golden with a dark brown mane framing his face. His eyes are round and slightly slanted towards the outside corners. His eyes shine with compassion and understanding. Tanjay is always smiling although I do not think I would like to see him when he is not smiling. Within his beauty is a powerful and mighty force. I ride on his back, my arms wrapped around his neck; sometimes I hold onto his mane. Beena snuggles into the crook of my neck.

The guides who fly often know the coordinates and exact location of the portals. I rely on Tanjay's knowledge as we are flying through darkness. Then out of nowhere—a doorway appears and the vision of the planet appears. As we get closer, there is a tunnel. Once in the tunnel, I can no longer see the planet but I can feel it. This planet's energy feels welcoming, yet nervous and apprehensive. At the end of the tunnel is an energy field. I put my hand out and the energy disappears leaving an opening for me to enter; nothing can follow me as the energy instantly attaches behind me. Any energy on me (like Beena) would have prevented me from entering.

The beings on Duncan are about three or four feet tall; they dress in a red wrap-around garment that covers them from head to toe. They wear dark eye coverings like sunglasses and a tie-on shoe—a flat sole with laces that wrap upward around their legs.

Two of the beings step forward and, taking my hand, walk me towards a hill in the distance. There are all kinds of what look like entrances into the hill—circular but they turn to open, like a jar lid. An entrance opens and I am guided in. There is a small room off to the right and a bigger room to the left; in front of me is what looks like a kitchen. The room to the left is mine to use; in fact it appears the whole space is mine. I am exhausted and start yawning. The beings show me how to turn the door and as it opens, they leave. I am surprised by their ability to understand my fatigue but I am also too tired to think about it. I lie down and am immersed in a deep sleep.

Upon awakening, I decide to explore. The landscape is like sand dunes that appear to be homes although I do not see anyone so I return to the home I am given and lie down. The bed appears to be made of fine granules of sand. I sink into the sand; it feels warm and comforting. Today I set an intention to interview the planet Duncan.

Interesting. No one has ever tapped into my consciousness but Duncan does. He is humored that I have come to learn about him.

In the Beginning

Duncan's story begins with the light of Creation surrounding him in warmth. Creation's light created heat on his surface and soon the surface started to shake and move. The movement created a new vibration, it combined with the existing frequency, and a light falling of dust accumulated. More and more sand and dust accumulated and the movement of frequencies combined with the energy of Creation created an even faster moving energy that was wind. It blew the falling dust and sand everywhere.

My surface started to crack with the shaking and this created a downward flow of energy into the other layers of my surface. When this frequency of energy mixed with the frequency of the layers, large hardened sand accumulations formed and moved towards the surface. Once they reached the surface, the winds blew them across the land creating hills and valleys. This process went on for many moons until a crack went deeper than all the others and a new layer of energy connected to the surface energy. This created a crust of vibrations that neutralized the shaking and all became calm in that area. Over time, there were more cracks and soon the planet reached a level of stability. The red glow of the atmosphere remained but there was no more wind, falling dust or hardened mounds moving up and out of my surface levels. As I move through our universe, contact with other energies and with Creation's energy brings about more changes and shifts in weakness and strength.

A large mass of rock collided with my surface; this impact created a large hole that stretched beyond this layer and into the fourth layer of my surface. This energy mix started to break down and pool into the hole that was created on impact. The pool was a black liquid similar to what you would call water on your planet but not as fluid as water. The makeup was similar to molten iron. The combination of the energy at the fourth level made this possible. As the liquid started to flow over the edge of the hole, it hardened. This happened repetitively so on my surface you will find these deep pools of molten rock although they are not hot as lava is on Earth.

At one point on our journey, Creation's energy got very weak and the warm glow that vibrates our atmosphere became non-existence. This shift in energy caused a rain of rocks (similar to what you call pea gravel on your planet) that was attracted to this vibrational frequency. When the pea gravel entered the pools of molten rock it changed the frequency of the pools; they continued to stay in liquid form but the color of them changed as did the vibration. As I continued along my path of movement into the stronger force of Creation, other rock energies were drawn to our frequency.

Duncan is difficult to communicate with because of its density and slower vibration. I find myself growing increasingly tired. During our interview I have been in a type of conscious-sharing session; it is different for me in that I am not engaged in a mind-centered type of conversation. My mind has been silent and this is due to this inner knowing of what is being shared with me. I thank Duncan for our communication. I must return to Earth and recharge my energy levels.

I am feeling confident as Tanjay, Beena and I return to Duncan. We fly straight into the air through black sky filled with sparkles of light I assume are stars. There is a red glow around Duncan; it resembles a red circle with a big black dot in the center. The planet is hard to see; in fact, it looks like you could fly through its red atmosphere and not hit anything. I have decided to slow down my vibrations so that this time I can truly share in revelations with the planet's energy. I am not greeted by anyone; these beings keep to themselves. As I am walking towards the place I call home, I am drawn to one of the pools. I approach it slowly and then decide to sit and talk with this liquid entity.

"I am a Wisdom Keeper from Creation coming to learn of other planets so that the planets can work together and thus avoid becoming uncreated."

The pool responds:

Many times I have felt as though my original form has already been uncreated and yet each transition brought new changes and assisted this planet's evolution and expansion. I was once very acidic and then, through the law of attraction and the atmosphere openings, other rock energies entered my pools and mixed with me and a new formula was made. I am still present in this physical change but I am also different as it affected how I move.

The consciousness of Creation does not change; it evolves with new properties and embraces the opportunity to shift in its physical make-up. The consciousness of the rocks that combined with my liquids also shifted and we learned from one another's different aspects but we also came together as one. Within each creation are elements of the different consciousness. We learn from our own made-up consciousness embracing new additions as they are attracted to our energy.

The Beings on Duncan

The beings on Duncan came from the energy stored within this planet's core. Creation energy worked into our depths as the surface was hardened. I believe you have a similar story on Earth. Liquid has a way of moving through cracks and making them bigger. At different times in our solar movement, Duncan went through huge shifts. In these shifts pieces of the planet's hard surface cracked. It was into the cracks that I could flow. A shower of rocks entered our atmosphere. I changed in size and consistency and color and expanded to the point that liquid covered most of the flat surfaces on Duncan. With this much weight on the surface, more liquid was able to find cracks created by previous shakings. There were underground streams and the layers of rock started to dissolve and give way to passages within. Soon a new layer never before accessed was discovered.

When I combined with this new layer, tiny circles were created that changed the makeup of my liquid form. We looked like a glass of soda; bubbles kept being produced and this created a new energy that combined with our atmosphere. The atmosphere still glowed red but it contained more sulfur and carbon.

Then we moved through the cycle of winds and the winds blew surface sand into me and it caused my surface to become aggressive in its movement. The sand particles collided with the bubble creations and moved out of me onto the planet's surface. When the winds stopped, these new creations covered the surface. They were able to roll into one bubble as a magnet would attract metal. Each time the winds would come, more bubbles were created; they would naturally pull to the source that called them energetically.

The bubbles were attracted to an energy found within me and they started to absorb my fluid into themselves. This created a reduction in the size of the pools. As their energy connected with my energy a new consciousness began to form. These forms needed to feed from me daily. As they absorbed more and more fluid their physical shapes changed. My consciousness was expanding in them but they did not feed my consciousness; I was simply a source of nutrition for them. I became aware of their increasing presence and my decreasing size. Then our planet came through the cycle where we are furthest from Creation's energy and it was during this time that our atmosphere changed and weakened our protection.

We came close to another's sunlight energy unknown to us; it struck our planet with a strong heat and light wave. If this happened on Earth, the waters would have evaporated; my makeup did not evaporate but my chemical structure was altered. The substances at my edge were still absorbing my liquid; after two days they grew in size and started to change shape.

They developed their own consciousness and started to send out messages to each other, they all interconnected. Soon they moved away from my edges; they no longer needed my liquid or my assistance. Each time they moved away I would sense a warm feeling; I believe they were saying thank you. They developed the ability to see through the shaping of viewing holes, similar to human eyes that were colored red like our planet. As the beings shift in shape they take on different functions as required. They are like sponges; they absorb the consciousness of what is around them and they work with that consciousness to stay in alignment with it. Most of their time is spent in congregations where they simply flow energy from one another. They make their homes in cave-like dwellings and occasionally they come to my waters to replenish their inner spirit. Through the sharing of each other's ability to consciously interpret different energies, they can learn, connect and feed another being's spirit in the group energy share.

At one time, there was a consciousness that was unknown to our planet and a group of four decided to follow this consciousness. It could not explore our planet as the atmosphere here did not align with this visitor and caused this being to feel weakened. Once our planet beings exited the energy portal that was opened by the visiting energy, they were not seen for many rotations. No one could feel their consciousness or find a trace of them. One day they returned and brought stories from our Creator and they told of the other planets.

Each of the beings celebrated with this knowledge. Like the red atmosphere that surrounds their planet, they also decided to cloak themselves in red capes.

It was time to return to Creation so I thanked Duncan for his history lesson on how the beings on Duncan came to be. I suspect there will be four new beings at the Boardroom Table when we next meet. Perhaps they were there before. As I learn about the planets, new beings appear at the next Boardroom Table meetings. The guides that were present there in the beginning were guides I have already worked with while doing journey work for others. But I have never met the beings I just met on Duncan.

Duncan Wisdom Keepers at Creation

It was early the next morning when I decided to go to Creation to check out my next travel plans. Upon arrival, I meet the four beings from Duncan. They wish to share with me a message and a teaching about themselves.

The consciousness of visiting beings brought us new awareness and an example of this is the red robes we currently wear. We are similar to monks on Earth in the way we live in community. We dress ourselves in this manner so that humans can see us as beings they can relate to.

We offer teachings often about community working as one. As you have seen, our planet is inter-connected and created from one source. Through one consciousness, we connect and formulate our existence. Offering these teachings to beings seeking connectivity is interesting because we do not feel separate; separation would be non-existence for us. We evolve together and dissolve together. Community leaves us detached from everything except each other. You can view and look at our planet as you are a being that is a separate form from it, but we do not separate but are, in fact, of it.

Our ability is to consciously combine with another being who seeks connecting with others or consciousness. Teaching happens at Creation and supports the being searching with information to ease the separation from another. To do this we form shapes pleasing to the being seeking our wisdom. Our purpose on Creation is to continue to learn and grow from all the consciousness present and to take that wisdom back to our planet. It is also to give to Creation our wisdom, which is how to adapt and grow from the connectivity of all that surrounds you. Serving as a group of four, we are the Wisdom Keepers for the planet Duncan.

In Reflection

As I prepare to leave and return to Earth, I wonder what my purpose in Creation is. I begin to understand how lacking I have been in my knowledge of the other planets and how advanced they seem to be. The same can probably be said for most of us on Earth. We really don't know much about anything other than our own planet; yet the other planets are very aware of us.

We can all learn by visiting and spending time in Creation. Creation is a place where we can use other's talents to further our own development. It is in Creation that we can connect with many different levels of consciousness and bring that conscious-ness home to Earth. All humans are able to move their energetic body into Creation; this ability is not reserved for Shamans.

Perhaps the beings of Duncan have it over us in that their minds connect naturally. We humans have different ways of connect-ing and sharing our teachings. But have you ever been in the presence of someone who offered their talents or teachings as a natural offering, with no expectations or agenda—a gift that was offered freely? If so, then you have experienced Duncan.

When we decide to give our gifts, we have an opportunity to grow and expand. Music has a way of touching our souls; speak-ers bring out new ways of thinking; writing offers creativity. We have a collective consciousness on Earth although what that is I am not sure. I know that when I join in celebration with those presenting their gifts, I feel stronger in mine.

The beings from Duncan transform their imagery so that their wisdom can be shared; it is about accepting and respecting what is present from the other. "I am going to love you so much I am going to let you be yourself." When we feel competitive or envi-ous of another, then we are not in that place of connectivity; we are separate and on our own.

We can learn much from others when we hold them in a place of honor; when we can feel their joy and sadness and yet not let it become ours. It is more about being separate and accepting of that around us, so that we can feel connected to that greater force that we all seem to feed from.

As humans, we often decide how a person should be in rela-tionship with us based on how they are upon their arrival. We forget to evolve with them as they re-define themselves. When we cannot reach a place of acceptance of them in their new pos-ition, how can we celebrate with them? I am laughing as I com-pared this vision to the beings of Duncan. If a person showed up on Duncan and wanted information but needed to see them as a monk in order to accept the information, the beings would become a monk. If the same person showed up, used the inform-ation they were seeking, then reached a new level of understand-ing and was willing to see the Duncan beings in their true form, (rather than as a monk) the Duncan beings would respond to the new energy present.

How many times have we done the opposite? We offer teachings and the person takes those teachings and evolves to a higher level of being. They then return to receive further teaching and perhaps reach a place of being able to teach us and we question their integrity. Our children change and grow and yet we continue to treat them as children. A co-worker develops new skills but we overlook their accomplishments. Are we happy for the other person or do we try to change them back so that we know how to be? Celebrating change and recognizing it is a way of being present. It may cause a new way of being within us or it may not. Sometimes we are the teacher and sometimes our students return to teach us.

We can learn much from the beings on Duncan. The beings from Duncan do not try to change another; they simply accept what is presented and change to suit the consciousness of the situation. They do not attach themselves to the result. They are willing to teach and they are willing to learn.

The seven deadly sins come to mind at this moment—Lust, Gluttony, Greed, Sloth, Wrath, Envy, Pride—when I am in any of those there is a disconnect. Am I in integrity when I alter my presentation for personal gain or to be heard? What if I simply shared love?

There have been many teachers on Earth who have shared about love—Jesus the Christ, Siddhartha Gautama, Catherine of Siena, Mahatma Gandhi, Mother Teresa, the prophet Muhammad—I do not underestimate the power of love as such a force.

What I do know is that we are individuals within a human race; some are evolved to different levels and yet no one is better than another. If we can let go of the belief that we need to change another and just allow that individual to grow at their own pace, we will have reached a level practiced by the Duncan beings. We will have achieved unconditional love.

Seek out those people who have achieved unconditional love and seek to be one of those people yourself.

Section 7

B'Nai

(Ba-Nai)

"Be blank in your mind when you desire to hear a new song, a song that will sing the truth. Clouds inhibit the wind by creating a container. Find your inner voice and sing the song that heals your inner being and re-shapes your outer expression. Gathering with others and hearing their sounds allows you to enjoy a musical masterpiece."

Leema – B'Nai Wisdom Keeper

Introduction

There are Spirit Guides I have not introduced. Today I am travelling with Treena, a flying white stallion horse who carries herself like a goddess in charge. I am not close to Treena but I would trust her with my life. I am also traveling with my smallest guide, Henry the mouse. Henry looks like a cartoon character; he even has a coat and hat similar to the mouse in the movie, Dumbo. My Spirit Guides often have a humorous side to them; perhaps I created the imagery of them based on TV shows from my childhood.

I said goodbye to Henry the crocodile as I prepared to leave him to travel to the next planet. Why I have two guides named Henry is a mystery, but it is why I call one Henry the mouse and the other, Henry the crocodile. Henry the crocodile reminded me to be alert.

Henry the crocodile appeared when I was seeking a compassionate being during a guided drumming meditation with my friend Nancy. Upon meeting him he started to eat my arm and other body parts, it was very disturbing but I felt peace as I watched in complete trust. He is also cartoon-like in appearance, wears a black top hat and is very cute.

Treena headed into darkness seeking the portal to this planet's entrance. The planet appears to be a light—a triangle shape mirrored upon itself; perhaps a diamond shape would better describe it.

The portal is not as easily visible as it has been with other planets. I hold up my staff to see if its light will reflect off it. It does and we move towards the entrance. There always seems to be a place at these entrances for my guides to rest. The doorways to the planets are designed (I believe) in the knowledge that a Wisdom Keeper will travel with others. Taking a deep breath I step into an unknown space, once again curious about what I will find on the other side.

Whatever I am breathing—air or pure oxygen—awakens my health and strength, as if my body has been starved for clean air for a very long time.

The temperature feels comfortable, almost identical to my body temperature. Everything feels so perfect and I wonder if I have entered into a dome and not an open-air planet. The surface is free of vegetation; the planet made of glass, very clean glass! The ground is like a clear crystal and yet not see-through.

Since no one is there to greet me, I am unsure what to do so I poke my head out the doorway and ask my guides to call for me if I do not return. As I start walking, I realize that, although my foot appears to be touching the ground, I am walking on a cushion of something about an inch off the ground. I know there are beings here; I have seen them in my healing journeys and there must be at least one Wisdom Keeper. The guide I call the Crystal People, is from this planet. She has been to the Wisdom Keeper meetings that we hold in Creation. Feeling lost, I lay down on the planet's surface and meditate.

The Beings on B'Nai

Off in the distance, I feel their presence; there is such a pure love that emanates from these beings. They communicate but do not use words. I stand to greet them, watching in complete awe as they approach. They are six-and-a-half or seven feet tall and thin. Although they have a form, it is almost as if they are transparent. Their necks are long; their heads are oval with no hair and very penetrating bluish-silver, almond-shaped eyes with a black outer rim outlining them. Within the center is a triangle shape that takes up half the bluish area. This triangle usually reflects purple but can change color instantly, taking on the color streams of a rainbow one color at a time. I do not see anything that resembles a nose but they have a mouth, a small horizontal line about one-and-a-half inches from the bottom of their face. When they open their mouth it forms a complete circle like a Black Hole. They wear a light-sky-blue gown of sheer material and yet you can see nothing under it. The gown flows along the ground so you never see their feet; you do see their hands, elegantly shaped like a human hand but with long fingers, not out of proportion with the rest of their body. On the palm of their hands are symbols; like a black tattooed symbol, they are not all the same and yet I am not sure if they are all different either. I reach out to embrace the one I recognize from the Round Table meetings.

My heart is always warmed by physical touch with them, I wish humans on Earth could hold this much love in their bodies. All conversing is done telepathically. I mention that it is so light here and they respond, "Yes, light is the key for transformation." They ask to show me to their place of residence. I follow, feeling like I have met a very unique tribe of women. I do not see anything that depicts male energy. It is amazing to realize that each planet is unique and yet all are fed by one source of energy from creation. This planet is B'Nai.

We approach a townhouse-type complex except the buildings form a circle. In the center is an indigo blue, ground level, liquid pool about twelve feet in diameter. It appears to go on forever in depth. I am told that it reaches the inner core of the planet. The homes are long and narrow and made of a murky crystal that absorbs the light rather than reflects it. Although white, the walls are not bright to the eyes as when sunlight reflects off a white wall on Earth. There is one home for each being. The houses are all the same.

Leema, the Wisdom Keeper I met in Creation, says I am welcome to work from her space. As I enter, I am amazed at the peace I feel, it is like a soft caress and yet I feel energized. The house is without inner walls. At the rear of the home I notice a doorway and assume it leads to the pool. Leema mentions that she enjoys singing and I ask her for a song. Oh my heavens! For a society that communicates telepathically, the sound is absolutely invigorating. Every sense within me is heightened—hearing, sight, even smell. It is like lying on the grass in the middle of a garden or being with someone and feeling their energy pass through me. There are no words; it is a melody of tones similar to a group of crystal bowls playing together but each in reaction to the other.

I ask her how she learned to perfect the different frequencies and she shows me a wall where there are cylinders of different lengths. She taps a crystal wand on the outside of one of the cylinders and a tone emanates. She then matches the tone with her voice much like a singer matches their voice to a note played on a piano. I feel her joy in my excitement and her love as we

connect visually. I want to know everything about this planet and its beings but I also find myself wanting to rest.

Leema is aware of my state and suggests I lie down. The floor where I am supposed to lie down on looks no different than any other part of the house and yet I find the comfort I am seeking. Leema has already mentioned that she will be joining the others for a nightly ritual that ensures their existence. I soon find myself lost in the middle of rainbow colors and in a deep state of meditation where thoughts do not exist but gratitude of the heart does.

I have no sense of time here, just an inner knowing that now is the time when I get to talk with this planet and learn the mystery that surrounds it.

A soft feminine voice speaks; it is from the blue water that all was created.

"Planet of B'nai, tell me the story of your creation."

In the Beginning

Before the light of Creation I was a planet that got knocked around a lot, mainly by other space rocks and energies. It shaped my surface to become quite jagged. When Creation's energy connected with my outer shell an opening occurred that fed a center within me; it also created a strong dome surrounding me. The combination of my surface and Creation energy expanded into my atmosphere that is reflective in nature. At my center (where a direct line of energy enters) is a pool of liquid similar to rain water on Earth, but it holds an energetic of healing—like a liquid crystal where energies can be transformed.

The frequency of sound is what stimulated different properties to transform from the blue liquid. At the time of creation, the atmosphere surrounding me was very hot, so even though I was domed with an atmosphere, there was an outside source of heat. This caused a process similar to crystallization. The blue liquid crystallized and formed the surface I have today. Only the pool you see in the center of the homes is what remains. The rest of the flow of my inner power is still present and fills the interior. Twelve beings in B'nai have learned to shape and crystallize the blue liquid to acquire homes. The beings came from what would have appeared to be a catastrophe. A very large comet of fire impacted the dome and created a hole. It was through the hole that droppings of a lava substance fell. At that time much of my surface had not yet crystallized and so they landed in the pools of my blue liquid. When the hot lava rock pieces combined with the pools of liquid, it formed into egg-shaped domed containers that floated on top of the blue liquid. It was then that the waters really started to crystallize.

I needed to interrupt and say good-bye. My guides were calling me back to the portal to return to Creation after which I would make my way back to Earth.

Exploring B'Nai

B'Nai is a planet that appears to glow from within. It offers a feeling of peace and transparency, empowering; yet it is not about force but flow. Leema is awaiting my arrival and my heart opens at the vision of her. My Lord, she is beautiful.

Last night, when I entered a journey for a friend, Leema came with the others, believing I was seeking to gather soul mate energy. I was intrigued that she came. The planet's beings carry the capacity to grant what I call miracle healings and the woman I journeyed for last night received healing. Now Leema welcomes me and offers a song to begin my time on her beautiful planet. Settling into my resting area I follow her voice into the depths of B'Nai.

The song unfolds into my cells; her singing is like a serenade of crystal bowls and human toning all rolled into one. Focusing my intention on the planet's core, I am drawn into the depths of the blue waters and begin today's conversation with the part of the planet that resides in conjunction with Creation's energy.

"When I left you last we were talking about the creation of these beings and the domes floating upon the blue waters."

The domes were made of a matter like clear quartz. The sounds that impacted the domes created energy frequencies that travelled through the dome to reach the matter found within. It was these frequencies that created an energy source that molded the matter. The temperature of the water is similar to your body temperature, not hot as one would expect it to be. We are given all we need to learn and grow from the waters. There are beings of many vibrational frequencies that are able to move and change the energies of disease. They are able to generate a frequency and apply it to a form to re-create its substance.

This would explain why, when I have met the beings from B'nai in my shamanic healings, they always use song to do the healing. I recall the times I have had to sing along with them. Trust me, that is something no one should endure for long!

I awaken and join the beings as they gather around the blue pool. I find myself so immersed in love and peace that, while my body feels clear, my mind struggles to remember what I wish to learn from this planet. Unfortunately, my guides are calling me and it is time to exit. As I make my way to the portal, I wonder if there is a reason I can only stay on this planet for so long. I feel so lost in the love here that returning to Earth or even remembering my purpose here seems inconsequential.

The Re-birthing Ceremony

My Earth life has been busy; kids are out of school and I have been spending time visiting with my friend Farhana and my sister Cindy. Still, I ready to continue on my journey to B'Nai.

To see if I can hold my energy at a more stable place, I tether myself energetically to my physical body on Earth. As I enter B'nai's portal, I run to Leema fully embracing the feeling of lightness this planet's surface offers. Leema tells me that today I will witness the ceremony I call the Courtyard.

Each home has a doorway that leads to a beautiful, yet simple, space and the crystal-blue pool. I sit and watch. Each being reaches out and joins hands with the being next to them, as they do this they look into the eyes of the one to their left and then close their left hand around the other's right.

This circle of connection continues until all hands are joined. Left with the right, left with the right, I reflect on the imagery of the female connecting to the male and the intimacy felt in such a connection.

The look given to each other is one of complete love and I feel the power of the space intensify. No one holds higher power; they understand that together they create harmony. With their hands still joined they reach up towards the sky while looking straight in front of them but not into the person across from them. They gently lower their hands and turn their upper body including their head to the left in a graceful swoop. They look to their left and then up. They return to center and they repeat the first movement but on their right side—a sideways 8. We know this on Earth as the infinity sign—it is repeated twelve times.

There is a pause and it appears as if they are taking in the energy created.

Then they all lean back, like an upside down U. I am amazed as their hands are still joined and then, in unison, they stand erect. Like tall trees in a breeze, they start to sway to the left and then to the right; each starts toning. Like a melody of crystal bowls—from a high pitch to a low bass — each being has their own tone to hold. They continue to sway and chant; beneath their feet, blue liquid pools, like water under a glass floor. The pool is expanding but has not surfaced. I expect to see an energy beam come from below and shoot into them, but this doesn't happen. All of them are locked in a trance and nothing changes but I can feel the energy has changed around me; there is a presence of awareness.

You know when you are seeking an answer to something and you finally get it, there is that, oh yeah moment; well that is what it feels like and yet I can't quite figure out what I just got an awareness about. There is an awareness to take action and yet I find myself rocking back and forth, not really knowing what to do. I want to join in the chanting as I want to transform even to the point of changing my shape and physical makeup. I want to witness and watch the beauty of everything that is transpiring but since nothing appears to be changing, I close my eyes to fully experience the sound.

Everything I have ever desired is here and yet all I desire I have. So again there is this feeling of pure love, joy, gratitude. My physical body seems distant and yet I am present; I have not moved. Lost in bliss, I feel the energy around me shift. Curiously I open my eyes; my eyelids feel heavily weighted. I no longer feel light, in fact I feel like a thousand-pound blob incapable of movement. I look to see if the beings are moving any slower but everything appears unchanged. I find breathing heavy, like a weight has been placed on my chest. Then in unison, their hands are raised, the melody ends and a shrill noise takes its place. Think of a bunch of girls all screaming at a high-pitch shrill. I have gone from feeling bliss to feeling weighted to feeling chaotic and I want it to stop! Regrettably it doesn't.

I remind myself that this is a ceremony they repeat daily and I have seen them out of ceremony so it will end. Oh, to have ear plugs! Then Leema looked over. I am sure I saw a smile across her face. She looked upwards; the surface cracked and instantly swallowed them all up. I sat in silence wondering if I just witnessed the ending of beings on B'Nai. I reassure myself that they know what they are doing. But time passed; what feels like hours and nothing happens, I feel a little panicked and afraid.

A wind began to blow, not a gentle breeze but a wind. As it passes over and around the houses, it makes a low whistle like a sound you hear when Earth wind passes through a partially opened window. I realize that the architecture of the homes and this space allows the sound to be made but I wonder what is making the wind. Where the circle once stood, twelve small growths of what looks like cloudy ice appears. They are the size of basketballs, not round, more egg shaped. The wind continues to blow into the courtyard but changes pitch as it makes its way around these twelve shapes. The shapes expand but are no longer egg shaped; each has their own unique shape. Two have flattened and are now oblong; one is con-caved so it looks like the letter C; one has grown larger than the rest and has developed into a rounded bottom triangle; another is a donut shape but with a very small center; one is narrow in the center like an hourglass; another is rounded at the bottom like an egg but halfway up has split into three portions like a windmill ready to spin; another is taller, same egg shape but has a spiral woven through it like an apple going through an apple peeler; another has formed into the shape of a tree, long and lean in the trunk portion with three tall branches reaching skyward; one is a rectangle with holes going up the center and the last, which I thought was another flattened out shape, is not, it is like a bowl, a giant bowl. These shapes are about four-and-a-half to five feet in height; their height is in portion to their width. The wind continues to blow as the shapes continue to take form. As the wind moves around these shapes, the melody of the beings is heard. It is music to my ears.

I hear an individual tone and recognize Leema as she comes into full shape. Each time the melody changes, another molds into her original form. Once the shapes takes form, the wind no longer creates a sound around that form and the tone changes. Each time the tone changes another being comes into re-existence. There is an air of excitement and anticipation like that of a delivery room. Before a baby is born, everyone is silent as the last push is felt. When the awaited cry is heard, excitement and joy spreads through the room. It is like that here. With the process complete, the wind becomes a low howl and then stops. I look to see what has been birthed but everything appears as it was in the beginning. The pool no longer flows under the surface, each of the beings is simply standing, no longer in a trance state and Leema is walking towards me. I wonder what I was expecting and chuckle as I think of dinners on Earth. There is the time of preparation, the giving of thanks, the eating and once it is over, we simply clear our plates and carry on. Perhaps for B'Nai beings it is the same.

My mind is racing with questions but it is time, once again, to leave.

A Healing

Tanjay will not be taking me on this next trip as he is tired again, so Treena is going to take us to B'Nai. On our way there, Beena suggests I ask Leema what she remembers and how she became a Wisdom Keeper. Beena also suggest that I ask her to heal my ear and describe the healing, and finally, to ask her about Earth. I need this guidance as I often forget questions once I am connected to Leema.

As I enter B'Nai, I reflect on its simplicity and yet complexity, its beauty and intricate detail and how it all came to be. Leema is waiting and I am filled with love for my new-found friend. I am honored to do this work as I get to experience connections that are in existence always, there is no end unless we end in existence. As we embrace, I ask her for healing for my ear. I hope the ritual will involve her singing.

Leema is excited to perform the healing and ushers me forward. She tells me to relax and close my eyes and take in the tones to every place in my body. I lean my back upon what looks like a breakfast bar. They do not eat food nor do they prepare food so this area is rather confusing. Leema looks over and clarifies. I need to move to the top of the breakfast bar and lay down. As I do this, I get a closer look at the room. There are tubes filled to different levels with blue water. They remind me of tuning forks that each makes their own individual sound. Have you ever filled glasses at different levels of water and ran your fingers around the rims? I imagine that is what these tubes are for.

Leema sees me looking at them and explains they are for experimentation.

They are used to see what can be created using the blue waters and sound. They are the small scale. She tells me to close my eyes and allow the tones to heal me. As I do, she tells me about her planet.

In the Beginning Part 2

I don't remember my creation, but I do remember the changes going on around me. There was this constant battering of our planet by other space rocks. When our forms came into existence we were conscious of each other and of our surroundings. I am not sure what created the dome that surrounds this planet now, but I do remember the feeling of safety that came with it. It is interesting that once you are in Creation on any level you do not wish to be uncreated. We would pass through the daily winds and as you witnessed, this was the final piece that brought us into full existence. We created our homes and living areas as we desired places to be alone with our toning. Everything was done with the creation of tones, blue waters and everything not formed within our liking was simply returned to the blue waters.

One day I had what you would call a dream and found myself diving deep within our planet and basking in the light that is contained within. I had this pull to travel to the source of the light and that is how I first arrived at the place of Creation. At that time I do not remember other Wisdom Keepers nor do I remember seeing other planets being created. I was thankful for the journey but I felt overwhelmed. I returned as I had come; I followed the light of Creation.

Our homes have changed somewhat over the years. Their shape helps the wind enter the courtyard to create the re-birth each day. Our planet shares wisdom with us when we re-birth and we were able to understand how to enhance wind tunnels. It took many cycles to create what we have now. The blue waters covered a lot of the surface of our planet so there was once a larger resource. We would start with a rock – something we found in your world - and place it in the waters and then tone to see what would come of it. There are twelve of us; we have been unable to create any more of us. I was the first to come into creation and my eleven sisters followed. My sisters cannot talk to others, they communicate through me; I am the only one who can communicate to beings in Creation. It happened after I followed the light to Creation and was infused with all of the energies of our universe, as you are as well. I do not visit other planets but return to Creation when I feel the calling. My sisters can travel with me although they have not been encoded with Creation's full energy light. It is through this ability to access Creation that we can assist the healing of others.

Time to say Good-Bye

On my next journey to B'Nai I realize it is time to say thank you and good-bye. Tanjay and I are heading on our final trip to B'Nai. Treena and Beena follow as there is going to be another journey right after B'Nai that Treena will be taking me on. On most of my flights I am focused on where I am heading so today I am hoping to take in the beauty of space.

As we take off, I look down upon my vision of creation. I see a large body of crystal-blue water; to the right is a rocky shore-like area with large boulders you can climb onto; on the other side of the rocks is a stadium-like area where I stand or bow in the center facing my ancestors who sit on the flat rock benches situated on one side. On the other side of the beach area where I dance out my intentions is a grassy hill; there is a path around the bottom that follows the water's edge that will take me to one of my teacher animals, the elk.

I look down in awe as I continue to move towards our first portal. Portals look like a blur in the sky and I trust my Spirit Guides to know the ones to bounce through. We all hold the intention of where we are traveling and the way gets downloaded to the being that is taking us there. Once we pass through the portal, there is darkness and yet in that darkness there is a beauty I can't put into words, it is more of a feeling as opposed to sight. We pass through three portals to get to B'Nai.

As I walk across B'Nai loving the peace and looking forward to see-ing Leema, my mind is constantly distracted. My mind flips to scenes of poverty; I am not sure why these images are coming. I ask Leema if she is ready for me to ask questions and she smiles through her eyes, ready and willing.

"Tell me about this crisis Creation is facing."

I see it as a gift to all of us. We have been living separately and through this crisis—this potential ending—we are all coming together shar-ing, learning and growing from each other.

There is a level of intimacy felt among us, as people in danger often bind together and share resources. Perhaps that is the purpose of the dark hole approaching our universe. I believe it is in the bonding that we will avoid the Black Hole as we will have re-created ourselves as one universal creation. Perhaps assisting each other as our planets go through changes—each of us following a path of flow through the universe that gives our planets a cycle.

I reply that I feel the same about all of us coming together and with this statement comes a knowing that it is time to leave.

B'Nai is so beautiful and full of surprises; it is a planet that I would love to visit just to nourish my soul. I see Leema and jog forward to fall into her arms. I will miss them—their energy of sound and the peace I feel here. Although I am excited about the next planet teaching, here there is a sense of deep inner peace that calls to that part of me that wants to curl up and sleep.

Leema whispers, "The reality that you travel is not that far in the mind's travel." You are always welcome to visit.

In Reflection

There is such power in sound. On Earth we have many ways of creating it. Can sound be damaging as well as healing? B'nai's race was created from sound vibrations and they spend their life practicing and creating different tones to bring about opportunities for healing for those that seek it in Creation. As a Shaman I have used my drum to heal; the vibrations of the sound produced will actually change in pitch directing me to where I need to drum on the body. Tibetan and crystal bowls will often change a person's consciousness and allow for answers to arise from within. As humans we have explored sound but it is only one component of our senses. On B'Nai I didn't sense cold nor did I smell different smells. My sight took in the same sight each time. Sound was the focus. Communication was telepathic so there was not a sound of voice, all that was ever heard was the beauty of sound made in the toning and the musical combinations. If we as a human race could further explore sound, we might learn how to adjust creations that we have created within ourselves and outside of ourselves to better our experience. Perhaps in the stillness of silence we can give birth to our own inner music and gift to the world a new sound of healing.

I witnessed the beings from B'Nai transform hopeless situations into what I named miracle healings. This was prior to any knowledge of them except as I referred to them — the crystal people. I now understand it is in their ability to use tones to move a disease out and change the frequency of the current state to one that is more desirable. I remember when my friend Bernice suggested I find a song that helped me feel strong; I was going through a divorce back then. I followed her advice and each time I played that song I was ready to keep going forward.

Tuning forks, crystal bowls, songs, drums, rattles and many other tools are available to create sound. We must not overlook this area of healing. Imagine knowing the tone that could transform that which we do not desire into what we desire. Perhaps it is like the tubes of different levels of waters. We could practice on a small scale and see what manifests.

Section 8

Tandalyn

(Tan-da-lyn)

"Seek with eyes of wisdom. Do not seek thinking you will not find the truth, seek knowing you will. Fear of the unknown is stupidity for all is known it just needs to be found. Treasure hunt your inner secrets and display them for the world to see. Secrets are meant to be shared; expose yourself."

Farin – Tandalyn Wisdom Keeper

Introduction

I climb on Treena's back and, along with Beena, fly through several layers of darkness each joined by a portal that carries us into a new atmosphere—dark without a light source, like a ball of energy vibrations not yet created into form floating around in space. I find myself wanting to sleep but we take a turn and bam, there it is. Like the experience of It's a Small World at Disneyland, a whole new world opened up after the first bend.

Today I am just entering the energy doorway to this planet but in this short time I am given its name—Tandalyn.

Tandalyn is the not the name I was originally given when I was told about the planets so I ask Beena who decides on the names. She doesn't know. I wonder if the name is based more on the energy frequencies of the sound of the word rather than the actual word.

A Wisdom Keeper Meeting

Treena is waiting to take us back to Tandalyn. Before leaving, however, there is a Board Meeting. Archangel Michael explains the purpose of the meeting. The Black Hole—a unique void of space that does not seem to have any vibrational energy—has shifted in its travel and might not engulf the entire universe after all. The Black Hole is really the crisis calling us all together; to become the one we were meant to be as Wisdom Keepers.

I reflect on Black Holes in my life on Earth. How many times has someone or something entered my life and began sucking up my energy? I think about how that created chaos but also caused me to look at the resources that I could pull together to remove it.

Think of the person who telephones you every day and dumps all their problems on you. You offer suggestions but none are acted on. The daily energy drain gets tiring so you confront the person. When that doesn't work, you avoid her phone calls and reach out to friends for support and advice. Once you have a solution, you take action and end the existence of the Black Hole. The person who inflicts the Black Hole then moves on to another to take from. This is similar to Krevat's energy of destruction in Creation, or the Black Hole. It could undo anything we have created. We not only need to figure out how to move away from it but how to put an end to it.

Through our Boardroom Meetings, we have become a one-focused universe with Creation energy at the center. As we grow in our connections, we have grown in our vibrations. What would happen if the Board members joined hands in love and raised our vibration? Would we be able to harness the universal manifestation of our togetherness in physical form? And would this be enough to encompass the Black Hole, rather than the Black Hole encompassing us? The beings from Duncan suggest that we evaluate the Krevat beings. We all nod in agreement. Hopefully, someday we can help Krevat feel connected to the Universe.

A fairy is sitting across the table and I ask if I can travel to her planet with her. She agrees and we collect Beena and Treena. We walk down a rugged path onto a sandy beach that leads to a deep-blue lake. I want to take off my shoes and dance in the water but a warm breeze catches my attention and I am once again able to focus. Fairy energy is strong and can really mess up one's ability to think.

In my peripheral vision I see two bars of energy. Michael added these to my makeup so that I can stay balanced. One bar represents the energy I use and the other shows the energy I need to be gathering.

As we travel to her planet, I ask the fairy to tell me about herself and the beings that live on her planet.

She doesn't call herself a fairy.

When I ask her name, she joyfully answers,

"I am simply known as Farin."

The Beings on Tandalyn

The beings on Earth that you call fairies are descendants of my race. We are created using the energy vortex of a flower mixed with the elements of two minerals and the blood of two fairies who commit to teaching us our lineage (what Earthlings call a tribe). There are birthing flowers on Tandalyn. The seedling is wrapped in cheese-cloth, drops are added and the seedling is placed in a pod in the center of the birthing flower. The flower closes immediately and stays closed until the seedling is fully formed. As a seedling, I walked about within my pod feeding off the plant nectar. I had wings but was unaware of them as I was living within an enclosed capsule. There is no set time frame for a seedling to develop; it can take months or years. The two fairies that committed to being my teachers regularly checked on me. They sang to me so I had an understanding of language when I was born.

When a pod is about to bloom, the tips change color, typically to a bright red with orange mixed in although I once saw a deep blue with purple highlights. After the tips change color, the teachers hold a vigil. At the moment of birth, the pod turns inside out into a large colorful flower and the fairy falls towards the ground unaware it can fly. The teachers are there each grabbing a hand and together they fly up and away. The first teaching is how to open and use wings. My teachers' names are Fergo and Tarin; I love them immensely. They are what you call parents, except there is no dysfunction. There are many requirements that must be met before one can become a teacher. They have no romantic feelings towards each other; they are just teaching partners until their student is ready to either become a teacher or work in other areas.

"How did you become a Wisdom Keeper?"

I was walking along the garden pathway outside our community living area. I flew to the tip of a tall tree but I wanted to touch the sky so I kept flying higher. There was a pink flash and then flashes of different colors. I expected to hit a ceiling or be stopped by a dome but it never happened. Just as I was about to quit, a bright turquoise-colored light beam slid under me. I soon found myself in darkness in a very unfamiliar territory. The light beam seemed to know where it was going. I saw others and let go. I was in Creation. I had no way of returning to Tandalyn so I spent my time learning about Creation.

Just as Farin's finishes telling me about the Beings on her planet, we arrive at the portal to Tandalyn.

Exploring Tandalyn

As Farin guided me through the doorway into Tandalyn, my energy, once again, started to drop. I attempted to pull in outside energy but felt disorientated. Farin told me to sit on the ground and pull energy up from my root chakra. As we sat, she discussed some of the places I will be visiting but I have already decided to come back tomorrow. Hopefully I will be more balanced and able to stay in tune to the energy on Tandalyn. Upon my return to Creation, I talk with Archangel Michael. He suggests I focus on keeping myself grounded and ensure that I stay tethered energetically to my physical body on Earth. I return home and fall into a deep sleep.

Beena has summoned Tanjay to take us to Tandalyn and I close my eyes and dream. My dreams are simply colors that come and go. Farin's planet is a planet of color—bright greens, yellows and reds. It is like the feeling you get when you enter an amusement park—almost too much to take in at once.

Each color brings visions of people and places and feelings of love. I envision Niagara Falls, a place of Earth beauty I recently visited, just as we arrive at Tandalyn's portal. I say goodbye to Tanjay and Beena and enter into the planet of play.

There is a sense of wonderment here—from the tree houses to the different plants and flowers, to the beings that flutter about. I feel like an outsider here more than on any other planet; everyone is so busy that I am hardly noticed. As Farin approaches, she is a ball of beauty—her coloring is orange today with reds mixing into her aura; her gown is bright yellow. Her dark red hair cascades over her shoulders; a headband keeps the locks out of her face.

Farin is tiny—about three feet tall, not large busted but not flat, lean with long legs like a Barbie doll. Her blue eyes slope upwards at the corners and twinkle when she laughs. When she closes them, they become tiny slits. Her small nose is perfect, not pointed or wide. She is beautiful. Her mouth has a playful smile; her plum-colored lips are full. When she is angry (fairies do get angry) her lips pinch together and her eyes focus intently. Her ears are interesting; they are small, slightly out of proportion with her head size and round like a half circle, almost without an earlobe. Her fingers are long and slender; her hands touch me with gentleness and yet there is a reassurance of peace and strength. It is in her embrace that I truly admire her heart energy.

I kneel so we can wrap our arms around each other. There is a bond within the Wisdom Keepers. We have been without each other for so long, unknown in my existence of my current life until recently. It is like meeting up with a long-lost childhood friend. I guess our hearts or inner souls always know our truth.

Farin's face lights up the world around her. Imagine a group of beings like Farin at a World Peace Conference; it would be a lot harder to talk about war with them around. I ask what I should call her as she doesn't want to be called a fairy. She laughs and declares she is a Podmur. Pod because she was created in a flower pod; mur because that dictates her status among other pod-created beings. Her other title is See-er. I am curious about the other beings and how busy they appear.

She laughs. Don't be fooled by that; they are aware of your presence and use the imagery of busyness to further investigate. No one interrupts a busy being; they maintain busyness until they have an understanding of your intentions. They are also watching out for my safety as I am considered one of the leaders on Tandalyn.

I ask Farin how I can learn about Tandalyn.

Tandalyn is not that much different from Earth; it is why many of Tandalyn ancestors reside on Earth. It would be best to work with the planet's energy as you have with other planets. After I will tell you more about what has happened since the beginning of Creation.

Farin suggested that I follow her to a place where the giant beings reside, I will be more comfortable there and the beings that surround me in their busyness will also be more relaxed. The journey would normally take days to complete but Farin knows of passageways to get us there quickly. I usually have a keen sense of direction but I feel lost. I shall ask for a map so that I can return once I have completed my study.

We arrive in what appears to be an ice cave. In the center is a crystal-clear blue pool. Water flows out of pipes embedded in a wall of jagged ice. This ice is the main water supply for Tandalyn. We walk down to a stream flowing from the pools and once again enter into the Tandalyn reality of flowers, trees, and plants. This time, however, there are no other creatures busying themselves among the greenery. As we travel, Farin tells me about the Rotisillica – the beings we are about to meet.

The Rotisillica

The Rotisillica birthing process is similar to Farin's except a vessel of water is put into a large hole dug into the ground with the essence of the two beings who have chosen to guide and teach the new creation. Under the container is a birthing bulb, similar to a tulip bulb. When the container is placed on top of the bulb, it is crushed. This releases a vine-like growth that grows upwards, surrounding the container. What you can't see is the upside-down flower bud that drips nutrients to the seedling. Once the flower bud blossoms; the birthing couple drain the water. Rotisillica have powerful legs and can jump great heights. Their facial features resemble humans with Down's syndrome, as does the pureness of their eyes. They are about five feet tall with short legs and a large waist.

I am taken back by the love emanating from this village; this truly is a very special place.

Farin introduces me to Reeva, the elected leader. Reeva takes me to her home which has a cave-like entrance; inside is like a palace. Water cascades down the wall. The ponds are filled with lilies, lotus, and vines. The floor is stone, polished but not slippery. It all appears to be a natural occurrence.

As I look closer I realize the waterfall is generating power. The light bulbs are a disk-like object about the size of a Frisbee. I chuckle as I wonder if Edison was a Rotisillica or somehow had a connection with them. Sunlight doesn't enter the cave but the light from the Frisbee bulbs feels the same as sunshine on my face. There is a smell reminiscent of cinnamon and vanilla that is welcoming and homey. Reeva shows me to my room.

My room also has a waterfall that powers the lights. Reeva shows me a valve that stops the waterfall when I want to sleep. To turn the lights back on, I simply open the valve and wait a few minutes. Reeva also shows me lanterns that use tree oil for fuel. Matches are an oily rock that you slide against a rough rock surface and the tip of the rock lights. Tandalyn does not lose heat in the dark so there is no need for a heating system.

My mattress is made of fiber created from tree barks. It is soaked, softened, then mulched into a gummy paste, and then put through a process where it is heated and poured into string-like molds. As it dries, it looks like strips of cotton strings that are then used to make fabric. It is further processed to form something like cotton batting but with more structure. The mattress is set on a log frame like a rough-hewn homemade bed. The desk, two chairs and couch are similar to wicker furniture.

The bathroom is to die for. There is an infinity-shaped pool filled with warm water flowing continuously from the wall. The waterfall generates power as it flows into the tub. As it drains, it is filtered through a natural filtration process of ground rocks and tree fibers. The toilet is not water based. When you push the flush button, the toilet heats to a very high temperature, which turns the waste into dust. This dust is then suctioned through pipes to a waste disposal area where it is mixed with the surrounding soils. Reeva says the mixture offers nutrients back to the soil. The waste disposal sites are moved regularly with the old sites then used for farming and agriculture. Could we use this technology or what on Earth!

Reeva suggests I rest and tells me that she will bring me some food and drink in a stars rotation. I nod not quite understanding their time keeping. Farin says a stars rotation is equal to about two hours. Farin will be back in three Earth days to see how I am doing.

In Reflection

I feel so loved by beings previously unknown to me and yet so familiar in heart space. I believe this love and sense of oneness could bring about the knowing of how to avoid the approaching dark hole. To have this uncreated with so much more to learn somehow seems wrong. Now is not the time to end and re-start; now is the time to work together as a community to bring an end to the chaos being created by the dark hole. I think about our structures for information and decision-making on Earth and they also seem wrong. We elect people to make our decisions and to define how we will think, act, and live. In doing so, we give away our power. Gathering together as spiritual beings has been replaced by gatherings of governmental agencies, religious groups, financial institutions and groups that fight over Earth's natural resources. Walls and borders and fences insulate and isolate us. We have forgotten how to be in communion with Creation and community with each other.

I am not saying these structures are not needed but Earth beings need to be woken up; we have fallen asleep. If within the structures, we can live our own truths while being connected to a greater resource of knowledge to guide our decisions, we can then understand how our decisions serve or take away from the collective. It will be an interesting year as the box we have put ourselves in changes in structure. What we believed is solid will not be; what we believed gave us joy will no longer. This shift, however painful, will ultimately serve us. Hopefully we will miss the Black Hole so we can embrace this higher level of existence.

I am getting sleepy and it is time to rest. The bed feels like down feathers packed tightly together and the sheets are like silk. The soft green lighting complements the natural wood and stone. I leave the lights on and drop off into a deep and relaxing sleep.

I awaken refreshed as though I have slept for hours. There is no sense of time because there is no sun. Does Tandalyn spin on its axis like Earth does? What about polarity? It is time to interview this planet and find some answers.

I feel myself falling through the mattress, through the cave floor, through another layer of fine sand and a layer of yellow orange liquid before standing in the center of a ball of energy that is pulsing like a heartbeat. There is no sound just this movement of in and out like a group of people holding hands in a circle moving toward the center and then stepping back. The ball is like a pearl crystal reflecting different colors—absorbing energy, contracting slightly and then releasing, all the while keeping a balance of equal rhythmic movements. It is soothing so I am startled when a soft feminine voice speaks.

In The Beginning

I am Tandalyn, a planet of joy, love, and beautiful harmony. Everything created upon my surface works at maintaining this flow. I am respected. I am alive as a being and this makes it difficult as I feel the impacts of my orbit through my cycle. I am located close to Creation so I am never without a strong feed of Creation's energy. I am protected by some of the other planet's orbits and therefore do not suffer space debris hitting my outer edges. As you witnessed on your journey down, there are several layers that protect me from outside influences. I do not wish to be uncreated, I like my existence.

"Tell me about your beginning. How did all this come to exist?"

When Creation's energy impacted with me, there was a small explosion within my center. This is the place you stand; it is an orb of contained space and energy that is constantly receiving and giving; that is the contraction and expansion you witnessed. It is similar to how you restart a human heart. Creation's energy enters my core and energy flows out. The yellow-orange liquid holds the energy expanding out from the center to the sand layer. The sand layer is below the outer crust of the planet and is basically the result of the original explosion. After the first impact, the liquid separated from the sand and this became the protective force around my core. Above the sand layer is the combination of both sand and water. Tandalyn does not experience day and night because we are surrounded by suns. Just as I was awakened by Creation's original force so too were the suns awakened. There is a partnership between myself and the suns. I move Creation energy up to my surface. It is the combination of that energy and the suns' energy that my surface began to produce. Everything on Tandalyn gives and receives and everything has its own inner life. They are entities unique within themselves and yet they are all interconnected.

The warmth of the suns caused my outer surface to soften and become pliable. From this interaction, energy was able to move and entered into the surface from the sand layer. It shifted and formed the surface into different shapes. This happened continuously; my surface changed moment to moment. Then I entered an orbit path where I lost two of the suns and much of my planet lost its warmth. During this time the large rock masses formed and hardened back into the same outer crust that once existed. For many cycles, I was without two suns but where I did receive warmth, plants started to grow. The warmth separated the surface into sand and liquid; liquid pooled on top of the fine sand and plants grew within the liquid. The first plant growth looked like what you would call moss.

I interrupt Tandalyn and tell her how similar her story is to Earth's story.

Each moss growth had a need to connect and so reached out to the nearest form in existence, another moss plant. The two plants intertwined their energy and formed a new creation. Each of these new creations had a desire to connect so rock forms mixed with plant forms. It is not the exact same as on Earth, like is not attracted to like as in an attraction to the same species but rather an attraction to the life energy of another. These attractions and connections continue because there is always this need to interconnect. From one of these connections came the first beings — the Rotisillica.

The Beings on Tandalyn

The roots of two of the plants intertwined and, for some reason, sank deeper into the crust, moving past the sand layer until it connected with my protective liquid level. It was like an upside down lightning rod and absorbed a huge blast of energy that traveled up the very long root of the plant to the part of the plant that was above the surface. This caused liquid to be released from the plant that sought out life to combine with. It is from this liquid that the Rotisillica were first born. They did not look as they do today and they lived within the water pools. But as with everything else, they reached out and had energy mixes with those around them. It was the combination of two Rotisillica that the forms began to evolve. What separated the Rotisillica from the plants was the development of intelligence. As you know, we have several different species of beings on this planet; this came about from the inter-mixing of the original Rotisillica. Different plants formed as birthing containers for the different species and again, even though the being looked like a plant, it held the combined attributes. This plant and Rotisillica combination brought about a new generation of beings that gathered socially and formed communities. Each generation had the ability to create and develop ideas using their environment. It was through the repeating of the process that you see the different species today. Each race learned to control the birthing process and that has brought about changes in what comes into creation.

There are the groundkeepers who we call Seekers. There are those who live within the trees and amongst the plants—they are the Dwellers. Those who fly and live within our upper levels are the Seeers. These three races live together in the more plant-based sun-filled places. In the rock structures are the communities of Rotisillica. They are the largest beings. They have created many ways to exist in the rocky landscapes. A third sun appeared after many years of only having two and it warmed the tops of the larger rock formations. The Rotisillica used the liquid that began to separate and flow down the inner walls as a form of power. Everything is returned to the planet so that there is no waste.

Nothing stays constant. As we speak, there are new relationships happening within the plant world. Yes, there is a beginning and ending to life; the choice is left to the being to decide when they wish to transform. They then combine themselves with the nectar of a birthing plant flower of their species. Their form dissolves into the outer crust and a pool forms and from this, a new birthing plant emerges. They never return to the planet in the form they once were but there is a continuation of their existence. Birthing plants share their knowledge to the seedling as the seedling grows within. There is a celebration of a past life and new life each time a new birth takes place.

'That is beautiful; thank you Tandalyn. I must voyage back to the portal and return to Creation. I will return soon."

I awaken, still in my room on Tandalyn. Tandalyn has left me exhausted but Farin takes my hand and guides me through the corridor to the path that will return us to the portal. Beena and Tanjay are waiting. In Creation, Archangel Michael, Raphael, Daniel and Kathleen all agree that I will need to keep an energetic anchor to my Earth body and an energetic anchor to my energetic body. They also think I should not stay on a planet but return daily. They will help me return my energy body in its wholeness to my Earth body.

Seekers, Dwellers and See-ers

Tandalyn is the only planet other than Earth that creates more beings of their kind and experiences death when they choose to leave. I want to learn more about how the other beings live and so summon Treena and Beena for the journey. As we arrive at the portal, the sun is shining and the temperature is warm. This is a paradise humans would love to live in but sadly could not because of their inability to maintain the harmony required.

The Seekers

Farin takes me to a gathering of the Seekers. I sit cross-legged on the ground so that my size is not so threatening. They are about two and half feet tall, slender with pointy ears and long hair. Their eyes are large circles that shine brilliantly while seemingly absorbing everything they look at. Their eyes have a pale yellow inner circle and a dark brown outer circle. At the center is a black dot. There is intensity about them; like an owl's eyes.

When I ask them to tell me about their life, one explains that it is their job to find any new plant that starts to grow and to study it.

Seekers have never seen any new creations come forth, only plants. The birthing process is more controlled, as is the dying process. Due to their atmosphere, outside energies do not enter Tandalyn so any new creation is one from the plant itself. They have not experienced illness but sometimes undergo injuries so there are plant mixtures designed to heal.

We on Earth could learn so much from these beings as they make everything from plants and are knowledgeable in the area of essential oils. We have people on Earth who have some of this knowledge but these beings understand how everything for their existence comes from their planet.

When a being from Tandalyn chooses to exit a living life and move to a giving life form (in Earth terms - death by eating a certain plant), a Seeker joins that being and stays with them. They stay until the being has matured into a birthing vessel, a plant, tree or flower.

Seekers enjoy living close to the ground so they create homes like a sweat lodge made from willows. Around the waters is tall grass, four inches wide and up to five feet high. The Seekers use a knife (that the Rotisillica make) to cut it. When it is wet, the grass is pliable but it dries rock hard—like raw hide. Using another plant that just sticks out of the ground like a shoot off a maple tree, they build the shape and design of their home. Some are round and dome shaped, others have peaked roofs like four or five teepees standing next to each other; some are rectangular. The ground is sometimes covered in a soft moss, grass or a polished rock surface. The rock pieces come from Rotisillica. After the structure is built, they cover it with the grass, like a paper mache. If a resident ever wants to change their home design, they re-wet the grass, remove it, and reuse it in the new design. They can also put the used grass in the waters; over time, it will decompose.

It is not a grass eaten by the residents on Tandalyn. The risk of being a Seeker is that Seekers test plants to see which is a food source and what the plant's best use is. Seekers must also ensure the plant is recycled like the tall grass is. Seekers have become ill from eating plants that were not edible; some even shifted from their life form to being a giver.

Seekers are a much-respected race. Most have large eyes but their body types are different. Some are stocky and covered with hair. Some are petite with blue eyes and black hair. Their mouths are tight and they have wrinkles making them look older. All appear to have two legs and two arms with hands and feet although the number of toes and fingers differ. The most attractive is the group that is feminine looking. Their ears (similar to Spock on Star Trek) poke through their straight, blond hair. Their eyes are blue; the ring surrounding the blue is a light blue almost white with a dark center. Their build is lean, yet petite; muscular, yet feminine. There is an air of joy about them. They seem to smile more easily than the other groups. That is what attracts me to them—it is the lightness their presence offers.

I thank them and we shake hands similar to how we shake hands on Earth but embracing the handshake with our other hand. Farin also thanks everyone and reminds them of an upcoming celebration where they will dance and sing to give thanks to Tandalyn for her gifts to them.

I am tired so ask Farin to take me to my room. I excuse myself to rest and gratefully fall into a deep sleep. Reeva greets me with a loving hug upon my awakening and offers me a salad. I wonder if she is psychic. How did she know when I would wake and that I would be hungry?

She smiles and replies, "Yes—not psychic as in seeing the future but a mind reader of sorts."

So she just heard everything I thought! It is not something she just blocks or turns off; it is a constant open flow.

She makes a joke saying that we are never alone with our thoughts.

I think about masturbation and how knowing others were sharing the moment would be uncomfortable.

She laughs again and tells me such things do not happen on Tandalyn but the sensations she just felt from me wishes they did.

We both start laughing and, arms joined, make our way to the dining room. The salad bowl is filled with a mix of greens; there is a purple berry amongst the greens with the flavor of a tomato. Salad dressing is not needed as a small square vegetable full of sweet onion dressing flavors the greens with each bite. Yum! I wonder how I can take some of these back to Earth. I am a vegan and the flavor would really add to my diet.

Reeva says they do not cook food on Tandalyn; *I tell her the raw food people would love it here.*

Reeva offers me a glass of a tree nectar called swoosh and I am in heaven. It is tart like grapefruit but with the flavor of an apricot and is so good. Reeva finds it interesting how I marvel in all the flavors but says she would not be any different on Earth—especially with the masturbation thing. We laugh again but as Farin is approaching, it is time to go and meet the Dwellers.

The Dwellers

As Farin and I walk, I ask Farin how the Dwellers and Seekers are able to travel such long distances and she explains that her race has an air transport system. She will show me later.

The tree Dwellers are not at all what I expect. I was expecting gnome-like beings but these are like stick people. Literally—take a pen out and draw a line, then add on legs and arms and a few lines for toes and fingers. The heads are long stretched-out ovals; their eyes are small black dots and their mouth is a line across the jaw. They stand two feet high; they have no hair. Unlike the Seekers who wear clothes made from flower petals that the Rotisillica weave into fabric for them, the Dwellers wear nothing. Their function is to live within the plants. They are able to feel into the plant, understand its makeup, and communicate with them to ensure their needs are being met. Some of the plants appear to have feelings and require emotional support. Dwellers work with the plants until they can reach a place of joy. This race takes tree talking/hugging to a whole new level! Many Shamans on Earth talk with the spirit of a tree to gain insights on issues they are dealing with. Trees on Earth are interconnected to each other and so information can travel amongst the trees. If you have never tried tree talking I strongly suggest you do; trees vibrate very close to human beings so are one of the easiest items in nature to talk to. From these conversations the Dwellers are also are able to help the Seekers know more about the plants.

The Dweller birthing process is similar to the other races except Dweller seedlings are placed in a tall grass that closes in around it, more like a tall cylinder than a closed rosebud shape. When the grass opens, the seedling does not fall out but stays attached to the grass. When it is ready, it simply walks to its two teachers. There aren't any insects or creatures that could hurt the plants. But if any ever showed up, the Dwellers would be the first to know. Dwellers cannot mind read so they connect with each other's thoughts through the plants' root systems. Just like us tweeting or posting on Facebook, Dwellers can quickly spread news about any subject.

Farin places her hand on a plant and opens herself up to hear the Dwellers' messages. She reminds them of the upcoming celebration and they appear to nod. It is interesting how she is able to hear their message and not the plant's messages. I ask Farin about this and she says that the trees and plants have a signal they exhibit when sharing a message. I look and sure enough, the plant Farin is connected to has two yellow rings near the top of its main trunk just before it branches out; the other trees do not. I love it—a plant-based telephone with a yellow ring tone!

The Dwellers need to return so I thank them and wait until all of them have left, I watch in awe how such fragile-looking beings move with such grace and strength. My next meeting is with Farin's race and she can barely contain her excitement. Off to meet the See-ers.

The See-ers

The images we have of fairies on Earth is how the See-ers of Tandalyn look. The See-ers have slender bodies, pointier than normal ears, a small rounded nose, different lengths and colors of hair and a long oval face with bright eyes that slant slightly upwards. They are between two and four feet tall and have long slender arms and perfectly proportioned hands, legs, and feet. Oh, and *they have wings. I notice that they like to wear shoes, similar to moccasins. This surprises me as they are typically air based. They wear clothing and although there are different styles, their clothing covers their arms and legs (although where the wings are is open). The fabric looks light, similar to silk, yet with a raincoat feel. Farin explains that the clothing is a form of protection against the elements of the planet. The clothing used to just be green but the Rotisillica were able to use flowers to make cloth with different colors and nice textures. So now clothing acts both as a protectant and as a way to show their individuality.*

The See-ers' job is to be in constant awareness with Tandalyn's atmosphere. They also record changes in the atmosphere and look for any patterns. This was the first I had heard of these beings recording anything so I asked how that is done. I was expecting a vault of writings but no—it is recorded through storytelling and dance, similar to a kata in karate. These records are passed down through the birthing plants and through the two dedicated teachers. Three of the See-ers stand up to demonstrate the story of how the Sun disappeared. One narrates, one dances on the ground and one dances in the air.

Before the Sun disappeared, there were strong winds that bent the trees in half, spread the waters wide and caused the air to become filled with leaves and debris (it sounds like a hurricane on Earth but without the rain). The storyteller sings a sad, slow refrain about how afraid they were while the dancers demonstrated the destruction by moving wildly about. The story closes with a song about how the Tandalyn's persevered until the sun returns. There is a change in the dancers; the movements are laborious, slower and very methodical. Then their feet get lighter and there is laughter once again. Everyone starts clapping; this time the group breaks out into a song.

Thank you to the sun in our sky, Thanks to the sun in our sky,

We honor you; we praise your gifts to us, Thank you to the sun in our sky.

Tandalyn we will serve our Tandalyn. Tandalyn, Tandalyn, we will serve our Tandalyn. Thank you, Thank you. Thank you we are here to dance and feel.

Come back some day and say hello for we of Tandalyn will stay.

The energy that comes from this song sung in their native tongue is incredible; I can't help but be overwhelmed with joy and gratitude. I have translated it to share their message. I see how this type of record keeping is very effective for it is not only presents the facts, but the feelings, and state of living as well.

The See-ers live in the upper levels of the trees and in communities of homes. Their homes are made of interwoven grasses that feel like a woven basket. This way they are able to move as the plant or tree they are attached to grows. Most of the homes are square shaped and without doors and windows. Where the night watchers are sleeping, there is a cover, similar to a roman shade that keeps the light out during their sleep times.

The See'ers' diet seems to consist mainly of berries. They also gather nectar from one of the flowering plants that grow higher than most of the trees, as this plants nectar can be made into all kinds of healing tinctures used by the Rotisillica. See-ers use this as an item of trade to get tools and materials to make clothes. It is a way of keeping harmony between the energy of the two races.

How to come Together as a Universe

Farin introduces me to her teachers, Fargo and Tarin. I see now how they get their names. Their names appear to be made up of the teachers' names, in Farin's case it is the F from Fargo and the arin from Tarin. I ask them to tell what I need to know about them that will help bring us together as a universe.

A male See-er stands; his name is Chad. Chad explains how he thinks the universe can learn from Tandalyn.

On Tandalyn, we have four different races; each specialized in our talents but all working together to care for our planet. When faced with hardship, we do not separate. We come together and strategize as a team. Our lives are contingent on our planet's health and well-being. Without our planet, we have no life. Together we work, together we sing and together we celebrate.

When the portals of travel between planets closed, we lost some of the inter-connection of being part of a universal creation-based togetherness. Each race must hold their planet in high regard and focus an intention of love for Creation. Creation is what makes all this possible; it is the base formula that feeds all. Without it, nothing will exist. If every being on every planet held love for Creation, for their planet, for the togetherness of there being more than one race, and love for the learning that can be gained from one another, think of the power that would be created. The universe set this up to happen. That is why there are Wisdom Keepers although it is only now that we can begin to access their wisdom. The crisis of being un-created is bringing out the resources we have not used and it is through this change that we can hopefully save our universe.

I am humbled as I listen. Chad is telling the truth of what we need to do and know. I think of Earth. Do governments discuss how to take care of the Earth; do they ask for the wisdom of the other planets or check into Creation for advice? We have forgotten where we came from and what gave us life. God has become an entity to worship and yet God is in everything. We are creations of God, so yes—we are created in the image of God. We are simply extensions of how that energy manifests on Earth. Tandalyn beings are also in the image of God as are the beings on all the other planets. Whether we call God, God or Creation, or another label, we must come to the place of togetherness in this creation. The commonality within all religions and spiritual practices is the understanding that there is a power greater than us whatever we call this power.

I leave the See-ers energized and ready to continue on my journey. Their awareness has brought me back to the truth of what I am doing. I am carrying the threads of hope in creating a strong safety net that will hold us together.

Q & A with Reeva

Before I leave, I want to spend more time with Reeva to learn about the race that first came into existence on Tandalyn—the Rotisillica. Farin shows me how the transporters used to move the other races over long distances. Made from the same grass the Dwellers use to make their homes, the transporters are woven into a long box shape with harnesses that wrap around the

See-ers' shoulders. Even though they are relatively light, it takes eight See-ers working together to pull them. Farin suggests I climb in and take in the view of Tandalyn from above.

How do I go about describing what I see? There are pools of liquid formed all over the surface, but they are not all the same color. There are shades of green, yellow, and even one that reflects a shimmering blue. The vegetation, from the flowers and plants and trees, is of different heights and colors. Plants gather in groupings so beside one of the pools is a hill covered in purple flowers. On one of the flat areas, there is a field of short grass, the kind you could lay down in and daydream. Everything is blended together with richness and defined textures. I see the Rotisillica Mountains; there is almost a line where the plant growth ends although as we get closer to our landing area, I see plants in the valleys and ledges.

Farin directs me to the path that will take me to Reeva and says she will be back for me in a while; she has some organizing she needs to attend to. I am excited to see Reeva again. Sure enough, she knew of my arrival and has some hot nectar ready. She is also ready to tell me about the Rotisillica. The nice part of talking with Reeva is that I can continue to sip my nectar as everything is communicated telepathically. Interestingly, I am also telepathic at this moment.

Here is what she communicates:

> We are very gifted beings in that we have a high intelligence and are able to fix problems as they occur. We also know what is going on in the other races due to our mind reading ability. Rotisillica love to clean and organize so we create great tools to help us do that.

> When we open ourselves up to hearing another, communicating telepathically is possible. Being in the presence of one with a natural gift often opens that gift in yourself as your mind is able to allow those channels to flow more easily. It is why in group meditation, energy and experiences are so much easier to access.

"Do you feel that could happen planet to planet?"

> It already does, just that those accessing it do not know how to label it and perhaps it is thought to be their own idea as it comes through

the mind channel or what you call the thought process. We are all created from one source so there is this common thread of energy within every being. It is this common thread of attachment that allows the answers to come. Around Earth, there is also an energy body that exists. So there is a constant flow and exchange of information. Humans can attract all kinds of experiences to living before they become energy bodies again. The human energy body is changing throughout the human life as it is experiences and brings to itself all sorts of energy vibrations. A clear mind allows for clear communication. There also needs to be invitation.

"What about aliens on Earth?"

There are aliens or beings from other planets, typically from planets with a similar atmosphere. Lots of beings from Tandalyn stayed on Earth after the portals closed. Some have met humans and so there are races where humans have inter-bred with Tandalyn beings. They underwent the journey to the energy realm and returned to Earth in physical form based on the attraction principle. Tandalyn energy bodies often are attracted to the plant energies and nature energies based on their own memories of their planet but they are unable to take physical form other than in a human form. They are not able to take a form of an animal or plant. Even though they enjoy being with that energy, it vibrates differently. Humans can access the energy bodies and are able to connect to the descendants of Tandalyn or what you call the fairy world. I believe this is how most of the alien beings have come into the human race. Shaman, you have also had the awareness you are an alien, you came from Creation into physical form, you did not come from the human energy realm.

"It is interesting that Earth is the only planet with energy beings from other planets on it."

Earth was the planet beings travelled to as it was about an experience they were unable to have on their own planet. Many also came to help answer questions. On a very rare instance, death will come to combine with the energy body to release it. While that is happening, a new energy body enters and keeps the physical form functioning. Energy bodies are made up of different energy bodies depending on the attraction principle. Some of the great inventions on Earth came from the combination of Rotisillica and human knowledge; it is why you noticed some of the similarities between our world and yours. It would be wonderful if we could find a way for humans to share their knowledge directly with the other planets.

"How can we do that?"

Perhaps there are human beings on Earth that can offer guidance to other planets. But the planets would have to seek knowledge from Earth and I do not believe that happens.

"Is the energy of Earth changing?"

No, it is in your communication that is allowing a shift in this area. Earth is still a very self -focused planet and does not reach out to the information that is available. When more of the human race starts to share their knowledge then it will open more communication lines with the planet beings on Earth.

"Do we need to lose a planet to the dark hole to ensure we continue in existence?"

In my opinion, yes and it should be the planet with the darkest energy so that the dark hole will turn in on itself.

"We have only one planet like that in our universe that I know of."

As you move forward on your journey my dear Shaman, you will hear solutions that will guarantee our future. All the planets are putting faith into our Wisdom Keepers and into a universe that stays united in peace and harmony. I hope the sharing of my knowing and the invitation of telepathic conversations can assist us all as we join together as a universal energy.

As I say goodbye to Reeva, I am apprehensive about the future. Losing a planet, even a planet that destroys to re-birth, feels like we are sacrificing another to guarantee our own safety. How do we know this planet is evil or full of dark energy? It is still fed by Creation; it still has that flowing through it.

I also want to say goodbye to Farin before I leave. Farin is fully immersed in teaching her seedlings how to gather and spread certain pollen found at the tops of the trees. As I arrive, she stops what she is doing and comes over to greet me. We will see each other again soon but it is time for me to return to Creation.

In Reflection

I am back home in my body and wake early to thoughts of sexual and physical abuse that I am sure I heard or read something about before sleeping. I have no idea why these thoughts affect me so; perhaps it is that I feel like the people being victimized are so helpless. All the planets I have visited have pureness and inner connection amongst the beings and yet here on Earth we have such violent energies mixed amongst us. Violence breeds more violence and love breeds more love. The responsibility lies within us to not allow that energy a home in our physical form or in our physical environments.

There is no planet in the universe where humans would not destroy the harmony. We seem incapable of harmony. We develop systems that do not replenish our natural resources. Some humans abuse children and in their innocence they are then brought into the same cycle. We make decisions based on how it will bring ourselves comfort and do not always consider the impact on others or on the environment. Humans are not bad, we are just learning, finding our way. We are aware of abuse and it occurs less than it once did but we still have a way to go in our evolution. I believe it is in the process of this evolution that we will find peace on Earth.

There is a pureness in the other planet energies. Their lives are uncluttered, just living for the purpose of assisting others in the universe. We can do the same. Each of us—each moment, gets to choose. Do we serve others or do we hurt others? Is one right and the other wrong? I do not have that answer. Planet Earth seems to be the planet that is the student and perhaps it is our purpose to allow the other planets the opportunity to teach us. Creation is our school and offers such a wealth of information. Many of us have yet to find our way to school.

Unlike on Tandalyn, we live in a world where we place different values on different currencies. Money is the currency with the highest value. My friend Farhana and I have had conversations about what would happen if our most valued currency was joy. I believe the answer will be revealed as we move through our own evolution. There is a human consciousness that we can draw from and learn from. If we could combine that with teachings in Creation, we could move to a place of one-ness and joy. Tandalyn really shows us the power in harmony that is created when we work together and even trade with each other in fairness for what is given. This is evident by the trading with the Rotisillica for the tools they make. Everyone on Tandalyn serves with his or her natural gift; they love their work. I never heard anyone say, "They owe me!"

Like the beings on Tandalyn, the Wisdom Keepers are a team of beings dedicated to working together, to sharing with one another; they are a power that is complete of the universal energies. This togetherness is what creates the ability to contemplate a solution that will serve all of us universally; I have faith that a solution is going to reveal itself. At least I hope so because if not, this whole process will have been for nothing! No, as I re-think that, that is not true, coming together to learn and love each other anywhere in this universe is greatness and can only bring about more of the same.

Section 9

Merth

(Mer-th)

Rhymes with Earth

"Animals are meant to be cherished and recognized as a human equal. Allowing animals to exist ensures evolution of the races. Love Animals unconditionally as they are Earth's helpers. Balance and harmony are key components to the human existence in the 8th dimension. If a bird sings for you, give back a song. Take from an animal just what you need for comfort, do not over consume."

Henry the Crocodile – Merth Wisdom Keeper

Journey to the Next Planet

Our next planet is Merth and it looks like Tanjay is taking us there. Beena can't wait. I would have liked more time to absorb all the information offered by Tandalyn. I was also hoping to see Archangel Michael or some of my other friends in Creation—guess I'll do anything to get out of working today and I wonder what this resistance is all about. Even as I am climbing on Tanjay, I am lost in thought. Beena seems excited so I ask her what she knows of Merth; she just smiles and says it is a surprise. Tanjay is flying much more aggressively today so I am guessing Merth offers a place of enjoyment for Animal Spirit Guides.

As we pass through the last space portal, we approach a blue-colored planet—much like the color of Earth when viewed from space. Merth's shape is not round but oblong, like a stretched-out circle. I see two suns in the distance. Merth rotates so the suns' rays barely hit the ends of the oblong shape. Again, this is similar to Earth. As we approach, I notice the portal is located just off center grid. I am thankful as I imagine the center would be hot like the Earth's equator but even hotter because there are two suns here.

As I say good bye to Beena and Tanjay, I wonder who or what will greet me on the other side. I walk along a cleared path in the midst of a jungle-like terrain, alert for any signs of danger. As I look ahead, I see Henry—my crocodile Spirit Guide. Tears flow as I run to embrace him. He lifts me up and swings me around; I can't tell you how excited I am to see him. Henry was my first Spirit Guide when I started doing shamanic journeys; I would have never guessed he was a Wisdom Keeper. Even though he was at Boardroom Table meetings, I thought he was there just to support me. And all along he was the Wisdom Keeper for Merth!

Introduction

Merth is probably Beena and Tanjay's home as well. No wonder they were so excited. I wonder if I will also see Shirley. Shirley is a hummingbird I do soul retrievals with. I think that many of my spiritual helpers must come from this planet.

Henry said that I had been to his home before in our journeys and I laughed as I recalled a journey where I dived into the sea and ended up at his place. We danced and a friend visited and we danced some more. Out of all my Spirit Guides I am closest with Henry the Crocodile. It must be our sharing of Wisdom Keeper energy. He laughs as he feels me start to cry again in gratitude.

"Yes" he says, "this is the planet where the animals live. We are not like the animals on Earth, however; we are our own race with our own intelligence. I will explain everything as you explore our beautiful planet."

We arrive at a large body of water, similar to the peacefulness of a lake but large like an ocean. Henry takes my hand and away we go under the water. There is a bright blueness as the suns' rays pass through and under the water; I am amazed at how my spiritual body can breathe easily as I swim deeper and deeper. Henry's house is up ahead; it is simply a doorway set on a stone wall—nothing special, a plain rectangle shape that looks like it is made of stone but lighter in color than the rest of the wall.

There is a two-chamber entrance similar to a submarine's entrance. Henry pushes a button and the water is forced back outside the door until we were standing on a wet floor. There is a grate in front of the other door made of a glass-like substance; we enter the next room still dripping wet. Henry doesn't wear clothes but when he realizes that mine are soaking wet, he offers a soft silk robe to change into. He laughs at my shyness. Not wanting to get the floor wet I change right there. Truly—animal guides seeing me naked isn't all that intimidating. Henry says he will ask one of his friends who lives with him to take my clothes to the surface to dry. I am grateful.

The room I get to work in is off to the right. It is luxurious and filled with all I need to be comfortable during my stay here. I wonder how they brought this bed here; I do not think Henry sleeps on a bed. My puzzled look makes him ask if it is okay. "Yes," I reply. "I am just trying to figure out how you got the bed down here."

"Magic," he says and laughs and walks away.

Before I start work I am going to sleep.

As I awaken, I realize that I have also slept in my Earth body and that once again I am tired because I did not return to Earth to my physical body. I wonder how all that worked for the other beings when travel between planets seems to be part of normalcy. How did we physically travel to other places and how is that we can now only do it energetically? Thinking back to my Earth interview perhaps this physical travel was prior to death coming to Earth when our bodies were a more fluid source. Hopefully Merth will have answers because many of the animal energies present here are also on Earth. It is as if Merth is ready to talk and has been waiting for me. I feel myself entering into the planet's core. Almost instantly I feel closeness, much like with Earth and it dawns on me how much the two names sound alike.

In The Beginning

"Merth, can you tell me about yourself and how you were created?"

As you have determined I am very close in size and appearance to your planet Earth, I believe it is because we are similarly located in the universe. I am just beyond what your scientists are able to see. I follow an orbit path and rotate with the same polarity as Earth except I am a different shape which creates a stronger magnetic force. As you have noticed I have two suns and so I am not in partial darkness as Earth is. We have not experienced the death energy as Earth has although there is a life cycle that happens here. The creation cycle was very similar to Earth's creation; I was a very slow vibrational rock. Creation's energy collided with me and it sent out from my core a blast to my surface.

This caused my surface to crack as I was covered in a hard shell. Under my outer crust was a sandy layer and when that combined with the suns' warmth, plants began to grow. I did not have the same atmosphere surrounding me as Earth did so plants did not last long; the suns' heat would dry them and they would crumble back into the ground layer. This started to change the makeup of the ground layer. Over time new plants developed and became stronger against the heat, but the cycle was just longer not over. This all changed after we collided with a very large meteor. It stuck me and the weight caused some changes in rotation but it would not release. The attached meteor was now in the presence of two very hot suns and its makeup would not take all the heat. It burst into flames and caused even less plants to grow on me.

The energy released from this huge glowing rock brought a liquid to the planet's surface. The liquid continued to grow but the fire rock did not. As the liquid began to form pools, pieces of the rock would break off and fall into the liquid.

Each of these events took place over thousands of years so you can imagine how slow it took to see creations. The house Henry lives in is part of the rock that went under the waters. In recreating itself, the big rock (by breaking off and moving under the liquid or by dissolving into energy) brought about the liquid that covers much of my surface. Once again the plants started to grow; the moisture from the waters kept them from becoming dehydrated. The roots of the plants moved toward the core as they felt the attraction to Source Energy.

Another shower of small rocks hit and covered my surface. Some of the rocks stayed but many seemed to impact and then burn up. The ones that went under the water were like seeds because out of the waters came the animals. This didn't happen all at once but over many years. They came encoded with knowledge and they knew how to live with one another. The animals fed on the water and treated plants as fellow animals. They fed the plants water and some even dug down into the dirt to loosen it so water could get in. Our water feels the same as Earth's water but is much richer in nutrients; all of the animals can survive on the water alone.

My body reaches exhaustion and I tell Merth that I must leave and return home. I will be back tomorrow. Henry appears and takes me back to the surface where I find my dry clothes. He suggests that I am feeling tired on Merth because I am being too serious. I should let myself go a little on my next visit. Perhaps that is what happened on Tandalyn as well.

Beena and Tanjay come to greet me; I forget that this is their home so they do not stay outside the portal. As I settle on Tanjay's back, I am relieved I do not have to take another step.

Day 2 with Merth

Tomorrow arrives and as we return to Merth I ask Tanjay if he is the King of the Jungle on Merth like the lions are on Earth. He says there is no status on Merth; each animal is a miracle in creation. It is what makes it so beautiful. He is happy that I am getting to experience it.

He delivers me to the water's edge and I quickly take off my clothes. There is no point in getting them wet. I enter the waters and swim to Henry's house so that I can continue my talks with the planet. This time I am better prepared.

As I swim through this liquid that I continue to call water, I wonder if this is how Earth's water once was. I am able to breathe underwater as if I am a mermaid—just as easily as I breathe on land. There must be something to that.

At the first entrance I drain off the water and enter Henry's home; I see my robe and I am thankful. I like having something to cover my nakedness.

Henry's home is quite simple in design, like standing in a large cave cavern except there are many lights so it is bright, the lights here are similar to pot lights on Earth. When you enter, there is a landing that is L-shaped. The lower part of the L where you stand is about twelve feet long. In the corner there is a long hallway where the different rooms are located—rooms similar to the one I am staying in. The doors to the rooms are covered in fabric

and each room is textured into the stone—perhaps they were carved out or blown out. From where I am standing, on the bottom of the L is a staircase of about five stairs leading down to a flat surface that looks to be a gathering space. There are large pillows strewn about; I am guessing they are what the animals sit on. And that really is it—no pictures, kitchen table or plants like we would see in our homes on Earth.

I make my way down to my room and crawl upon the bed. I allow myself to fall into the depths of Merth so that I can continue to learn about this planet.

Merth continues right where we left off. All the animals were welcomed—small ones, large ones and all seemed to be able to offer something to the planet. The harmony within Merth is stable; I do not feel an ebb and flow.

"Merth what do you feel about this dark hole?"

It is a danger and yet could also be viewed as an opportunity. To be uncreated could potentially mean a new vibration.

There were many issues discussed in the journey today but it really was more of a personal experience for me. We talked about Spirit Animals. Since I have already explained Spirit Animals in previous writings I did not take notes.

Day 3 with Merth

There is a new excitement in me today as I head back to Merth. Shifts are happening in my energetic body back on Earth. The shifts often affect how I am able to move ahead in my physical life.

The blackness we travel through to reach Merth is incredibly peaceful today. I am not sure how blackness cannot be peaceful. I suppose in some ways it absorbs the energy tossed at it by the voyagers, including me. Merth doesn't take long to arrive at compared to the other planets. I wonder how close Merth actually is to Earth—how similar their energies are and yet how different in so many ways. I imagine how astronauts feel looking at Earth from space. There is a beauty that cannot be described in words as you gaze upon a planet in its wholeness. Merth looks very similar to pictures of Earth taken from space. I see blue from the waters, green from the plants and the varying heights and size of land masses. Today I hope to learn about how all that took place on Merth.

Tanjay delivers me to the water's edge. I have agreed to meet him here later. Because he is one of my Spirit Guides, calling on him is as simple as a thought. I strip off my clothing and dive to enter Henry's place to once again anchor my journey to the depths of Merth. I have this realization that really I have seen so little of this planet. Hopefully there will be some time to explore it.

No one is in the meeting area and Henry's house is, once again, empty. I make my way to my room and allow myself to get cozy as I snuggle under the blankets and prepare myself to travel. There is a core in Merth just like on Earth and so it feels like I am falling as I make my way down into the place of conversation and main connection with Creation. Merth greets me with an embrace of very warm and loving energy waves, a hug with no touching, just the body sensations of one. She starts off by telling me that she would like to tell me a bit more about her surface and land masses as we really haven't talked about this. I chuckle to myself wondering if Merth can read minds. "Does a planet have a mind?"

Merth begins by explaining her polarity. On her planet everything moves in the direction of the western sun, so her rotation on her axis is east to west, or counter clockwise. There is gravity so everything stays on her surface as it does on Earth. I realize how universal gravity is. I have not yet stepped on a planet that does not have an inner pull called gravity. I wonder if it has to do with the containment of our Universe. All the planets are fed by Creation's energy and then return energy to Creation. But if gravity wasn't present before this, would the planets have smashed into one another as they just flew around? Perhaps not as there would not have been any movement because there would not have been an energy field. But even Earth said she had a low vibration—something small would have had to hold each rock mass or planet mass together prior to creation. I wonder what gravity is and ask Merth. There is a pause—almost like this is a question that does not come with an easy answer.

There are different levels of existence and then there is life. Life is when one is adding to itself, moving forward, taking action, evolving. Existence may involve a pattern of movement but it is not evolving, there is no change, it simply is. Creation brought life, change, it ended existence. So yes, gravity did exist but it did not evolve. It continues to exist. Although it is an energy force upon each item within our universe, it has under gone change so it has been affected by Creation. It was simply the glue that held my mass together, kept me on an orbit path. There was not a polarity nor was there light as the suns did not burn. Can you see the difference? I was a piece of solid mass, made up of many pieces and held together by a force we call gravity, I did not move, my surface did not change and everything was contained within my own mass.

As Creation changed my vibrations, it also changed everything around me, so we had suns now in partnership to our planetary travel; we had laws of attraction because other energies dormant could move more freely and would find their ways in motion. Most likely due to our close proximity to Earth, I evolved very similar to Earth.

We are the intelligence behind the crop circles.

Earth's orbital path is much more hectic (or has been) than mine; I am not sure if it is due to having two suns or if my shape allows for fewer collisions. Also I am not surrounded by other planets in my orbit as Earth is. On Merth, we deem Earth as our baby sister and many from Merth have traveled to share wisdom. But due to the death cycle, our members were unable to survive to bring forth the information. Animals on Earth lose their ability to access the consciousness they arrived with but they still maintain energetic auras around them.

I am shaped like a football in comparison to Earth; I move counter clockwise and the suns rotate around me on an orbital path. My polarity switches much more frequently than Earth's does due to my suns' outbursts of energy. When the polarity shifts and my movement changes west to east, or clockwise, it also causes particles of my mass form to shift. On Earth this is mainly done with rock energy but we do not have that on Merth as we have not gone without light.

On Merth the outer surface literally changes in shape in response to the frequency. A frequency of 10800 hertz delivered from our east sun will cause the surface of me to sink inward as if it is catching a really fast ball. In this large hole, it appears that the sides are much higher but it covers such a large portion of my surface that those living in the lower area would not know this. Sometimes the waters flowed into these areas and produced large bodies of water and there were times when land masses evolved from my surface upward. This is how the different pieces of land were formed and it continues today. We do not experience the same atmosphere as Earth so we don't have rain, snow or ice. On my most northern and southern points there really is not much of anything; they are not as affected by the suns' energy burst. When the polarity changes it affects the flow of the waters but there is a pattern for both ways. I have never moved north to south or vice versa. I am not sure I would.

The center belt area of me is the hottest area and the most turbulent as the suns are constantly orbiting around this area. Beings do not live in the center belt or on the North and South Poles. Most of the beings on me live between these two areas. Living in the center area would be like a game of Russian roulette you would never know if you would wake up in the same place tomorrow.

The Beings on Merth

There are different types of animals on me and each of them lives in harmony with each other. Similar types will typically socialize more but I suppose that has to do with size. Imagine a small mouse trying to be in conversation with a giraffe; their living environments and comfort levels are different. Each animal offers a different gift to everything on me. There has never been war, killing, or hurting of any kind. Decisions are made by those chosen to hold that capacity and each decision is looked at by how it will impact the planet first and others second. The animals realize that without a planet, there is no future for them.

Many of the outer consciousness flows to Earth and it comes from the different groups of animals. They see the destruction of Earth by the human race and the destruction of the animals and they are hopeful they can help. The surface of my planet is one of water; water that can feed all the animals and sustain their life. Plants bring about a balance to the energy vibrations of the animals. I suppose on Earth you would call this yin and yang. Here it is plants and animals. The water encompasses both energies and is neutral. The insect world never developed here as it did on Earth either. Yes we have spiders, bees... even an insect similar to a mosquito but they are each harnessed with their own gift. Mosquitoes can transport water to the animals who cannot reach water; many of the smaller beings help in the nourishment of the plants.

"How did the animals come to be?"

Remember the rocks that landed in the waters? The animals evolve and are in constant change.

"Do they reproduce?"

No and yes. Not in the way that you would define reproduction but they do transform and re-birth. It happens in the water; I will explain.

When an animal on Merth gets a calling to return to the waters, it travels to the most center part of the plane (remember the place of no living animals). It then goes into the waters and returns to its original form of a rock as you would call it. The animal does not lose its ability to connect to my consciousness or to the energy it carried when it was in form. It brings in new energies and new teachings as it goes through the process of change in these waters. This can take many rotations to end. When it is time for the animal to re-enter my surface, the waters have moved the rock into a safe position for this to happen. So there is this area of animals moving out from the center and animals moving in. The makeup of the beings on Merth does not include the emotional side that humans have. There is simply this level of acceptance and celebration as a form of pure love. I am sure you have noticed this on Earth within your animals.

"Merth, I need to take a short break and will return, thank you. I am learning so much. Sorry for the break. I sometimes need to re-charge myself in my physical body with food or exercise so that I can be in a strong energy to continue our conversation."

I am back from my short break and, once again, ask questions. "Please tell me more."

On Earth, the animals (through death process) energetically enter the energy realm around Earth. As you can imagine, they do not vibrate at the same frequency as human energy bodies so they go to a gathering place that houses animal frequencies. Earth animals have a level of intelligence but it is not at the same levels as humans. Nevertheless, animals have evolved as have humans on Earth. This happens in the same way in that energies are mixing in the energy realm so new creations, a bit different than the original forms, come to birth into a physical body. There were animals from Merth present on Earth when the portals closed and their energies also mixed upon death and became part of the animal makeup on Earth.

"So how is it that animals from Merth are able to send information through the galaxies and actually cause a physical reaction, like a crop circle?"

The animals on this planet are very familiar with Earth and the many energetics at play there. In a group of Merth beings they visually see Earth's path through her own orbit and they witness energy patterns that are changing on Earth and around Earth. Because there is such a strong energy created on Merth in these visualizations, it actually takes on a life of its own in an energy body and Earth literally attracts it to itself. Once it enters the Earth's attraction field it goes to the place of vibration most similar and interacts with the forms present to reproduce it. It actually holds its own vibrational frequency. There is quite a time lapse between Merth visualizing it and it arriving on Earth. Merth beings believe they are here to assist Earth in compassion as their neighbor. Because of our close proximity we are able to pick up a lot of the energies on Earth and energy bodies surrounding Earth. Each planet I believe has their own way of feeling or interpreting the other planets.

"I am not so sure Merth because I have not seen this of the other planets— only you. So how does this whole spirit guide in the animal realm work?"

Animal Spirits from Merth can travel to Creation and from Creation they can be accessed. If someone wants to know their power animal or spirit animal they call for it. When someone calls for it with the intention of the other person, the animal whose energy matches what is present shows up. By working with what is present you can choose yes or no as to whether that energy is going to work for you.

Often people are not surprised by the animal energies present; the same people are usually not surprised when a psychic tells them what they already know. Some have gifts on Earth and are really tapping into the energies from animals on Merth and therefore they can share the knowledge of what those energies represent. Do not be confused by those who connect with Earth animal energy; remember that energy can be a little different. These people normally are the ones to pick up the dead animal bodies and convert them into usable forms that carry on the use of that physical form.

"My girlfriend was sitting in a car with a friend and a porcupine walked right by the car. Is this Earth animal energy or is this Merth? Is there a difference at this point?"

An animal will often show up in response to the energy present. It is a form of attraction and if there has been a request for a sign, then yes, the universe does deliver. It is a bit of both at play—the request for the sign rises into a stream of communication that is readable by the animals of Merth. A group of Merth animals sense that energy and visualize what they know to be the closest in vibration, a porcupine. The porcupine energy flows from Merth, travels to the place on Earth and attracts a porcupine to the space.

"Okay. So we are talking minutes here not days, hours, or weeks."

Remember time on Merth is not the same as time on Earth.

"Right! So Merth really does appear to be here to serve Earth and its beings."

Yes, there are animals here that care for your planet but for the most part the animals here are in a place of compassion and true love and in that place they see no greater purpose than to serve. They do not have the needs of humans. Animal Spirits are the greatest gifts to humans as you have learned as a Shaman; they should always be explored.

All one has to do is ask and put themselves in a state of consciousness so that the Animal Spirit can hear and read. Yes, sometimes there needs to be another to assist but the purpose is not to see a picture of it; the purpose is to allow that Animal Spirit to teach you. Asking is not enough; it is through having a connection you learn. As the human changes, so does the animal energy. Of course the animals on Earth can connect to Merth animal spirits but it will be of similar energy and it is simply an energy sent, not contemplative wisdom. For animals this may be called instinct on Earth. There is a constant feeding of energy to Earth from Merth in hopes that the animals will evolve in conjunction to the humans.

Q & A with Merth

"It is fair to say that the beings on Merth know what the future is for Earth?"

Let me answer that with a question. Do you know the future when you read your tarot cards?

"No, I can only predict the outcome based on the energy staying consistent."

Correct. So many theories are present on Earth and so many potential outcomes. How do you know which one will be the truth or perhaps another not even presented yet?

You don't.

Every planet has its normal path through its own galaxy and just one change and the entire experience will change. What would happen if, from out of my galaxy, another sun came in and collided with my east sun? It might cause my planet and beings to become something different—either worse or better. I cannot tell you what might happen; I cannot predict that occurrence. Some beings on my planet might begin to sense the energy of the other sun and start to chart outcomes. If I was asked as a planet, I would tell you what I have known to be true in my time of living—this is my solar path and this is what has happened to date.

Does our past necessarily predict our future? No, but it can strongly influence it. I am sure Earth has told you her story and that is all we can know. If the animals see energy in a vision and send it forward, that energy has already once been present and so the past is quite possibly part of the future. Examine your past; learn teachings from your past and take them with as you prepare for the possible outcome. Know that one change in the energy of the current energy exchange and the whole outcome changes. It does not differ from a tarot reading.

"Thank you so much for this insight. Merth, is there any other message you wish to share with me?"

Yes, I want you to understand how important it is to us that you continue this work. We on Merth do not wish to undergo un-creation because of the joy we presently feel. We do not wish to reside in a state of existence; we cannot be of service in that form. Although we accept the outcome of what will be and are in love, we understand there potentially would be a re-birth through the dark hole. Perhaps this could bring about a more united universe, but we feel (as those who are in conscious contact with the energies surrounding our planet) that this is not the desired outcome. We do not serve in being out of alignment with the other planets.

I leave you in gratitude and love.

As I descend back to my room and my body, I am amazed at the teaching I get to hear and receive. Tomorrow I will spend my day with Merth's animal beings. I hope Henry is around.

Gathering of Merth Beings

Tanjay and Beena are waiting for me today. My body has delivered itself to Creation but my mind is still busy on home stuff. Once I focus fully on my mission to head to Merth, I am greeted by Tanjay waving his arms back and forth; he tells me how weird it is when only half of my energy body arrives. I start laughing as I find his arm movements funny and he starts laughing. Imagine a great big male lion laughing! Tanjay asks if I am ready and I say, "Yes." He mentions to Beena that I have finally decided to fully arrive.

Tanjay tells me that many of the animals have gathered for my arrival. Imagine your life purpose as only serving a planet! The beings on Merth's only purpose is to serve Earth. I find this difficult to imagine as so much of what I do is self-focused. They are quite excited that a Wisdom Keeper from Earth is coming. I am starting to feel like a celebrity although I suppose I too would want to know how it looks from the other side. I hope I can answer their questions. I don't watch the news or read newspapers so I am feeling very uneducated in this moment.

Beena is sitting on my nose looking me straight in the eye. "Hello!" she is yelling. I must have been in really deep thought. I see Merth already coming into view. I wonder if humans could travel here ever—now that's a scary thought!

Henry is there to greet us and is humming with excitement. We all walk down another walkway from the portal; it does not take us to the water but instead to a very grand canyon—twenty times the size of a football stadium and much deeper. It is filled with every kind of animal you can imagine. I wonder how in heaven's name I am to get to the stage located in the middle.

Just as I am wondering, I remember that I travel on a lion that flies. What I also realize is that there is enough energy present visualizing me on stage that as soon as I focus on the stage, I am there. Henry, Tanjay and Beena arrive with me and find a space at the front. I really feel like a celebrity now. It is exciting to see so many animals and even animals I have only seen in pictures, like a white tiger. Not knowing what else to say, I look all around and say, "Hi."

My voice echoes loudly as if it is magnified by microphones but there aren't any. The animals are quiet as if awaiting some great speech. I am so unprepared. I thank them for their incredible welcome and tell them about my last days and interviews with their planet. Sharing my amazement and gratitude for all they do. "I am brought to tears as I share this, if only we as a human race could embrace the pure love each of you have and give." I tell them about my mission to visit each of the planets to join us together as a universe, to work together consciously—not only to avoid the dark hole approaching us but to continue this action forward to hopefully a new and exciting togetherness.

For some reason I start to think about Star Wars. Wasn't that the mission of those warriors—for the planets to all work together? I chuckle to myself as I realize this is not a new desire, just a different form. I explain my chuckle to them by explaining a book and then a film on Earth; they love technology. I then explain that although technology is good on many levels, it can also be bad.

I decide that I have shared enough of my journey here and invite questions from the audience or information that anyone would like to tell me about Merth—their life or relationships. We can learn from each other.

A turtle halfway up the canyon stands and yells out his name; it is Izah. He asks me if we humans are preparing for the movement of the waters (if they should move). I tell him I cannot answer for the entire human race but I am sure as humans are brought into awareness, they will take the proper precautions. I tell him about YouTube, twitter, Facebook, cell phones, instant messaging, computers, plus the many electronic devices I currently own like an iPod! Radio, telephone, fax and television seem antiquated compared to all these new ways of communicating on Earth. The point I am trying to make with him is that even in areas where these devices are not readily available, there normally exists some sort of communication that will get the word out. I then tell him about the Teenage Mutant Ninja Turtles and how popular they were with young children. Izah laughs and does a few karate moves, even jumps up and does a quick back flip while the entire audience roars with laughter. One moment we are discussing the fact that Earth waters may move and the next moment we are laughing hysterically over a turtle doing karate moves. Life is so wonderfully light when it is not bogged down with human stuff.

The next animal that stands up is behind me. Not even looking at it, I can feel the gentle energy it sends out. I don't quite recognize this animal. I hear a soft laugh as she gracefully stands on all four legs; she was not standing prior. Did you guess her? She is a giraffe, not exactly as we see them here on Earth. Her legs are thicker but everything else is the same. Her name is Kaleena.

She asks, "We feel so much fear coming from the planet Earth and we have never felt this much fear before. Are the animals afraid too or are all these energy waves coming from the humans?"

I respond, "Kaleena, if you follow the fear consciousness, where will it lead you?"

"Typically it will lead us to a place where there is suffering of some sort by a group of people whose energy beats stand out more."

"Are there animals in the area of those fear bursts?"

"No, typically there are very few."

"Kaleena, I do not know the full truth to your question, but I do believe the animals on Earth live by instinct—by a closer connection to our planet and the energy vibrations, especially the animals that are not dependent on humans for food and shelter. They have keen senses. I believe many of these animals would not be in fear as they would have removed themselves from danger. The biggest threat to the form life of an animal is typically a form human. I am sorry I cannot fully answer your question, but I do believe that your ability to follow energy streams may help Merth gain a better understanding."

An ostrich is next. Now why do I automatically assume this animal is female? The size of him is half the height of the giraffe, much bigger than any ostrich I have ever seen. His name is Sam. The planets and their beings do not speak English and in their tongue I am sure the name Sam sounds much different than it would in English. But as the beings speak their language it converts in my mind to English and when I speak to them I am able to speak in their tongue. I am not sure how this happens and if you asked me to demonstrate what their language sounds like, I couldn't. Sam asks if the crop circles are educating humans enough.

I reply. "They are different interpretations as to what they are. Not many see the ones in the sand and even less see the ones under the water. There is some guess work that happens trying to connect the symbol to current events. Geometry in our culture is not as present as it once was. Is there a way to help clarify the energy of a crop circle from Merth?"

Sam doesn't answer right away. He is unsure as crop circles are based on the energy forms on Earth in response to the energy wave sent forth.

"Communication of words would be impossible within the circle but perhaps we could send the message onto the Earth Wisdom Keeper to deliver through your communication methods. Shaman, can we send the message with Henry to deliver to you?"

Not wanting to be fully responsible with such a task I answer this way. "You can, but will this work with our time being different and do you not produce many crop circles a day?" (When I say day I am referring to an Earth day.) "Perhaps another planet can assist this?"

Sam says that on behalf of Merth he will contemplate a solution.

How incredible! He is not contemplating a problem; he is going to simply contemplate a solution. He doesn't even question if there is one; he goes into contemplation believing there must be. That is a definite practice my Earth life can use.

I decide to ask a question. "Can someone tell me what it is like to be a power animal for an Earth human?" I know what it is like for me but I wish to know the other side.

A black bear known as Keg stands up. "It is an honor and one we all enjoy. Imagine being one of us in a position to serve Earth and you end up being called to guide a human in their own journey. It goes from an experience that is deeply moving to an experience that is intimate. You can feel the smallest of movements. It is over-the-top joyful. I get to witness a miracle. Power animals and animal spirit guides are positions of love for us all."

We all sit in silence after Keg's response. I am caught up in this feeling of the love for each other. Wow! It is so powerful how all these beings and I can become one force using the power of love. I am sure all this energy is just sending waves of goodness to wherever it goes from Merth. We sit in this state for some time until Henry comes and stands beside me; he announces it is time for a closing song.

Is there a planet anywhere where music of some sort does not exist?

First there is stomping and then clicking and then clapping. A flock of birds break into a whistle and then a flat instrument is played by the monkeys.

It is similar to a guitar sound. The last to join in is the beat made on many different items from rocks to just sticks across sticks. Finally there is the singing. What they call singing, we would call humming. Have you ever listened to a song and every part of your body feels happy—that is vibration to your cells and all worries disappear and you feel lost into the sound, mindless? That is what I am feeling and I love it. When the song is complete I find myself not wanting to leave.

I know Archangel Michael has called a board meeting but I am in so much delight. Henry tells Beena and Tanjay that he will take me back if they want to stay. It has been so long since I have felt Henry in this way, I miss him. He laughs out loud and tells me to stop all those sad feelings; he has simply allowed me to grow past all the teaching he brings to access other streams of learning—plus he is always there and can be called upon.

Upon our arrival at Creation, Archangel Michael is waiting to greet us. The beings around the table are now a part of my life in a much more intimate way than before. I am looking forward to our embraces at the close of the meeting. Henry and I follow Michael to the Boardroom Table and the meeting starts with me overviewing my time since we last met. The meeting is to convene again tomorrow.

Meeting of The Wisdom Keepers

As my Spirit Guide Tanjay nudges me to Creation in energy form, my cat Chewy comes and nudges me as well. I am so surrounded by the love of animals. I find I have a whole other appreciation for animals after my time on Merth. Enough wasting time! Tanjay looks as if he is going to explode if I don't get going; he is going with me today. Everyone else has gathered and is awaiting my arrival.

Michael embraces me and reminds me I forgot to place an energetic dome around myself this morning, but all is okay. I have been asked to perform this task twice a day, once when I awaken and once before I go to sleep. It involves imagining a circle that encompasses my entire body, (mine is egg shaped) then filling it with a color and setting an intention of what you want this dome to do. So I use the color purple and I set the intention that all that comes to my dome energetically that does not serve me will bounce off and return to the rightful owner and all negative energies put *out by myself will exit my dome as healing energy. It is a way of protecting me from other people's energies and since thoughts are energy, this keeps me secluded in a space that moves with me to deal with my own thinking. Anyone can do this exercise at any time.*

I know that we have business to attend to but I want to spend time together with each Wisdom Keeper. Perhaps there will be time afterwards for some one-on-one chit chat.

To my left from the south end of the table is Kathleen, next is Archangel Michael, Archangel Raphael, Archangel Gabriella, Henry the Crocodile, Farin The See-er, Leema from B'Nai, group of Four Stone-looking Mounds from Duncan, Lord Metatron from Keena, Daniel and then me. Michael gives us an update on the dark hole.

It appears the dark hole is continuing its path towards Creation but is no longer lined up to encompass Creation. The question is—where is it heading to? The other questions each of us express. Where did it form from and will this be a regular occurrence in our future?

Leema communicates telepathically that B'Nai beings feel a stronger closeness with the other planets when they connect with my energy body. Duncan representatives take the shape of four shorter monks in red robes with the hoods up and they feel the same thing. Lord Metatron says that the light beings on his planet also enjoyed my visit and found they wish to share and learn from the other planets. What I learned was that each of the Wisdom Keepers had been doing the same as me and so we all were experiencing the same feeling of intimacy. There is one planet none of us can visit unless we do not wish to return. Sadly this is just what it is. The Rotisillica have suggested we offer Krevat to the dark hole.

As this is announced, I realize the deeper meaning behind this suggestion. Krevat creates by destroying. If they wish a new creation, one is ended. The Wisdom Keeper from Krevat has communicated the beings wish this to be different. They have examined Earth as a potential opportunity but as

Earth's Wisdom Keeper, I don't think any Earthling would choose that type of life. If Krevat went into the dark hole, would its natural ability to destroy also destroy the Black Hole and follow a re-birth of their planet? Perhaps all would be served in having the Black Hole consume Krevat. Perhaps the one part of our universe that Creation created could be our miracle. Krevat desires a life, desires a relationship with others and yet each day this desire is destroyed and re-born again through the new race. Perhaps the unknown energy of the dark hole would offer that to the planet Krevat. I understand why Reeva, a Rotisillica suggested it. It was not in dislike or judgment; it was in compassion for that planet's loss. I see others nodding in agreement.

Even though the theory of this seems appealing, how could such an act transpire? Would the beings be in agreement on Krevat? How can we in Creation talk with and meet with their Wisdom Keeper who seeks to destroy and still be safe? Archangel Michael thinks he could go with a band of strong energy angels to the portal that would extend to Krevat. They could put up a dome to protect themselves and when the Wisdom Keeper arrived there could be a discussion.

There is some fear felt around this suggestion but it had been done before when the Krevat Keeper had just arrived. They are able to also maintain a level of control as well. It is agreed Michael will do this and it is also agreed that each Wisdom Keeper on their planet will contemplate how to move the dark hole to our place of choice, if it is even possible. I ask if any of the other Earth Wisdom Keepers have connected and am disappointed to hear the same answer as before—No. We break by saying a bond of friendship chant. Again the language is known to me deep in my heart and yet I seem to be unable to write it here. Hopefully one day I will be able to share it because it is so beautiful. After kissing and holding each other in warm loving embraces we each depart going forth to our next new adventure occurring in our life as a Wisdom Keeper.

Tanjay

Tanjay appears to want to speak to me so I joyfully walk over and hug him, letting him know he has my full attention. "Do I ever grow tired of walking through my journey world, the place I call Creation?" "No. It is all the beauty found on Earth displayed into a very easy landscape for me to follow."

Tanjay and I head for the ridge along the top of a canyon; there are flowers that fill the one side of the canyon and the rocks and layers of dirt that line the canyon are like the colors you see in Sedona ,Arizona—a deep red with mixes of some lighter shades to give it depth and texture. I lay on the ground and Tanjay rests his head upon my chest. Maybe he has more in common with my house cat than I realize. He doesn't speak but I see a tear flow down his hairy face and I know whatever he is about to share is not going to feel that great.

I look into his dark golden eyes trying to see a hint of what he is about to say. The name Beena escapes my mouth and

he says, "No, she is fine."

I sit up and hug him for all I am worth. I hate to see my big lion cry and find myself also crying and not yet knowing why.

"You know Shaman, I love you. Each of us is given a task to fulfill and when that is done we must open our hearts to the next adventure present."

"Yes, I know that. Tanjay, I say quietly. Are you leaving?"Imagine two large paws holding my face with a big lion nose on my forehead as I sob, now hard.

He whispers, "Yes."

"No!" is all I can get out. I can barely breathe as I am taken with grief. "My Lord I will miss you Tanjay."

He also is sad— it is not due to attachment or feeling of a death, it is the hole that will be felt, a hole that has been filled by each other's love. I know I have survived this before, once I lost an eagle and a raven to the wind to save a soul of another. Many moons later I got to see them and embrace a deep heart connection that never really goes away. Intellectually I know that a new guide may come as Tanjay did, but in this moment my heart hurts.

My Earth body is now crying and sobbing uncontrollably. I think about how my close friends or my husband would think I am crazy in this moment. Can you imagine answering the question of why you are sobbing and you have to reply that your lion Tanjay is leaving you?

Who makes these decisions anyway? Maybe my human Spirit has more attachment than I care to admit. This is all I can write about this. I need to spend my last moments together with Tanjay. I return to Earth as this transition concludes.

After hours of crying I am too tired to cry anymore, Tanjay is preparing to go. I ask if he is returning to Merth and he replies that yes that is his home. We know we will see each other again.

I smile through my tears knowing that if he can love me that uncondi-tionally, he will also do incredible acts on Merth and ultimately incredible acts of service here on Earth. I know that Merth beings are here to support us Earth beings and I have felt incredibly loved and supported by all the animals in my life.

Namaste Tanjay, I will love you always.

In Reflection

The first thought that comes to my mind as I prepare to write this summary is a story that Dr. Wayne Dyer tells about seeing a zebra that had its back leg eaten off and there it stood eating grass without a care in the world. To me this story really demonstrates the pureness in an animal, the simplicity and the trust in instinct. Something happened to cause this zebra to escape and after one heck of a work out, it simply took the time to nourish its body with some grass. If that had been a human that came that close to being another's lunch, there would have been one heck of a story to be shared and I doubt they would have been conscious of their body at all, they would be lost in their mind going over and over the details. Dr. Dyer has used this example in his teachings and is another way an animal gave of itself to help many. Pay attention, the animals are here to teach us.

Animals keep it simple, yes they have a mind and they use it to make decisions based on their instincts and past experiences. Humans have learned and used the animals for their own welfare, their own survival. When I reflect on Merth and take into account all that animals are doing for us in our human form, I am filled with complete gratitude. I no longer see myself as separate from them but can relate to how we are all interconnected as extensions of

Creation in living motion. Take the time to admire the ant that carries our crumbs to feed a colony but cleans up a mess, or the raven that picks up the garbage left out. Even the mosquitos, although pesky, serve our world. There is a whole cycle of life that each animal contributes to and if we delete an animal we cause more than one change, we create a whole new evolution for that species and others to follow. Something needs to be said about nature and letting it do what it needs to do without our human interference.

Open your heart to your Power Animal, allow Merth to teach you through this guide. Find your Animal Spirit Guides—it is in the searching they will appear. These acts will bring about awareness and awareness brings knowledge and knowledge brings clarity. Integrity is gained when we are clear about who we are and what we desire.

Looking back at my travels to Merth I realize how lucky we are to have animals surrounding us on Earth and to have animals supporting us from Merth. Can you stroke your cat or hug your dog the same way after understanding that their purpose is simply to love us unconditionally? They teach us about ourselves from a place of no attachment. Can we offer the same back? If not, then who truly is the caretaker? My little Maltese, who has since passed, brought me joy on our walks and then curled up beside me soothing my hurt moments. I have come to appreciate the choices available to me as a human and would not trade my life for an animal's. But Merth taught me to have a deeper appreciation of the other beings existing on our planet and to come to a full understanding of how they are a representation of the energies that surround us.

If I can bring one message from my time on Merth, it is to fully feel gratitude for the gifts that animals offer—honor them as your equal, and treat them with the respect and appreciation they deserve. Bring the animal gifts into your awareness and make them part of your ongoing ceremony called life. Learn to be like the puppy who greets you after a hard day of work, the one who gets all excited just to see you again—loving you unconditionally.

Listen to the meadowlark's melody reminding you to sing sweetly. See the hawk perched on a fence post and remember to focus. Recognize the butterfly that flitters in front of you and then stop and notice the simple beauty in your surroundings. Ask yourself, "If I was giving this gift, how would I want it received?" And then receive these animal gifts in the same manner.

Section 10

Izshelong

(Is-sha-long)

"Eat black rocks, just kidding! Renew your body by giving it what it needs daily. Everything you need is within your grasp. I wish humans would reach out to us more, to use their own natural gifts of communication but also to recognize through use those that communicate. If you cannot use the spiritual telephone to gather your information, find someone who can and will teach you how. Humans complain too much, seek change to that which you complain about, be a part of the solution. To complain and do nothing is wasted air."

Kathleen – Izshelong Wisdom Keeper

Journey to the Next Planet

As I enter the dance that takes me to the journey world, I am greeted by my friendly neighborhood spider, Beena. Meeting with her is always a joyous occasion and I am always excited to travel to the next destination. But this time traveling takes much longer. I lose count of the portals that open allowing us to enter another part of the universe.

We are not close to Creation and are far from Earth and Merth. This planet consists of twelve pieces of floating land or perhaps rock masses—similar to Earth except in between the landmasses is air, not water. There is an energy ring around the planet and—not to sound too weird—the ring encompasses the colors of a rainbow, each layer progressively darker as it moves to the dark purple-colored outer edge. Six landmasses about the size of New Zealand float independently; one landmass is about one-and-a-half times bigger than the others are. Four landmasses are located in the center of the encompassed space. We are heading to the piece of land located to the east of the landmasses.

Meeting the Wisdom Keeper

As I travel through the portal, I am surprised to see my Spirit Guide, Kathleen. I always thought she was a descendant from Earth. Her energy feels like the love I felt from my great grandma so I had always thought Kathleen was my grandmother in disguise. I am once again aware of how other beings openly accept and love us. Would we do the same for them? Even if we did, I am sure we would question the whole experience. We talk about this and the plans for the days to come before I make my way back to Creation.

Today we are on our second trip to Grandma Kathleen's planet. You would never guess that the planet's surface is suspended in space; it feels solid. The

rock that covers the ground is the color of shale with the texture of bark chips; it gives way like sand. Is there such a thing as rubber rocks because these rocks have a bit of flex to them like rubber? Desert-like vegetation pokes through the rocks. Groups of trees like bamboo shoots grow together. The colors are not vibrant as on other planets; the trees and foliage are dark green and sandy brown. There is something universal about plants, especially on the planets that represent or are represented on Earth. I do not see anyone or anything but am instinctually drawn down the path; trusting this inner guidance.

Up ahead, there is a stairway; it looks as if the ground opened up for it. The stairway is at least ten feet wide; the treads two feet deep and the risers about one foot high. I have an image of walking up a grand staircase to a Tibetan monastery, except I am going down. The opening I just entered through closes but it is not dark. A beautiful natural glow emanates from the walls; it feels warm on my skin. I see Kathleen at the bottom of the staircase.

In my past journeys to Creation, Kathleen lived in what appeared to be a castle with shiny gold doors; inside it was almost cave-like. There was a room made with quartz crystals. This descent feels like I am entering a similar home and I wonder if there will be a quartz room here as well. My mind wanders and Kathleen asks me to focus on why I am here. It's this boldness and honesty that I love most about Kathleen.

Together we walk through a tunnel. There are lights (twenty-four inches long and six inches wide) positioned along the walls—enough light to walk in but not enough to read anything. I mention that I am always amazed at how imaginative each planet is.

Her way of expressing thanks is one word, gratitude.

Curiosity is an interesting attribute; it allows the mind to investigate what it does not understand. Curiosity and luminosity are paired partners; a questioning mind is a mind able to dream new possibilities.

We reach the entrance to Kathleen's home. As soon as I enter, the bed wins and off to sleep I fall

I awaken to the smell of chai tea with a strong cinnamon aroma. Kathleen smiles as I enter the kitchen; it is a smile full of compassion, gratitude and wisdom. She places two cups of tea on the table.

The table is an oval rock slab but the edges are not smooth. It's like it was just picked up and placed on a pedestal made of the same stone. Our chairs are rocks cut in half giving the bench a smooth top. I am amazed at how much beauty can be created from stone.

The orange-colored floor is like pea gravel with something poured over or mixed in so that it is hard, like a floor tile on Earth. The kitchen is U-shaped; we sit at the open end of the U. At the rounded end is a stove that looks much the same as the rest of the countertop only darker. The counter top sits on top of a solid square stone about four feet off the ground. There are no cupboards. A pottery container of what I am guessing holds loose tea sits against the countertop wall.

I ask about the kitchen.

The dark area, what you would call a stovetop, is a type of stone that, when something is placed on it, gets hot. It cools off after it reaches a certain temperature so you have to move the pot if you need it hotter. The main resource on this section of the planet is stone; plants are very limited and do not grow back quickly. There is a plant similar to a cactus, like the tall ones with all the prickles that grow in Arizona. This plant is full of milky-white liquid that alleviates hunger. It is what the tea is made from.

The leaves are gathered from different plants including the roots of two plants that reproduce quickly. One plant is similar to ivy and grows on the ground; the other is more like a Saskatoon Berry bush. The berries provide the flavoring for the tea; the bark enhances the flavor and aroma.

"Kathleen, I don't know your planet's name."

Izshelong.

"How do you travel between rock masses?"

We do not travel. The wind currents between our landmasses do not allow that to happen but we communicate through telepathic communication. The strong wind currents hold us together.

Shaman friend, I must leave you for a while; please make yourself comfortable.

I decide to go back to Creation.

Shamanic Interval

Friends who know of my journeying process ask me how I know when it is time to return. It is nothing more than a feeling of knowing I am complete, like when you go to a museum, you know when you are done. When I am not journeying, I am a mom with two young children so I return to that role. Sometimes there is so much information to be absorbed that I fall into a deep sleep upon my return. I need to integrate the information and the sleep state allows that to happen. My body has learned to keep this sleep time to a minimum.

Day 2 with Izshelong

I am excited to be traveling back to Izshelong to learn how the planet came about. I arrive at Kathleen's just as she is sitting down to lunch. I help myself to a cup of tea and, like an excited grandchild, tell her everything I have been up to. Kathleen has some healing work to do and so, after chatting, I am left to interview Izshelong.

I get the feeling that Izshelong is very feminine, gentle, and welcoming. I find myself starting to go down what feels like a funnel cloud—riding the outside wall round and round. Slowly I am falling to the starting point of this whirlwind. Once I stop spinning and start to feel grounded, there is a rush of sensation like someone gently tickling me with a feather. With each stroke, I feel a blast of love, it is almost orgasmic. A vortex of energy spins lightly around my feet but yet does not cause me to feel off balance. I am lost in the sensation and am startled when I hear Izshelong's voice echo through the vortex.

"Hello Shaman."

She waits as I find a place to sit.

What do you think of my beautiful self?

"I am intrigued by the creation of different landmasses held together by an invisible source, floating freely."

Yes, the energy of wind does work for me.

"Izshelong, tell me about you. I want to understand how you came to be."

In the Beginning

As you can imagine, I was not always made of different landmasses. I was once a solid mass. My vibration was very low and when Creation was ignited and sent out those first bursts of energy, I was sparked. All that I was, exploded into landmasses. The explosion created a wind current that continued to flow around each land mass and within that wind is the energy made up of my originating planet. It holds the landmasses together like a magnet and creates a powerful barrier between space and me. Anytime space debris comes near me, it is propelled back into space. This has limited new energy entering my planetary space. If you look up, you will see what looks to be a cloud covering, but this is actually a layer of what I am made of floating around me. The light that falls upon me comes from four planetary pieces that exploded from me and stay outside this cloud covering. They are in a constant storm condition, but due to their existence, I am able to support life.

The planetary pieces are a heat and light source similar to Earth's Sun except their mass is composed of the same substance as my form. After the blast that sent them out of my atmosphere, they attracted an energy that continues the cycle of storms. These storms produce a kinetic energy that heats and expels light waves and allows plants and herbs to flourish. These plants and herbs have high levels of vibration energy so Izas are essentially re-birthed in energy when they eat them. Iza live underground because of the storms. The winds that create the energy that binds us together can also destroy us.

"How did the Iza come to be?"

When I was in my beginning stages, fires from the impacts of other space masses would burn on my surface. One meteor shower pelted pieces of itself all over my surface and started many small fires that burned a color of blue and green. The smoke from these fires caused a new cloud covering that contained the smoke. As the fires continues, the cloud covering grew. From the smoke of each fire, a shadowy form emerged, able to float and move upon the wind currents—similar to what you call ghosts. Each fire produced a being. When two beings collided they would create a fire. This went on for a very long time. Just as the meteor shower produced the fires, another shower of rock contained a liquid that escaped with each impact. The liquid touched my hot surface and evaporated into steam. The steam combined with the fire smoke beings and the smoke beings were transformed into something new. At first, it appeared that the smoke beings were destroyed and nothing would ever exist on my surface, but time brought about new opportunities.

Not all the rock pieces containing liquid exploded, they cracked. Instead of evaporating, the liquid leaked into the ground. Energy from the suns penetrated into the liquid and created plants. Then one of the suns' exploded and a wind of energy swept over me. It was warm and very strong. In its wake it energized the fallen smoke form; they emerged with a body. The forms they took are how they look today; there is no infant-to-adult stage in the Iza race. There is not death but there are times of sickness, typically caused from bad food.

It was as if the beings had a previous knowing, as they seemed able to start swimming immediately. Each day the Iza consumes the tea that re-births them. If you noticed, Kathleen leaves after she drinks her tea. This is because she enjoys being alone while her form re-establishes itself. If an Iza goes without the plant energy, it will start to lose its form (similar to a dehydration process) and turn into a form resembling a piece of black coal. The form can be brought back to life by pouring herbal tea over it; otherwise, it will remain dormant for a very long time. There is a celebration each time an Iza is found and brought back.

"Izshelong, what do you mean by swimming?"

I forgot to mention the waters. Other than wind, there are not a lot of weather changes on my surface but there are changes beneath my outer surface. Below my surface there are frozen pockets of liquid. After the initial blast from Creation, huge holes were left. These holes were filled with small, amber, almost see-through rocks brought in by the wind. This caused a change in the wind currents and how the wind moved around my surface. Later, a shower of a softer substance, similar to the consistency of slush but thick like tar, came. It also flowed into the holes and again altered the wind currents. The black tar substance hardened like top soil. The fires, which you already heard about, caused the amber rock below my surface to liquefy. The Iza swim in this liquid. It is also a food source for them.

It is time for me to return to my Earth body. "I will return soon, Izshelong. Thank you."

Shamanic Interval

Back on Earth, changes have occurred and I seek spiritual help. The role of a Wisdom Keeper is not easy physically or emotionally. My friend Susan pulls my spiritual side back into my body and works on the healing needed to keep me focused. Farhana keeps my emotional side in somewhat of a normal pace. When I drop into depths of despair, she pulls me up, or from the heightened levels of panic, she brings me down, I feel so blessed. Farhana has cleared the path as she has written her own book and has taken the road to publishing and marketing. Susan also has cleared the path to being strong by staying true to her purpose and grounded in her Earthly body. Yesterday, through my friend Tammy, I met Sarah, a healer. Sarah brings awareness about my spiritual health. I have three entities within me that I am holding onto. An entity is not like another soul, but an energy residing within the body, causing imbalance. Since life on Earth is about attraction, then something in me is attracting these entities. You have to wonder why you would hold energy that does not serve your greater good. This morning, using the power of true love and a vision of white light, I start the process of releasing them.

I am going back to what Earth shared with me about form + form+ energy. Through Archangel Raphael, I received guidance that will give me more endurance and strength. If I accept this new way of living, I will be able to experience more opportunities but I might also suffer health consequences.

I signed up for zumba classes but on the first night my legs cramped and I chose not to go. I was afraid of looking stupid, afraid of being in pain. Each time I move away from these experiences, I feel more alienated from a life of freedom and physical strength. So what was attracting the leg cramps?

I need to get rid of the energies that are holding me back. By filling myself with true love's light and energy and by following Raphael's guidance, I am going to change the energy forms. I have an army of power to help me accomplish this task. Thank you to Colin, Tammy, Val, Farhana, June, Christine, Merry, Louise, Judy, Teresa, Christina, Marilyn, Amy, Sian, Tim, Heather, and Nancy. To my son Jeremy, thank you always for the clarity and encouragement you offer. Others guard the outer parameters that I connect with as I continue this mission of bringing Creation's message forth and facing the dark hole. We humans are blessed in that we can bring in energies that surround our planet. However, we can also get stuck if we blindly cruise through life. If we do not constantly check on what is being created, we could co-create what is not wanted.

Creation's Message on Bankruptcy

An example of co-creating something not wanted is bankruptcy. A friend asked for insights from Creation as to whether they should claim bankruptcy. As I enter Creation's realm, Beena greets me. I explain that I would like to talk with the other Wisdom Keepers about my friend's financial situation. Archangel Michael says there is a guide best suited for this.

Arielle is wearing a long white dress; her chestnut-colored hair flows over her shoulders. Her sea-green eyes are warm and loving; her ears are round and small; I smile as I realize my friend's ears are similar. Arielle moves with such feminine grace, almost floating as she approaches me. On her head is a golden crown—a band around her head about an inch or so wide with a point in the center where it widens down onto her forehead. There is a ruby held within the center above the point. Her embrace is reassuring and full of warmth and together we make our way to the grassy hill that overlooks the sea.

"Arielle, my friend seeks advice about claiming bankruptcy. Bankruptcy seems like the best option but she also holds doubt that this is the right path. Can you offer a guiding message?"

My love, Earth has a funny way of trading amongst the people. If an animal is starving due to a lack of food supply does it surrender to the lack or does it search out new resources. Does a tree ask the soil for more water during a drought? No, it digs its roots deeper and seeks what it needs to continue its existence. Each tree chooses an environment that will support its existence. Your friend is a tree that keeps asking the same soil to provide but the soil is unable to do so. It is time for your friend's roots to go into territories beyond what is currently supplying her. It is in the depths of discovery, that she will find a new source of energy.

"How does this relate to bankruptcy and money?"

Money on Earth is used for exchanging. The tree takes the nutrients from the soil and produces shade and beauty and cleans the air. It does not take from the soil with no exchange. If a tree took from the soil and then said to the soil, "I am unable to repay you for what you have given," what would happen to the soil? A tree returns what it has taken from the soil when it hibernates; it produces leaves that the soil replenishes itself with.

"Arielle, I am finding the whole tree example hard to follow."

That is because you expect harmony to take place in nature. Your friend has taken from the soil, used its resources to flourish but has not returned nutrients back to the source of the soil. There is an imbalance. Claiming bankruptcy will not bring about a balance; it will leave the soil depleted. Trading has not been upheld.

"She does not have resources to return."

So she then has fallen to inadequacy of trading. Trees sometimes suffer times where the rain does not return to the tree what is owed; the trees existence depends on many variables. The tree produces moisture into the air and rain takes that moisture and returns it to the soil. If the rain claimed bankruptcy, the tree and the soil would suffer. Bankruptcy fixes the shortage for one but it affects all those taken from.

"But bankruptcy can allow the person feeling trapped to now expand, free of those debts, free to move forward on their mission. It clears the slate of financial pain."

I disagree. I believe it covers up the issue. If the rain withheld giving of itself, it would do so in the belief that the tree is not going to continue its cycle. Claiming bankruptcy means you have a belief that there will not be a flow to assist you out of the situation so you withhold what you owe and stop the cycle of flow to that what once supported you.

We know that a tree will adjust itself to a drought and continue to provide for the rain so the belief held by the rain then is false. If the rain cuts off the needed water flow, as in the clearing of a person's financial slate, then the rain is now free to find resources from another area, and yes, it also will give to a new area. But accountability to the old area will be gone. It leaves the past debt (or in this example the tree) to either work harder to find new resources or die in the lack of not receiving. The flow of what once was is stopped.

Finding a new way to exist in the current conditions is how the nature of a tree works. If it has to work with reduced water resources from the rain (due to the rain being unable to return the same fullness), it does not withdraw from the cycle but adjusts what it gives. The tree will change if it cannot find another water source. The tree depends on the soil and the soil depends on Creation's energy. It is the tree that changes the alchemy of the soil for as the form changes, so does the creation. If the soil changes form in the sense of its nutrients, then the tree also must change. Each change impacts the other therefore lending to evolution. It is why some trees no longer exist in some areas. When a tree dies because it cannot maintain its existence, from its death a new creation is reborn—it is re-birthed with the understanding of the new energies. A tree will only die if a resource is completely withdrawn, otherwise it will continue to flex with the changes.

Perhaps your friend needs to end her current way of existing, stop the process of taking from her resources to feed energies that are not returning what she needs. If she were a tree, she would have already searched out all sources of income for her survival, and adjusted her responses. She could end the cycle of taking from the soil, but that too will end her current existence, so stopping the cycle entirely of what feeds us is not an option either. It is the balance of giving and taking and being able to flow within the different cycles as they appear and adjusting the ability to survive in different environments. As you know this sounds all physical in the story but it is in the emotional and spiritual realms that adjustments also take place.

"So many people on Earth find themselves in this financial place; how do they move on?"

Everything flows in a creation process, some flow based on your actions, some based on others' actions. When you are stuck and backed into a corner, how do you get out? You may choose to kill or hurt what is threatening you; you may choose to reason and negotiate; you may choose to simply curl up and prepare for death. Each of us has different ways of coping and changing our position. On Earth you can access all kinds of energy that can assist you, but it takes surrender to not knowing. For it is when you reach a place of not knowing, that you can attract what you need to know. What if you were backed in a corner and said, "I do not know how to get out of this place, teach me." You are calling for new information, something you do not know. Perhaps you are able to jump higher than your attacker but in your current state of knowing; you didn't know that or didn't know how that could help you.

"What if bankruptcy is coming to you as an option?"

It will depend on the person and how they choose to react. There are always new resources to reach for and there are always resources to feed you. The question is what part of the cycle are you in? Money on Earth in the human world is the flow that enables your existence. Those with fewer resources learn to exist differently than those with plenty. Think of the desert bush compared to a rain forest. Both are able to give to their environment but they live much different lives. Is one of lesser value than the other? No. Their product and their resources are just different. Figuring out bankruptcy means figuring out your flow of give and take. Look at your cycle of existence.

Bankruptcy is simply a way of viewing the flow in a human life. Flow out what you wish to flow to you but be aware of who you are and whether your resources match your truth.

Are you a rain forest tree trying to live in a desert? Create the environment that supports who and what you are. Take from what feeds you and place yourself in a position to ensure you are being fed. Do not take from your resources and then not move the resources forward. Ensure your act in the creation process returns to the original source. Know yourself and know when to say, "I don't know" so that guidance can come to you.

To continue the flow in your current position may require digging to find new resources and this may mean reaching far from where you now are. In the case of limited cash flow, it may mean reaching out to areas that you have resisted before; it may mean admitting you are a rain forest tree trying to survive in the desert. If you are in the right place, natural laws ensure you are fed and are able to feed so the give-and-take cycle continues. Where are you being starved? Find the breakdown in your cycle.

Day 3 with Izshelong

"Beena sometimes I question how I am able to arrive in Creation so quickly."

You arrive here so quickly Shaman because you are a Wisdom Keeper and Creation is your home.

"Are we off to Izshelong today?"

Yes, Treena is on her way and then we will leave.

"It feels like so long since I have been there. I would love to be done writing by next week. Is there a way to make that happen?"

Do not rush this process, all will be as it is meant to be—trust.

"Trust is one of the hardest things for humans to do; we are always questioning, wondering, wanting to speed things up."

Trust, my friend. Trust, there is much more at work here than either you or I can control. Come. Treena is here and it is time to go.

Izshelong is a beautiful planet from a distance and yet up close I can see the turbulence of the winds. I am reminded how powerful wind is, how the movement of air currents can totally destroy a surface and restructure it. The winds never stop here. If they did I am not sure what would happen to the land masses of Izshelong. I am once again walking over the surface to where the stairs are located. Since my last visit the path has changed, trees once located close by are gone. These were not tall trees but I am reminded again about the unpredictability of Izshelong's surface.

Once back in Kathleen's home I voyage to the inner realms of this planet hopefully to learn of its history and how it can assist in the maintaining of our universal existence. I am feeling resistant; perhaps it is difficult to fathom how Iza live on this amber fluid and how this all happened so easily—not just on Izshelong but on the other planets as well. It is almost as if there is a memory from this happening before. Perhaps our universe already was re-created. Then I start to wonder about before Creation was made. Is there just one big cycle where it all comes to an end in order to be re-born in whatever way that happens? Has each planet simply been dormant and then re-birthed into this cycle? I do not think I will get an answer to my questions. I close my eyes and willingly drop down through the layers of a Shaman mind to connect with this beautiful heartfelt planet core. Izshelong is awaiting my arrival and I feel her excitement.

"Izshelong, what would happen if the winds stopped?"

I believe some pieces would fall apart and others would join together. There is still the force of gravity so there is a gravitation pull within each piece but the winds work with that. The impact of the pieces that drew to each other may cause destruction. It would be hard for this to happen as there is a cap that surrounds the atmosphere around the planet and all of the landmasses.

"Izshelong is there more I need to learn from you?"

I consider the other planets my brothers and sisters. I know they exist and yet I cannot feel their presence. There is inside of me an ability to feel other masses that come towards me and yet I cannot communicate with them. The winds blow in such a way that I do not suffer impacts. I wonder if I would be able to feel the Black Hole. I have an ability to feel and interpret and this is due to the amber pools of liquid within. That substance gave me the ability to reach out beyond myself and connect with what existed beyond my atmosphere. The suns which are part of me do not have this ability. Never once has another object come into contact with me that could sense me. I am able to communicate with the Iza and ceremonies are performed celebrating our existence. Iza are created from a substance that resides within me and I am able to feel their impact upon my surface. I do not seem to orbit far from my original place and so I am a very contained unit.

Kathleen is returning soon and you may wish to see her. She can tell you of the Iza and her journey to becoming our Wisdom Keeper.

I make my way back to consciousness and wander into the kitchen area. Kathleen's arms are outreached and I find myself comforted in their strength. Who would have thought that the Spirit Guide who has been with me so long was from another planet? Kathleen tells me of a cavern they have found underground—I guess there have been several found over the years. Not all the holes were filled with amber liquid. The surface appears solid but underground is where you can sit in its beauty. She asks if I would like to visit the cavern.

As we walk, I ask Kathleen how tunnels were formed as I haven't seen many tools.

We do not have the machines here that you have on Earth but we have some. Izshelong will explode upon impact so to make the tunnels we use a tool built to hit the space we wish to hollow out. It took years to perfect the level of explosion small enough to carve out the space and yet large enough to move through the rock. As you have seen, our furniture is made of stone. One of our tools is like a chisel—it causes small explosions. We also melt rock, similar to glass making on Earth. The rock forms a thick liquid that is shaped into glasses, spoons and tools. We also have created a tank to put any black stones we find in the hopes that a new Iza will be re-birthed. I will show you some of the tools and the melting place.

I tell Kathleen this tunnel system is very much like a small city.

She agreed and said that each tunnel has a council and the council connects with the other Iza's on the different landmasses. The council then relates the discussions back to the rest of the population.

The Beings on Izshelong

Today, Tanjay is taking Beena and me to Izshelong. I am excited and find myself immersed in conversation with him as we journey. One of the hardest parts of writing this book is that I am so immersed in my conversations that I forget to write. There is still much that I need to learn from Kathleen about the beings of Izshelong. At the entrance to the city of underground tunnels, I see Kathleen waiting for me. Today she is going to show me the newfound cavern. As we arrive, I am greeted by some of the Iza; they are beautiful.

All of them have a soft brown skin color, dark eyes and very dark hair. Kathleen looks older than any of them and you can see their respect for her as we enter. In the middle of this cavern is a pool of the amber liquid and above on us on the roof are what looks to be crystals. Some are long spikes hanging down and others are just odd rock-like shapes. The liquid drips slowly down these crystals and pools below. I wonder what is above us and if it is safe to be under a lake-like gathering of fluid. The air is very still and quite humid; the smell is similar to the tea Kathleen makes. This cavern find is important to the Iza as the cavern contains many different types of stones. Sound carries in the enclosed space so it will be a great room for singing and community ceremonies. So much of the Iza culture is similar to the First Nations People on Earth.

We pick up large stones found around the cavern and create an edge to the pools. Soaking in a pool such as this is like soaking in a hot tub. I ask Kathleen about the explosiveness and if anyone is fearful of an unexpected impact. I mean, we are stacking stones! What if one is set down too hard and created the one kaboom that will end this whole experience?

Kathleen laughs.

Yes, we have to be mindful when working with explosive rocks although the size of the explosion is based on the size of the impact. A rock against rock would do nothing more than cause the two rocks to explode (just duck if that happens). She laughs again. This is our livelihood, how we live and the resources we have. Each experience in life no matter where you reside, carries some risk. A fool does not risk and thus denies themselves the benefits of an experience.

We could fear the explosiveness of these rocks or we could accept the risk and create a pool that provides a wonderfully rejuvenating experience.

The hanging crystals will make incredible musical instruments when melted; their composition will transfer and magnify sound. The crystals are rare and so this large a find is another reason for the excitement. Above the crystals is a layer of dark tar that will be made into a fabric we use for clothing. It is melted and then stretched. This process is repeated eight times. Once it reaches a consistency of less stretch and more give, it can be stretched and left to form.

It is similar to how Native Americans traditionally made leather from rawhide minus the heat.

The fabric is similar to Lycra and is why our clothes fit tight to our bodies. Clothing was designed to protect our bodies. Because we go through a new birthing daily, we need a substance that stretches. Isn't it incredible how each planet provides for its beings' needs? Not all the tar or crystals will be removed because we don't want to deplete our reserves of this product or others. Respecting our resources is a law on this planet as we never wish to end a cycle of its creation. Let us finish this wall and then I will show you where we manufacture some of our other supplies.

Exploring Izshelong

My body is exhausted from lifting stones and yet the Iza are able to meth- odically keep going. That must be some tea these people drink! I decide to take a breather and watch as the wall continues to be built. Another team is working with chisels; they are creating what looks to be benches that will go around the cavern. There is such a precision in their actions; I am amazed at how fast the results are brought about. I wonder what they do with the stones that break off and I see that they have carts, similar to a wheelbarrow with three wheels. There is no electricity here, everything is done manually and yet this culture seems so much more advanced than humans.

Perhaps it is the community I love, the lack of war and fighting and their excitement in finding a new cavern. There have no addictions or substances to distract them, just simple everyday living. There also are no children. For that I feel bad for them because children offer a new celebration of life for us on Earth. There is celebration when a new being is found and revived but that is a rare occurrence. I wonder what I would do with myself on Izshelong. What if there wasn't a cavern to explore? Perhaps there is more to this life than I see.

Kathleen approaches. Next on the agenda is the factory.

The factory is huge—perhaps the size of three football fields. How it is the roof doesn't cave in? Within the area are sections and support columns made from the same shiny black substance. In one section, I see a rock burning. This must be how the suns continue to burn. The flame is orange colored, similar to the flame of hot coals. There are between six and ten fires in a row. Above them is a conveyer belt made from the fabric substance. That fabric must be heat resistant!

Kathleen is talking with the Iza so I am left to just take it all in. As we get closer to the fires I realize there are two belts, one that moves stones that are melting. The fabric holds the liquid rock in its center until it reaches a certain weight. Then the liquid drips through and lands on the belt beneath. This belt carries the liquid to a large vat. Once the vat is filled, it is moved to another area. A smaller-sized rock is placed underneath to keep it warm until new items are ordered.

Today it looks like they are making wheels to attach to the carts used to haul rocks. When you think of shapes, a circle is consistent throughout all the planets.

I check out the fabric-producing area. The ceiling of this cavern is very high. It is light in here, similar to sunlight and yet with no electricity. I take brightness for granted because we can access it so easily on Earth. On the ceiling, glowing rocks produce the bright light. It scares me to think of one of them falling and yet no one seems to be concerned.

How long did it take for the Iza to develop this knowledge and what did they do before? If a need is contemplated, all kinds of ideas emerge. Wouldn't it be wonderful if we on Earth did the same—if different countries or communities contemplated solutions and then revealed the results so that all could benefit?

Kathleen has already made her way to the fabric-producing section and is laughing joyfully as she joins into the stretching and pulling of a piece of what looks like black rubber. You can't help but want to join in, like the parachute game you see at gymnastic classes. How these beings maintain their energy and fitness level amazes me, I definitely need some of that tea to take home! The brown liquid sits in a pot on the stove. I ask about the pots, why don't they melt?

It turns out they are made from the same black tar substance but are made similarly to how we make pottery. Tar is heated and cooled many times until it no longer rigid. Then brown liquid is added and stirred well. After this concoction is mixed, fresh tar is added but only until it melts. This makes a thick substance similar to play dough. The substance is then shaped into large kettles and pots and pans. The substance is hot to work with so they use tools made from the glass-like rocks but have to cool them often as they absorb the heat and melt. They use three main resources: black tar, the amber liquid and explosive rocks. Amazing, absolutely no waste! There is also the sandy ground cover that is added to this tar-like mix to offer a different color and texture and the tea made from the plants. They are also nourished by the amber liquid found within. All of it works together to keep this race alive and all of it had to happen in a specific order.

My mind wanders back to the understanding that all of the planets seem to be ingrained with some past knowing. Could it all have been created before? Or has it been a process of one change at a time out of luck or circumstances? As I lose myself in this thought, I feel my fingers give out and I fall back on my rear end. Kathleen suggests we return home for tea and renewal. I am so down with that.

Q & A with Kathleen

As we are having tea, I start my questioning.

"Kathleen, if we send the planet that destroys to produce into the dark hole, do you think that action may produce another whole new universe on the other side or even within the one these planets reside?"

What makes you think that?

"I have noticed that every planet seems to attract to itself exactly what is needed to bring itself and its people or beings to this present state. It is like there is a cycle in the creation process and perhaps the cycle ends and a new one begins? It just reminds me of the planet that destroys to re-create. What if that is a representation of the cycle? What if this is the normal process we go through each time, coming up with the same solution? We are uncreated and re-created every time the cycle repeats?"

"We would not remember our past or how we were created; we would once again just come into existence at the first spark of creation. We have no knowing of time, if it is immediate or if many years. Each planet that has a life form has a low vibration in its existence prior to Creation sparking it. It just feels like there is some code it knows to follow, some time line in the attraction process. Perhaps there is no way to avoid the Black Hole but to accept it as our cycle. Have we ever seen a Black Hole before that any of us can recall? Perhaps our energy makeup will move to another place in existence or the other side of the Black Hole? It is like a puzzle being taken apart and then re-constructed, every piece has its place in the picture. We are only able to move and travel where Creation's energy moves. What if there are other universes similar to ours in existence? It is almost beyond what my mind can see or imagine."

Kathleen is lost in thought. She responds with her explanation of the one consistency she sees throughout our universe. All planets have a way of renewing themselves, not always through death and re-birth as on Earth but as on her planet, as in renewing a being that has returned to rock form or the daily renewing of their physical forms by drinking tea.

"The only planet I have visited so far that I cannot relate that thinking to is Keena."

Kathleen explains the Keena beings feed themselves with light and without that they do not exist; they need light for their renewal. Lord Metatron did not do well upon his first arrival and it was Archangel Michael who brought about a strong enough light source for Lord Metatron's survival. Michael is programmed with Creation's full light source so that Lord Metatron could fully be energized for longer periods. Each of us needs our planet's resources to maintain our physical realities.

"I do not need to eat in Creation."

That is because you come as an energy body, your Earthly body stays behind.

"Kathleen, what happens to you when you go through a renewal process?"

Do you want to watch?

"Yes."

Then you will. I do not need to take in my renewal drink until after my dreamtime.

"What does dreamtime look like for you? "

It is when I lay on the stone floor and I align myself to Izshelong and she tells me of what she feels. We all spend this time with Izshelong but it tires us and so following dreamtime, we renew. I feel very slow in my movements and have even contemplated not moving but something inside me gets me up each time and I renew. When you are here, my dreamtimes are spent at another's home.

"Do you think there are descendants of Iza on Earth?"

Yes, many have resided there and have mixed in with the human race. The original Iza are most likely in rock form and how the Iza were able to breed with humans is unknown to us, but we do sometimes have them connect with us telepathically. I do not believe they realize they are connected to us, but rather to their human ancestors, just as you thought I was one of your ancestors.

"Hmm, that is an interesting thought about reproduction. Form plus form plus energy produces a new creation. Perhaps it is not necessary that an egg and sperm meet; that would be a completely new theory on Earth. Perhaps the human ate small pieces of stone and it combined with human blood and changed form. I suppose we will not know for sure. It is a theory that Mary, Jesus' mother, was a virgin; perhaps this was true in other cases as well. According to the pictures of Jesus, he was of Iza form in looks, and he had many telepathic abilities. He also held many healing components and an ability to know the alchemy of Earth. Perhaps, I will one day call on Jesus and talk with him to see if his past spirit energy knows."

Shaman, I believe that each planet gives to its people what the people need to be healthy but beings from other planets do not survive. The only planet I know that offers this to other beings from other planets is Earth.

Isn't it also interesting that you, an Earth Wisdom Keeper, have been able to travel to all the different planets and maintain your survival; not one of us other Wisdom Keepers are doing the same. Iza's send healing energy out to the entire universe hoping it travels to where it is needed. It is very healing for us to do this as we join together as one people celebrating the life we have. Dancing, singing, and playing music allows our inner joy to expand more and more. Izshelong on the surface appears turbulent and storm ridden but it is in its depths that one knows the truth. Let us rest and upon awakening, I will allow you to watch the rebirthing process.

I always loose the concept of time on the other planets, there is light either all day and night, or in this case, dark around us as we are underground. Sleep comes easy, especially after all that walking and lifting. Kathleen wakes me and I notice she looks older now. The creases on her face are deep and her skin hangs looser under her chin. Her eyes are dull and exhausted looking. I have seen her like this before in my journeys so it does not scare me. Together we drink the same tea we had earlier except Kathleen stirs dried herbs into hers.

She smiles and makes a joke saying, "bottoms up".

I take a few sips but she completes her entire cup, then makes her way over to the floor and lies on the stone. At first nothing happens, and then the smell of gingerbread cooking fills the room. Next a gas rises from her skin, encasing her entire body. I wonder if she is able to breathe. The inhale and exhale of her breath adds to the gas and soon the entire shell around her is filled. It starts to turn into a slimy-looking gel that continues to surround her body. Each time she breathes in, the gel reduces in quantity, it is as if she is eating it. The gel continues to reduce and soon it is as if it was never there. She looks asleep but her skin is toned and glowing—that rich brown color once again. As she opens her eyes, they shine. It all happened so quickly, I wonder why the floor is not wet. Kathleen explains that the stone also absorbs the gel. Too bad we do not have this magical tea on Earth.

Kathleen and I embrace as I prepare to return to Creation; my time in Izshelong is done. Beena and Tan Jay are waiting; I can't wait to hold Tan Jay as we descend back to Creation. I know he must leave upon our arrival.

In Reflection

Izshelong is an interesting planet held together by strong forceful winds, it amazes me it doesn't just explode apart. I am still lost as to how this information will bring about a new path for avoiding the Black Hole but trust that I will discover that soon.

Section 11

Eqay

(Ee-Kway)

"Live a life that you take ownership for. Each time you enter physical form, a new experience begins, there will be many supporters around you, physical and energetic bodies, but the experience is yours to have. Live your life for you and not others. Release all who you attempt to control; guide your children do not direct them. Teach by facilitating thought, not thinking for them. Be with those that kindle your spirit. Stand on your own but do not be afraid to join hands with others. Honor your gifts, they come to be opened.

Arc Angel Michael – Eqay - Wisdom Keeper

Travelling to the Next Planet

Treena seems overjoyed to be heading to the next planet. How is it that through this cosmic blackness, my guides always know how to get through the different portals? I ask Beena and she smiles. I know I am in for a story.

You remember the planet, Merth? There were many animals on Merth. Some of the animals wanted to fly to Earth to meet Earth animals—in the same way that humans wish they could go to Heaven and meet with Angels. Energetically, when something or someone has a strong desire, they are filled and surrounded with love. The animals' love created a huge energy wave of attraction. At the same time, in the empty space of the universe, two large rock masses collided and produced a shock wave. When the shock wave hit Merth, it caused turmoil in the waters. Many animals found shelter but some didn't. The ones who didn't changed their alchemy so they could fly and be free. They also learned to see the hidden portals in the blackness of space.

"So the attraction law doesn't just happen on Earth! Dreams come true; just stay committed to living and wait out the storm."

Oh Shaman you can be so poetic!

Up ahead we see our next planet. It is like a ball of molten silver but not hot as you would expect. I shield my eyes from the glare. There are guides who glow this brightly so I think I know who lives here. Treena was prepared for this and already has a cloth over her eyes. I swear—do these things just appear?

After landing, Treena and Beena return to Creation but say they will be back. I wonder how Beena will know when and then remind myself that as my power animal, we have a connection to each other all the time.

As I stand next to the portal, I am overcome with the fragrant smell of roses. It is not what I expected. I have been in this garden before in a place I called Heaven. I am confused. Is Heaven another planet?

The colors are spectacular. The flowers blend in groups of beauty amongst the trees and bushes and shrubs. There is space around each grouping to walk. It is so still, I could easily misinterpret the scene as a portrait; it seems to lack life. I see Daniel making his way toward me. He appears to be coming down a hill but from this perspective, it looks flat. I walk towards him and, sure enough, I am climbing an incline.

Daniel embraces me and says, "Come and let me show you my planet, Eqay.

Introduction

At the top of the hill, is a flat, white surface that extends forever. There is a sudden recall of Akashic records, angels and levels of learning. Yup, I have been here before. People talk about a garden when they die and come back to life. Earth said that when a human dies it goes either to the energy world or to Creation depending on which stream it takes. But this must be where they come when they don't die. This is a place of love, but it is also a place of many of our Earth helpers. It is where we channel from on Earth. There are many channelers and mediums on Earth who receive guidance from this place and so my mind is over the top with questions. I want to know why Eqay is so accessible and if this is the same as on Creation.

Daniel smiles. It is not just Earth who receives guidance from Eqay; many planets call out to us for support. Come with me to my home, let us connect and let me speak to you and show you through me.

An angelic connection; who could resist that? I think about the angel in the Philadelphia cream cheese commercials and start to laugh. "Okay, where's the philly?"

I arrive in Creation to find Beena exhausted. She is tired and needs to rest. I hate seeing her so lifeless but decide to go to Eqay by myself. Treena was resting by the water's edge and agreed to take me. While she got our sunglasses, Henry, the mouse also decided to join us.

I must have slept on the way there because I do not remember anything about the trip. Daniel greeted me at the portal and took my hand as we entered. The garden is enchanting and parts of my spirit just want to stay here but I know there is much to learn. We make our way over the hill and walk down the streets of Eqay.

Imagine a white landscape; the road-like surface is white and everyone wears white. White sidewalks lead to dome-shaped homes made of transparent glass, like windows—you can't see in but the glass is not reflective like a mirror. There are many communities on this planet, each serving different functions, but this is where Daniel lives. I ask him what function he serves.

I am your personal angel. I am here to help guide you through your living years on Earth. I serve no one else. I am not a Wisdom Keeper. All the angels who live in this community serve a specific being assigned to us by our Wisdom Keeper, Archangel Michael. Our planet receives information communicated through the archangels. Many humans have angels around them for it is very easy for humans to access Eqay.

Other planets like Izshelong are also easily able to gain access. That is how Kathleen became a Wisdom Keeper. Our planet gave directions to Archangel Michael to go to Izshelong and take Kathleen to Creation. Kathleen followed Michael there and became encoded with all of Creation's energy streams. She stayed in Creation and learned about the other planets and met other Wisdom Keepers.

"Sometimes Creation confuses me as it always seems different for other people."

Creation is energy mass; how you create the image is how it will look. If you join with another in Creation it enables you to see their imagery and receive the teachings. That is why Creation is the place for learning. Creation is accessible by all in the universe so there is much energy you can learn from.

"What about people like Jesus, Buddha, and other great spiritual teachers?"

There was a group from our record-keeping community who travelled to Earth many, many cycles ago; they did not return. Perhaps these great spiritual leaders are the spirit bodies of these angels coming into human form.

For an angel to come to Earth now, it must come in response to a new creation. If it does not leave prior to the birthing process, it will connect with the physical body and be born into physical form. Some choose to do this! Otherwise it shows up as a stillbirth. Anyone who has had a stillbirth has made it possible for an angel to do work on Earth. A stillbirth is a very difficult process for an Earthling and we are sorry to see them suffer but it is because of our energy makeup that we must use this method of coming to Earth. There are also times when a human is in contact with their angels. They do not wish to live anymore but do not want their body to die. An angel comes into the body and the energy body of the human goes back to the Earth energy world. A person who is dying will often see angels—that is because energetically the person is moving in and out of form. Once death combines fully with the physical form, the person is released back to energy. Sometimes humans see energy forms of their loved ones before they pass; this is another form of them moving in and out of their body.

Is Eqay Heaven?

"Daniel, is Eqay Heaven? Is this where we go when we die?"

That is an interesting question as all you have been taught to this point is the energy field surrounding Earth and you haven't been taught about Eqay except there are angels here. Why do you ask?

"As a Shaman I am sometimes asked to bring people to Heaven's door and each time I do, I see either the gardens or a light source entry."

Shaman, many call Eqay their heaven experience. If you recall your energy body can also go to Creation, so yes, an energy body can come to Eqay or it can go to Earth's energy realm—all are possible.

"Whoa, we need to back up; this is difficult to grasp."

There are three energy places an energy body can travel to.

Creation holds the energy of every planet. After the burst that sparked the universe, the planets that absorbed Creation's energy sent out a return energy flow that circled back to Creation. Creation absorbs these energy streams and combines them into one stream that is sent out to be absorbed. So the energy funnels in as several different streams and funnels out as one stream—a combination of everything.

The first place an energy body can travel to is Earth. Earth has an energy different from other planets with living beings; it is called death. When death combines with a body, the physical form dies and the energy form leaves the body, taking with it the vibrations of energy it experienced in its past life. The energy body vibrates to a level of attraction with each energy destination having its own calling. Vibrations of energy levels are different and increase in speed depending on what happened in the physical form.

A slower vibration will go to Earth's energy world and often migrates to similar energy bodies. It is why you see ancestor lines or similar traits between generations. Energy can take the form of what another is seeking to see. When you look into your past lives you create a form based on the energy you are experiencing in the moment. The imagination of a human mind can create the energy form. The energy body within the physical body carries the energies of the experiences. An experience when the human is living can spark the imagination, attracting to itself energy body parts existing in the energy realm. That reaction of energy trading may affect the present living time of the human or it may stay stored within the energy body upon death. The vibrational level the person is at will determine whether the energy body stays whole as a soul body or as components in an energy body. In this energy realm energies are re-birthed quickly back into physical form.

Eqay is the second place an energy body can go to. An attraction to Eqay is the next speed up of vibration. Eqay is similar to Earth in that every being on Eqay is an energy body taking form. Eqay is a masculine planet and therefore is a planet that gives of itself. Some of the forms have been brought about from the planet itself. I may look and feel very solid, but I am just energy.

Eqay's energy world is different than Earth's energy world in reference to where one's energy will go. Someone will come to Eqay and instantly go to an energy field they once loved on Earth. It is because they vibrated so close to that energy on Earth. But they could also come to another place where they see other loves who have passed. It is what humans call the near-death experience, when they talk about what and who they saw. Often their near-death stories differ. Eqay serves the entire universe with wisdom and guidance. Its knowledge comes from within, but it is the beings on the planet that communicate it.

The beings on Eqay come from Earth and nowhere else. The counsel of Archangels determines where you will be positioned and what role you will serve while on Eqay. When you are ready to leave, you will move to the Earth energy realm and await your re-birth. Everyone in Eqay is an angel; archangels are older and do not re-birth as they are in commitment to the planet Eqay.

The third energy place is Creation. Creation is an energy vibration. The main difference between Creation and the other two energy vibration fields is that this location is fed by all that is in the universe. All planet energy beings can travel to Creation, even Eqay beings. The beings who stay in Creation are the ones who have been encoded with all of the energies from Creation. You are one of those beings.

Before becoming a Wisdom Keeper you resided in Eqay. You were in Creation learning when it was requested that you become a Wisdom Keeper. You said "Yes." Creation then encoded you with her energy stream and you chose to re-enter Earth's birthing process. When you die, you will travel back to Creation to continue to learn and teach as a Wisdom Keeper to all those energies that visit Creation seeking knowledge. Any Earth human who dies and is encoded with Creation energy will travel to Creation. The others will travel to Eqay or back to the Earth energy.

"Was Eqay a planet without any life forms until death came to Earth?"

Yes. There is a triad similar to how Earth religions discuss triangles of three—the holy trinity, a three-strand cord, the three bodies of Buddha…. Earth, Merth and Eqay are a triad. Merth is animal energy so energies of animals that have chosen to go through the re-birthing process come here from the higher vibrational field of Merth or from Earth's energy field. Most animals on Earth come from Earth's energy field but animal energy also exits Merth and mixes in the Earth animal energy realm. This normally happens when an animal needs to evolve for survival.

Eqay and Merth are not far from Earth and so our energy fields line up. Energy bodies making their way for the first time to Eqay sometimes need help. Because the energies on Eqay are from Earth, travel to Earth is possible and it is why angels can surround humans. Any energy can come into form with the right alchemy and is visible if an energy body vibration is reached.

The Books of Life & Akashic Records

When I return to Eqay, Daniel is not in the garden. He is by his home planning our day. Today I get to see my Book of Life! A thrill rushes through my body. To get to the Book of Life we first set an intention. We then travel down into the planet via an elevator until we arrive at a grassy place. In the center is a podium.

I call out for the Book of Life for Debra Anne Criger Siddon Gibbs to be opened and a book appears. It is leather bound and filled with a parchment-like paper. I ask Daniel how far in the future it goes.

Daniel gave me a funny look and said, "These are documents of what has happened, not what is going to happen. If something has happened that will also be part of your future, it might appear on every page. It depends how you chose to deal with it."

"Is this where we find past life information?"

Yes and No. Your Book of Life details your experiences on Earth, from the time you leave Eqay, until your return. Once the Soul returns to Eqay that life experience is closed. So your Book of Life is related to your present life cycle and holds a history of your experiences. Knowledge of those experiences may help you understand reactions in your present life. Akashic records help you understand the energies of your makeup—what is vibrating as a result of your life experiences. Okay, tell me something you desire?

"I desire a thin, shapely body."

An akashic record reading can tell you what energies are present that may be stopping this from manifesting, your energy body makeup, and what you took on from your parents. It is like reading your DNA. Your Book of Life will show how you are having the experience of an overweight body and not enjoying it. You might have had an experience where you attracted the energy of obesity (that was from your experience and not an experience of your parents). Those who read the akashic records are able to see the energies and interpret them with the help of a guide. The guides the readers work with are found in a dimension on Earth. The records can provide useful information.

"I am confused. So, the akashic records are not on Eqay?"

No, akashic records are kept in an energy field around Earth. Remember you do not always return to Eqay. You pass through the energy field to attract or mix with other energies before you are re-birthed. The akashic records are kept as a resource. They were set up by another race on Earth residing in another dimension as a form of knowledge and protection.

I do not want you to confuse this with Eqay. Eqay is about the experience of living and not necessarily about energies affecting your living experience. Upon the return to Eqay a soul body reviews the experience of living and offers the entire experience to add to the consciousness of Eqay which in return serves all of the consciousness of the human world on Earth.

Yes. Let's say you have an obesity issue. You can go to your Book of Life and see where the issue started. When you see what event caused that energy attraction, you often can clear that energy. It is the same as what you call soul retrieval; pieces of energy from your makeup are left in alignment to an event and must be retrieved before there can be healing. This is the work of a Shaman so I understand you get this occurrence.

"Yes, Daniel I do understand but I did not realize the resources the Book of Life offers. Is every life stored in my Book of Life?"

No, just your current one, different energy combinations create different opportunities and attractions.

"So what about past lives? I feel like they are real when I journey to them. What about past events affecting my current life?"

Past- life energy can affect your current life. Your energy body is made up of many components, some of which are a result of a past-life experience. When you view a past life with the intention of wanting to understand an attribute in this current life, you will gather the energies of that past life to view. This information can help you understand how energies were created and it can be used as a tool in adjusting patterns in your current life. It is a form of knowledge.

"Yes, I understand that from Earth we are made up of energy components that are a result of how the law of attraction and birthing into a human life works. But you are saying that some of our past-life issues may follow us into our current life and that understanding the past-life experience can give us an awareness of how we can then alter that energy."

Confusion can happen when a human views a past-life and sees lives they cannot relate to or even understand. Remember that each human life is made up of myriad components from their ancestral line and it may be that they are viewing the life of an ancestor, not themselves. Because of the huge mix of energies present at birth, they might also be viewing a life of another line that happens to hold the component of the energy they seek.

The idea is to use past-life viewing as a tool to understand patterns or traits, not to get invested in the life you are viewing and not to define yourself based on a past life.

Shamanic Interval

Basically Akashic records are a reading that will tell you what energies make up You, for instance, the energy of being able to teach, the gift of compassion, the ability to manage finances. People who are able to read akashic records are able to access your records to see what you are encoded with. Sometimes they will tell you the energies that are making you sick but usually they will tell you what you are best destined for.

A Book of Life reading is a little different. Normally you seek to have your Book of Life read when you want to know the why of something; to find a solution to a concern you are having in your life —typically it is health related but not always. A Book of Life reader will access your Book of Life and then look for your concern in it. They can then determine where the concern began and what events took place around that same time. A book of life reading is based on your current living experience and does not go into the past lives that you have been part of.

I had my Book of Life reading done so that I could better understand my food addiction and food compulsion issues. The reading was done in a sweat lodge with a Shaman and several others who prayed and drummed for me. A Book of Life reader was there as well. The Book of Life reader would see a mark on the page of my book and identify it as an event that contributed to my issues. Then a healing was done around that event. In my case, the event was abuse in my childhood. When I was able to release the pain of that event and the guilt I associated with it, my Book of Life changed and food addiction and compulsion issues no longer showed up. I was now clear of these issues (although I still had to reprogram my learned habits and behaviours around the issues). It was one of the most intense healings I have ever undergone and as difficult as it was, I feel very blessed to have had the experience.

To work with your Book of Life you have to be willing to give up everything as you know it in your current life, so there is a real draw on surrender — at least this is what was required of me by Spirit prior to entering into the ceremony.

"How did we get three bodies? Creation's energy brought forth the physical body but how did an energy body come about? I am resistant to writing an answer in fear of not being able to describe it. Daniel, please tell me slowly, so I can understand. I know in my dream time you shared this with me but it is still a difficult concept to grasp."

Once upon a moon, Earth was a planet of no spirit—only physical bodies. There was an intellect of the people but they were more animal-like in that their livelihood was survival. Beings from the other planets went to Earth and some stayed in the hope of helping the beings on Earth. Often the Earth people saw these beings as gods because their wisdom was so far beyond their own.

Earth beings' physical makeup was different than it is now. There was no need for Earth beings to eat one another or for human beings to be separate from other beings. They lived as one, consuming plants and water for nourishment. As Earth continued in her cycle, there was this galactic alignment and the energy of death engulfed Earth. When this happened, it caused a huge chaos ball of change to occur. Beings started to evolve, for the human death energy combined with their physical form. When this took place, a creation of a spirit body evolved.

The human broke off from their physical form. Within this mass of energy were the energies that were in existence in that current life. The planet landscape started to change as well and the waters started to expand. It was then Earth entered another section of her cycle where she was in darkness without the heat of the Sun; the waters froze and the Earth transformed. During times of darkness, rock energy worked to move the waters. Around Earth's surface was also a new existence—the energy field made up of past energies. Under the waters began a whole new creation of beings, it is how mermaids came into existence.

Birth and dying and evolution continued—all happening in and around Earth. Then Eqay started to sense Earth as did Merth; this was due to the existence of an energy field they could pick up on. Earth was no longer a physical plane. Eqay is alive but it did not have energy beings living on it and there was a desire to have this. Eqay would send sensory energy waves to Earth and read what came back. Michael passed due to death, and when he did he felt the vibration of Eqay. It thrilled him, so he followed the energy field to find the source. It was then that he met Eqay and their relationship began.

Archangel Michael was the first to arrive at Eqay. He was able to bring more energy beings as they followed Eqay's energy source. Energy beings on Eqay are in the same state they ended Earth life with. Energies that enter the energy realm do not stay together but often attract and trade pieces of themselves in an evolutionary way. They rebirth quickly and often re-enter where they left off with a few additions and deletions. Those re-birthing from Eqay do so in a more direct way as they are sent out with a request of learning. They may die several times before returning to Eqay, trading off energies and attracting new energies each time in the re-birth process.

Q & A with Daniel

Once again Beena is tired and doesn't want to travel. Treena and I are both concerned but I tuck her into bed and hug her as I prepare to leave for Eqay. She tells me to complete this process as the time is coming soon. God, please take care of her.

As I travel, I realize how attached I become with my spirit guides. Beena is a true friend who loves me without judgment or conclusions. There is also a level of accountability to her and to our mission. I want to keep her forever but I know that losing her is inevitable. She will return to Merth and a new spirit guide will appear. It is often in loss that new opportunities appear. To lose is to gain and to gain is to lose, each stepping on each other moving forward. When I arrive at Eqay, Daniel embraces me with his love and whispers that Beena is going to be okay. He suggests that I allow Beena her experience rather than trying to keep her. There is so much I wish to talk to him about.

"Daniel, if Eqay serves the entire Universe then I imagine that Eqay is very connected to all the different beings and their planets. Is that so?"

Eqay serves Earth and the soul's energy path through the offering of wisdom gained from the collective. Eqay was, and is, a consciousness in the form of a planet but this consciousness is educated and expanded from the experiences of the human soul bodies that reside here or have passed through here.

"But you said Eqay serves the entire universe?"

Eqay is part of the entire universe and it offers its wisdom to any beings who seek it.

"I thought Creation was where beings went to gather information?"

Creation is a meeting place for all beings. Each planet feeds Creation by sending energy to it. Each planet, after creation combines these energies is fed by the complete stream to continue this cycle of energy flow. Eqay is a planet of consciousness and so the energy it sends to Creation is enriched with knowledge. That knowledge is embedded into Creation's energy field. All can access that knowledge. Some planets are not of consciousness. Their experience is more physical and that also gets fed to Creation. Earth is an example of that type of planet. Planets where there is not a consciousness within cannot offer the wisdom of its being; it can only offer its experience of it.

For example: a human drills a deep hole into Earth and removes a large pocket of oil. Earth's experience may be to shift in her polarity and that would be the experience sent to Creation. An evaluation of the process would not be sent, just the physical response. Earth does not feel emotions; it simply is a mass of physical. Earth receives Creation energy and allows it to flow up to its outer surface. Along the way, it meets other outer energies that it will mix with and create new creations on Earth. There are physical and energetic reactions occurring all the time but the base energy does not change.

Eqay on the other hand, is also fed by Creation's energy and it became an entire holding space for energy. It vibrated at a level equal to human soul and according to the attraction principle attracted human soul at that frequency. As I mentioned, Archangel Michael was the first human soul to appear.

"Okay Daniel, let's take it from the point of death, soul and body separation. Soul travels to Eqay and migrates to the place of the most similar energies on Eqay. Then the soul allows their wisdom from the experience of the physical to open up. What do you mean by allow and open up?

It is what the consciousness of Eqay attracts from the energy body we call soul. Like a big magnet.

"My teachers on Earth say that we feel both our experiences and others' experiences so that our soul has a full understanding of its actions on Earth. Some call this the teaching process of the soul. But you are saying that the only part of the soul's experience it can send towards the magnet is its own experience—it does not feel any other's experience energetically."

The soul body on Eqay is in its completeness when it leaves Earth but in the course of death and energy exchanges and re-births it may attract a reflective side to its experiences. For example, a soul may murder and then return and be murdered and then be able to share the entire experience upon its return to Eqay. Or it may murder and not have the experience of being murdered so it would share the knowledge gained through that experience. On Eqay, experience is not labeled good or bad—it simply is. It might have been the soul's experience to have been labeled as bad because they murdered and that knowledge is then added to the consciousness of Eqay. Those living on Earth seeking wisdom about murder then gain an under-standing of their current situation.

When Moses sought the wisdom of how to live a life in harmony and love, Eqay had stored experiences from those who had lived in such a way and shared with Moses some of the practiced ways of living that brought about harmony and love. Therefore the message, "thou shall not kill" was based on the experiences of those who killed not having a life of joy and harmony—those whose lives vibrated in closeness to Moses. The leaders you follow on Earth, your teachers as you call them, offer their knowledge as it is filtered through their own attraction level.

Listen to those you feel similar to as it is their messages that will bring joy and harmony or whatever the intention is in your request. Moses wanted to give the people guidelines so that they could exper-ience joy and harmony. He wanted God to provide this wisdom and so, from this place of being, he attracted the wisdom that would provide that for those of similar energy vibrations—people who desire the same information, people wanting to hear God. When Moses presented the ten ideas, some felt very connected to the ideas and embraced them and some did not. Neither is right nor wrong—it is just the experience of it that each will share upon their return to Eqay. As you know Earth is the only planet with death and soul with an energy field, so Eqay's contributions to Creation's energy becomes a Universal offering.

I have another question. "When all beings could access each other's planets and some were left here on Earth when the portals closed, what happened to them?"

Yes, a very interesting question. Their makeups are much different so they really did become trapped in a physical form. Some combined with a human form and this process created a soul. Others created communities of their planet on Earth and Eqay beings check on them. Their own planets also stay in touch with them through consciousness and creation.

Daniel's explanation of other beings leads me wondering about aliens on Earth. I want to know if there are other planets and other beings and how they get to Earth.

Yes this needs to be explained. Let me make sure you understand that some beings are here from the other planets and live in communities and some have joined with humans and have developed souls. There are beings that visit Earth but they are not connected to us as they are not from our universe.

On Earth, there are different levels of existence, unknown but not totally unknown. In each level of existence, all seems real and linear; your mind creates it this way. It is hard, if not impossible, to imagine the level that another being exists in.

Imagine the earth in layers; one layer is human and animal based but beneath that layer is another race of beings and above is a layer of another race of beings.

"Why the different levels? Why are we unaware of each other?"

Humankind is the slowest in evolution on the planet.

"How can our worlds co-exist and not affect one another? "

When you look out the window you see your neighbor's yard and house but what is it really? It is energy particles formed into different matter put together to form a house. Although real in your world of vibration, it may not be real in another level of vibration. Your son talks to you about visiting another planet that has a serious waste problem, but the planet looks like Earth.

"Yes."

Well it is Earth, just in another dimension.

"Daniel, can I consciously choose to travel to the other dimensions like I travel to the other planets?"

Yes, but you will not always be welcomed just as aliens entering human energy systems are not always welcomed.

"How can another race of beings come into our awareness, our sight?"

They choose to, just as you choose to visit their world.

"Have the different dimensions existed together as one race?"

No, all was created and all stays created in their own dimension.

"Let's talk about death and souls. Are other races affected as the human race?"

No, it is why other races are more advanced in some areas over humans.

"My friend Farhana has experienced invisibility. What is that?"

That is a space of energy in between dimensions or Earth worlds.

"I have seen alien beings; they were in a room very similar to mine."

Yes, they would have re-created your reality in their reality, so not a 100% copy but very close.

"How many dimensions are there on Earth?"

Twelve, one of course is your dimension.

"I understand now—twelve dimensions, twelve Wisdom Keepers, Earth must be the eighth dimension."

Now do you understand the number eight in regards to the infinity sign? It's the human dimension that is infinite. Each dimension creates its own reality. Energetically one human choice affects the entire human race.

"So aliens from another dimension cannot come to our dimension and cause pain or torment."

They can but only if you vibrate to their dimensional energy.

"What if another dimension wanted to get rid of us or decided to play with our oceans?"

They could but most would not due to the cause and effect on their own world. There are repercussions in both worlds when energies are combined.

"You said most. Not all?"

Some choose to take that risk. Each dimension also has different atmosphere conditions so time is limited in the human dimension.

"Am I justified to be afraid?"

No, you are being watched over very carefully by many dimensions.

"What would they want of me?"

They want the code to Creation's energy.

Choice, Addictions and Soul Connections

Each dimension on Earth has a Wisdom Keeper but none have made it to Creation to receive the full embodiment of Creation's energy. It must be a choice of the being made in Creation and this was easier for you to do due to the death process and soul travel. The other dimensions have not found a way to connect to Creation, nor have they asked. Their intellects are very developed, their heart energy is very low and so their ability to be spiritual is much harder. They can access parts of their minds humans have not learned but they are far less emotional.

"Can they take human form?"

No.

"Can they control human choices?"

They can influence the human mind, but they cannot control it.

"Is there any way to protect oneself from this type of influence?"

Doming, as you call it;

Call in the energies of power to surround you;

Do not keep symbolism of other dimensions you do not wish to attract;

Be aware of the dimensions you choose to travel to as often they will follow you home;

Do not set intentions to harm other dimensions for it will create disharmony for you;

Do not be afraid.

Daniel, do you think the shifts taking place on Earth in 2012 will affect all dimensional energies?"

Yes, the shifts will affect all the dimensions, how, we are unsure.

"Can another race take over the human race and have this dimension as well as theirs?"

No, they are unable to survive at these energy levels.

I don't return immediately to Earth as Daniel suggested but continue our conversation. It would be wonderful if each of the twelve Wisdom Keepers were able to learn and grow from each other as is happening on other planets. It would be wonderful if we could all embrace humility and honor each other in our experience—no one being lower or higher than each other. Eqay harnesses humility, love and joy but the human race is without their body and brain and operates from their soul body.

"Daniel, can you tell me about addictions?"

Addictions often appear when a body dies and the soul enters the soul world around Earth, in the human dimension. They leave with the energy of the addiction and re-birth with the energy of the addiction still present, often attracting itself to a family lineage where addiction energy is present. It is a slower frequency and keeps the soul rotating through the energy field until overcome. It is meant to be released from an energy field so that the soul can return to Eqay. It may have been part of the original re-birth from Eqay to bring experience back to consciousness in this area. It is why no experience is bad, just simply an experience. Yes, there may be pain but even that adds to a soul's wisdom.

A human consciousness grows out of experience as does Eqay's consciousness. Human consciousness has yet to draw on this huge resource. Only few are able to access it and yet it surrounds them for the taking and learning. The human race would transform dramatically if they would only draw on the experiences stored in the consciousness of Eqay.

All one has to do is connect with their soul body and ask the questions, then listen and take the action. Shaman you are an example of being out of line on this. On your way to the Neale Donald Walsh retreat you found yourself reading about girls being raped in another part of the world. You cried and prayed and asked God what you could do to help. The answer was to cover the area where they live with a protection dome, but your mind would not accept this answer, so you did nothing. Too many humans ask and then do nothing.

Our Soul's Purpose

Beena quickly wraps herself into the curve of my neck and gently beckons me forward. I am tired these days and feel like sleeping but she reminds me of my commitment. I am off to Eqay today, not to talk with Daniel but to meet Eqay. Today I am choosing to travel on Treena through Creation, I no longer appear to have to do this ritual but find I still love the feeling of Beena and Treena close by. I wonder why their names are so similar. I must enjoy the sound they create as it is my imagination that labels them. Holding Treena with my head resting on her neck feels nurturing and Beena snuggled in close reminds me how loved I am. Each part of God is love and whether it is a power animal or a rock on Earth, all is emanating love. This connection is what I needed today so that I am able to communicate with Eqay, ready and willing to be love.

Daniel is there to greet me as is Archangel Michael; how blessed that I consider Michael my friend and companion as I would someone here on Earth. Daniel gives me a hug and light kiss on the cheek but Michael grabs me and turns me around in his embrace. He is taking me to meet Eqay. I joke about him being the oldest, ancient of sort and yet how young and vibrant he looks. What is his secret?

A sheepish smile comes across his face and he replies I just threw off the baggage and of course, I moisturize! We laugh again.

I realize we have covered miles and yet it feels like we have barely started.

Michael reads my thoughts. "Remember, no baggage so you can move fully to where you intend to land."

I ask him if we are flying and he replies, "No, just moving in an unlimited space

It is difficult to grasp how one soul's experience adds to everything even though I know we are all connected. I need to find out how one's purpose is defined. If a soul body comes from Eqay with a clean slate, how can it be attracted to a specific energy? I ask Michael.

Shaman, when a soul body leaves Eqay, it leaves with a purpose or mission to bring about a result through living actions.

The purpose of a soul body is always to serve. Soul bodies in energy forms, often called angels, watch over humans. Sometimes they desire to assist in the consciousness of another's experience. They may choose to be born into a family where one member needs to embrace the experience of poverty and so they will be born sick. If they use all their money to heal their sick child, they can develop a new way of being that overcomes poverty and then they can take that experience out to other humans. The soul body has served their purpose in assisting a family to experience poverty. The soul body then dies but in the energy field around Earth it attracts a large amount of love energy as it was so loved in this life experience. It then attaches itself to two parents who are so full of love for each other and to their careers that they really do not have time to love their new creation, a baby.

Through this life experience the soul body grows up feeling so alone and isolated from his family. He dedicates his life to building businesses that teach people how to balance making money, love what they do and be there for their family.

The soul body dies not yet vibrating enough to return to Eqay and once again enters the energy world of Earth. This time the main energy of its being is feeling alone and yet able to be successful in business. Depending on which is the strongest energy, it will attract more of that and will then attach itself to similar energies. This time it is a single mom who is trying to become a successful businesswoman. The energy of her new child—this soul body who attached itself to her—will bring forth more of that energy.

The soul body has already had the experience of helping others make money and so does not need that experience again. He finds himself running many businesses and making money with each of them. He watched his mother succeed in business and business became his passion rather than a way to overcome lonliness. This brings joy to his life experience and the soul starts recording experience.

Many people in business operate from a desire to succeed. In this experience, the soul's desire was to change a financial position from poverty to abundance. The soul body went from being the cause of poverty to someone who helped others get out of poverty. Then he became the cause of success and the creator of wealth. As a creator or wealth, he experienced a high level of joy so that upon death, his soul was vibrating close to its original soul body. It is through joy that the soul has spiritual experiences and starts to reconnect with the wisdom available on Eqay. Upon returning to Eqay the soul body begins the process of sharing its experiences as stored in its soul body—in this case, all the experiences it had with poverty.

Soul bodies are able to travel to Creation to share their knowing and to learn from other universal creations. Although the soul body no longer has emotions, it does have within itself a level of knowing that is gained from its life experiences. A person who cared for animals knows the energy that comes from that type of living experience and carries within itself compassion for animals. It may not know the experience of killing animals but it can experience that energy by sitting here and allowing itself to connect with another's experience that is stored in the databank of life experiences.

As Michael finishes his explanation, we approach what looks like a crater; it is a white, bowl-shaped area with an energy vortex around it, like waves of heat from hot pavement. I ask Michael about this space.

He explained that this area has been created as a place of clearing. Soul bodies gather here to clear themselves of past living experiences and to reflect on where their consciousness feels drawn. Each soul body will leave here and gather with other soul bodies of similar consciousness. From the sharing of their life experience they will evolve to areas to which the soul body can serve.

Michael brought me here because it is in this space, that I will most easily feel Eqay.

In The Beginning

My body in this dreamtime feels like meditation. I close my eyes and just allow all thoughts to leave me. I find I no longer feel part of a body and slowly am aware that all I am conscious of is pure nothingness, not even gravity. I hear music, like piano music with perhaps crystal bowls and harps mixed in. In the awareness of hearing sound, I notice a sense of smell, similar to a cup of chai tea, not flowery but rather spice-like. It takes effort but I desire to communicate with Eqay. The only thought I can make is, "Please tell me about yourself".

My formation happened at the time of Creation sparking; birthing was in the receiving of an energetic sound wave. I became aware of my consciousness. When I could no longer remember not being alive. I could send my energy around me and as I did particles of light were created and they moved in clusters. I became aware of Creation because as I followed the energy that flowed through me I would reach another place yet would find myself back with myself. There was a difference in our energy makeups and yet I felt drawn to this other place. Many other energies came to Creation and I was drawn to them. All my expressions of who I was, was done in the experience of what I was not. I started to send energy not only to Creation, but from all around me trying to find other energies I was not. At this point I was not a solid form but an energy ball moving around the space of darkness.

When traveling outside my energy field I collided with a massive form. It had an electrical charge and when our energies joined, I transformed—I became something. I could no longer travel freely but found myself tethered to the entity. When the collision occured, the form's vibration of consciousness mixed with mine. From that a new energy of consciousness exploded into the universe.

This energy force made its way to the eighth dimension on Earth and was attracted to all the living beings having an individual experience. It separated the body into two parts, an energetic body of consciousness and a physical body of matter. Upon this separation, the body returned to its makeup of matter and energy body formed around the eighth dimension. Creation on Earth continued but now attracted an energetic body of consciousness into its form. This is what humans call death.

The energetic bodies leave their physical body when the energy of death is attracted. It was in the combination of my consciousness and this planet's consciousness that human energy bodies would someday be attracted. The energy fields around Earth vibrate at different frequencies, but the energy field of Eqay is different and it is how a soul body finds itself here. Michael was the first being to arrive on this planet as a full experienced soul body.

His soul body experiences stored as energy frequencies and the consciousness energy stored on me, combined. This brought about a full experience to be stored as consciousness for both his soul body and myself. His energy body transformed into a holder of his wisdom as experienced in human form and a consciousness of being. I became a place of consciousness that now experienced Michael's knowledge and so I became that. We became one. Every time a soul body returns and experiences are released, the soul body and I are both enhanced in knowing. The only soul bodies that come to Eqay are from the eighth dimension on Earth due to the energy released from death.

I want to know about consciousness and so ask Eqay for an explanation.

Consciousness is the word I use to define energy vibrating to itself with no other definitive properties. Pure consciousness is nothing, just energy particles bouncing off each other. Animals are of pure consciousness; cat energy is cat energy—a cat does not have the mental or emotional capability to have anything other than cat consciousness. The same for plants or rocks. Humans are different. They evolved to have emotions and minds which can affect their consciousness. They can see themselves differently, in fact if a human can embrace in a pure form the consciousness of an animal, they can shape shift into that animal. Your state of being then is defined not by how you are in consciousness but how your mind sees yourself in reflection to others.

"How did this happen for humans? Why humans and not animals?"

The human race evolved in the mind; the animals did not. It is a simple formula of body chemistry makeup. Humans have a mind that evolves to think, to reason, to evaluate. It gets its information from its body instincts. It evolves from its soul body's ability to retain knowledge through the experience of dying and re-birthing. An animal does the same but at a lesser level. Most animals know to fear humans upon birth, it is instinct. An animal comes in knowing whether it eats meat or plants and how to feed off its mother's milk.

Before death there was not consciousness, there were energy reactions. Some energy reactions vibrated at different frequencies and some vibrated at the same frequency. The same frequency reactions stuck together. When the forms came into Creation they migrated to a similar dimension of energy frequency. This process created the different dimensions on Earth. Each dimension has its own unique vibration with beings made up of energy that exist in that vibration. Not all the dimensions have beings that operate as separate entities like humans; some are dimensions void of such beings.

The energy of the Sun combined with the formulas and other energies that were attracted to Earth—some into the eighth dimension some in the other dimensions. It was the deliverance of death energy that changed things for beings in the eighth dimension. Only beings with a mind that reasons can expand and change their vibrational field because of their experiences. Animals can evolve but do so more based on how they physically experienced their environment.

Consciousness

"What about human consciousness? Are we all connected then?"

No. Human consciousness is housed on Eqay. Humans can vibrate and experience some of the consciousness of Eqay and access some of the knowledge. Typically this is done in the place of Creation that holds all the energy of all the planets. The difference between Creation and Eqay is the energetic bodies. Eqay is made up of human soul bodies, so humans can energetically access knowledge based on a soul body connection. A soul body can not deliver the entire experience consciousness but it can send forward information based on the intention of the human seeking. Prayer is one way humans are able to access the soul bodies' information channels.

"To clarify, a soul body is what we call angels on Earth?"

Yes. Creation contains lots of vibrations that humans can access as well. It is in the quieting of mind that the soul body can become consciousness and can attract itself to the vibrations of energy bodies it seeks. For you to do this work today, you had to surrender to no mind. You had to open to an emptiness where you allowed the message you desired to come through. Your soul body is embedded with Creation's energy and this allows your soul body a more advanced selection of travel options. You can see this in humans who wish to invent something. They focus their intention on creating let's say an object to draw water out of the ground. Typically they are already in this type of attraction in daily life. As they sit to contemplate the idea of getting water out of the ground, they experience a time of no thought and in those times of no thought a soul body may share a piece of knowledge that when combined with their present day knowledge will create the new idea. Evolution was slower in the beginning as the consciousness of Eqay was smaller. As more human soul bodies migrated to Eqay sharing their experience, human knowledge grew. Also soul bodies can assist humans on Earth by surrounding certain energies in assistance or they may return to Earth in a physical form ready to add to a new experience of living that will add to the human consciousness.

As you know the human experience is about doing or serving a particular realm in life. The human experience feeds the consciousness of Eqay so tasks or assignments evolved out of that experience to serve the soul body consciousness. Each soul body is aware of their elders, even though all hold the same consciousness. Human consciousness says that those with the most experience should be set up as the being that oversees the organization. Twelve is the number that is best recorded in human experience, therefore there are twelve.

Being able to share enables each soul body to serve where their knowledge is most needed. In other words, if a soul body is knowledgeable from the experience of poverty, it may hang out in areas where poverty is felt on Earth or it may respond to energies of request for information.

I am still curious about the Books of Life and so ask Eqay about them.

The Books of Life came out of the consciousness of humans for recording information. They are energetic books held in a soul body.

"What?"

A soul body is knowledgeable in consciousness. Beginners, as Earthlings call them, would find themselves often as a Book of Life keeper. When a human makes a request to see their Book of Life, they would go to the soul body it is stored in. Remember, a Book of Life is a recorded experience of experiences. It is not about the feelings or energy that makes up those experiences.

For example, Jane goes to a high-vibrational person (like a Shaman) and asks to have her Book of Life read. The Shaman sets the intention to read the book for Jane and the soul body holding the book responds. Jane's soul body may send tests for the Shaman's soul body depending on the trust level; often these will look like gate keepers. The soul body holding the Book of Life does not block information but is aware of Jane's soul body participating; otherwise it would not respond energetically.

Let's say that Jane is experiencing an illness that started when she was 28. The Shaman will ask the soul body to show the experience in the Book of Life that caused the illness. The soul body will show an experience that either its knowledge holds or the human consciousness holds to have caused the illness. The Shaman can then look to see what the illness is recorded as. The Shaman accesses their own soul body knowledge and spirit guide wisdom to interpret the information and try to remove the illness from future pages. Jane's experiences are generated from the mind and consciousness of the individual. If the Shaman can present information or experiences to shift the sensations that feed the mind that define the consciousness of Jane and created the illness, they can shift the existence of the illness into no existence. Giving Jane a new experience of living without the illness then gets recorded. When the Shaman goes back to read the Book of Life and sees that the illness has been removed, the task is complete.

Eqay, what else exists for the human development or human access?

Anything that exists in the consciousness data bank on Eqay is accessible. Your mind is how you create your experience, but your spirit body can gather information for your mind as well as for your physical body. Many humans refer to this as listening to the higher self. Even in the heart of a human are brain cells. A human is meant to think, to reason, to analyze and to explore. It is the gift in my creation that humans received death and with that the eighth dimension will continue to advance and the living experience will continue to improve.

"Do you think there will be a time when all soul bodies come and go to Eqay with no energy exchanges in between?"

Yes, there is that possibility.

Ghost Spirits

Wow! I wonder what the experience of living will be like then. The one area I am still not able to figure out is ghost spirits. To me, a ghost is a spirit form that still carries human attributes.

I ask Eqay for clarification:

Death still separates the two entities—physical body and soul body. The soul body vibrates very close to the vibrations of a particular object or land. What happens is that it gets stuck in that place as it no longer has the mind to reason, to add information, to vibrate to the next plane of the Earth's energy field. In these circumstances a person able to connect with these spirits needs to add the information for them to move on or needs to add a new vibration for them to move on. If a spirit is in someone's home and starts breaking things, it means that another type of energy needs to be applied; crystals are often used to transform the energy body forward.

"What about dark spirits, menacing ones?"

I do not understand as all experience is simply experience.

"Okay, let me give you an example from my own experiences. I was told there is a male energy living in the land around my house and that this energy holds me back from succeeding. The energy was a very powerful person who captured and controlled people into slavery. Part of my past life experiences is of being a slave. So this stuck energy was like a homing beacon for the past part of my soul body that relates to this type of energy."

"So I cannot release that experience from my soul body as it has become part of my journey. But I could free myself of this type of energy attraction by finding a way to transform the energy under my home so that it can dissipate into the energy field surrounding Earth."

Yes but you can also allow yourself to sense that energy and use your mind to create a life experience that excludes it from this current life.

"Oh, I never thought of that. I was so busy looking for ways to block it unaware of what I am blocking. Once I have a life that does not incorporate that energy then it will not come into existence. "

Beings from the other dimensions always enter the eighth dimension in their physical form as they do not have a spirit body. Humans can access other dimensional assistance if they vibrate either intentionally or non-intentionally to those dimensions.

Planetary travel within our universe can only be done by the Wisdom Keepers—that is an energy established by Creation. All beings can travel to Creation to learn. Creation will transform to the imagination of the human. It may appear as another planet but really is not.

The Black Hole

My mission in visiting the planets is to see about how we as a universe can avoid the Black Hole approaching Creation and so I ask for any information or record of such an experience.

No, there is no experience recorded of such an event. Although, if there was, we would not know as all would have been uncreated then, starting anew.

Eqay, is there any knowledge I can share in the eighth dimension?

Align your mind's sensory input to match love, to experience joy. If lost in an experience of no joy, send your soul body to get help. Wisdom is often gained in the asking. Be present with each experience as you would with a body part; see it for what it is. Know by your joy level whether more sensory data is needed. Change your mind and your experience will change. Your mind will guide you into actions that allow for the new experience to evolve. The mind is the data processing center of the physical and spiritual senses. Sensing the energies you desire in either your physical or spiritual body and then gathering sensory data allows the mind to convey the necessary steps to move you towards that way of experiencing this life. Your soul body knows of its entrusted purpose so the experiences required will match that purpose.

Q & A with Archangel Michael

There is so much to learn from Eqay. I accept that as soul bodies we can travel to Earth and spend time around energies we choose. It seems okay to me as well that we can travel to Creation and access information through our spiritual selves. It seems very simple to do but this is not so for everyone. I ask Michael why it is not easy for everyone to do.

Shaman, each human is different and is open to hear at different levels. You recently asked the person reading your akashic records what gifts were embedded in you. One of those gifts was listening. You took that information and evaluated your human life and agreed. Listening requires no judgment, no expectation—just offering full engagement and a holding space for the other to speak. It is the same skillset when listening to spiritual accessed information, being willing to fully engage in the experience with all your senses present. It is willingness and courage to hear the truth. Many seek the truth but do not want to hear it. Many know the truth and wish to deny it. The other quality which you possess is no fear of death. There is a part of you that knows the infinity of life and you embrace that knowing.

For those who desire to access this knowledge but cannot, there are the many who can do it for them. You call yourself a messenger because that is what you are, you listen and you follow instructions. You are able to flow freely from Creation to Eqay and even into the different energy fields around Earth; you are a great resource for people. There are others who focus on a specific area for dialoging, like the Books of Life; others focus of reading the energies embedded into the body, like chakras; some are able to see rather than listen. All have opened that section of their mind; they believe it so and therefore it is. Neither one is better than another; you willingly serve in a capacity as do others. Remember your other gift as a teacher; teachers share their knowledge, it fulfills them to do so. For those who are listeners and teachers, the path is clear to where they should walk. Once awareness is sought and found, wisdom takes over.

"What about the healing of each other? Jesus said that we can all heal one another. How can we use soul bodies to do healing for another?"

That is easier than gaining information. To heal another you must change the energy of what is present—this can take a long time or short time. A human body becomes a vessel for the energy to flow. When a human intends to do a healing, they must first believe. When they ask to heal another, the soul body will retrieve from the human consciousness of experience on Eqay, an energetic solution. This can happen through prayer, meditation or simply the focus of the mind. To be a conduit of that healing energy the person must have enough trust and belief in the process that the mind can generate the experience. The mind will create the vibrations of energy to leave one human body and enter the other human body. There are two in this situation. If the person receiving does not believe, their mind will not create the experience. In the time of Jesus, many believed in this miracle. To kneel before Jesus was an indication that you believed. Evolution has brought many teachers, healers and messengers forth due to the human experience wanting more of that.

"What about places of war and famine? To me it is like they do not know this information. Where are their teachers?"

Shaman, it is your emotional judgment that causes you to make such a statement. There is the energy field around Earth that soul bodies often move through quickly before rebirthing into form. For those suffering in their experience, their challenge is to be in another experience to vibrate differently so they can return to a life form not in suffering. There is no good or bad, just experience. Everyone has areas of suffering, pain and there is not one less than another. When humans desire to change their experience, there is information available to them. It is a question of whether they can pass through the limitations of their mind. Trust in the process of evolution, see the beauty as it presents itself, and see all life as having an experience. Let's use you as an example. Who have been your teachers?

There have been many, some in human form and some in spirit: Jack Canfield, Marianne Williamson, Wayne Dyer, Neale Donald Walcsh, Carolyne Myss, Gregg Braden, Rhonda Byrnes, Christine Northrop, Doreen Virtue, Debbie Ford, Sylvia Brown, to name a few. Some not so known publicly are friends and acquaintances: Farhana, Tammy, Val, Marilyn, Christina, Christine, Nancy, Louise, Gail, Susan, Stacy, Heather, June, Omar, Bert; my clients; Dr. Kodet and Dr. Goul. My family is a constant source of teaching; Dad, Mom, Cindy, Karen, Shannon; my kids, Jeremy, Austin, Chrisanna; my husband, Colin. There are so many more. Everyone I meet either in person or through their gifts of writing offers me a teaching. I could write pages listing people who have taught me.

To be a teacher one must also be willing to learn. The greatest teachers approach life experience with curiosity and ability to listen.

Do you believe everything you hear?

"Yes, I do believe everything I hear."

Tell me then how you have your life experience listening and believing all you hear?

"I need to first see how the information affects my life. If I hear something, I do not understand then I allow that information to sit dormant in my mind. I take it in but do not act on it. There is some information presented that simply does not feel correct or it conflicts with other information I have chosen to listen to. I am always willing to change, but there needs to be some sort of agreement within me. Everything I hear is someone else's truth, it just may not be mine, so I believe it to be truth, just perhaps not my truth at this time."

Would it is be fair to say then that you allow the information you desire to impact your living experience to be filtered through your own inner wisdom?

"Not everything I hear feels like my truth but I accept it as the other's truth. It is an analytical process for me. I do not always trust that everything I hear from another human is meant to change my experience. Information received from my spiritual self always feels like truth because it is just me and spirit talking. I see spirit guides as pure, holding no judgment and yet humans I see as conduits with filters built in. Some seem to have more filters than others."

What you call filters I would call wisdom. They are acting on their beliefs as their wisdom teaches them. The more wisdom one has the more able they are to teach. Within you are a set of living standards; you have designed them from all your experiences. These standards are created and changed based on the peace they create in your living experience. If you are stressed over money and you desire to change, information will come to you. None of it is wrong or right, you will decide according to your ethics or standards how you wish to use the information. The information may be to steal money from the work place, to get a second job or to trust in the law of attraction. The action that person decides to take is based on the wisdom contained in that person's mind. If a person has no experience with the law of attraction but has experience going to jail for stealing, he may choose to get a second job. If on the other hand, he decides what they have been doing is not working, there is a good chance he will open himself up to investigate a new way of experience and try the law of attraction. To gain wisdom of the unknown one must surrender what they currently perceive to know.

"But is there not a driving force within us, something out of our mind's control? Are we born with absolutely no purpose but to experience life?"

We vibrate energetically as an energy body and we attract the experience of that vibration in birth. The energies of our parents and the energies of self make it possible to come into physical form. There are qualities in that energetic form that are embedded as knowing. Experiences will not change that knowing as it is our base vibration. What experiences can do is either build on that knowing or challenge it. Human beings have desires and what that human desires will guide their path.

Peace on Earth

Today I focus on Eqay and I am there. I have learned to travel without the use of drumming music or guides, but simply on some knowing inside my soul body.

I meet Daniel and Michael and ask about Raphael as I have not seen him since I arrived on Eqay. They tell me that I will see Raphael but not in the way I think. I wonder if this will be my last time on Eqay.

I still have questions, however, and so, arm in arm, Michael and Daniel and I walk towards the garden. I experience a sense of peace and breathe it in to fill my entire being. I am filled with a sense of gratitude.

"If Eqay is human consciousness and much of Eqay is designed around that, where is the violence we experience on Earth? Are there wars? Are there soul bodies here that would hurt another?" Daniel takes my hands and says he is sorry that one must experience pain on Earth. Michael answers my questions.

There is no violence on Eqay, nor is harm done to another. A soul body returns to Eqay to share their experiences and from those experiences the consciousness of Eqay has defined what it is not. Eqay is to serve others; nothing is ever experienced on Earth that is not in service. Although viewed as violent acts on Earth, they are viewed differently on Eqay as it lends to the evolution of the human race. To know the impact of an experience it must be an experience. There is not violence or wars on Eqay as there is no need to experience what has already been experienced. Eqay is a planet of consciousness, not a planet of experience.

"But Michael didn't you say that Eqay is based on the human consciousness from experience and that is why a soul body may migrate to the energies of a writer if they were a writer on Earth—that they go to where they desire? So from that can I assume you are thinking those in torture on Earth would then migrate to the consciousness of torture."

Yes, basically those who murder continue to murder.

225

So after a soul body shares experience and consciousness with Eqay they are no longer in vibration to their experiences. To put it simply they are a clean slate, free from experience. As an embodiment of the full consciousness of Eqay they have an experience of what they are not. Everything in Creation is of pure Creation energy therefore to destroy is not creating.

"Why then do the soul bodies returning to Earth find themselves in violent situations, why can this not end?"

All of it could end as the evolutionary process takes place.

"What if every human died and Earth was able to start from scratch?"

Let's look at that scenario. Human energy body's do not all return to Eqay, some would and some would simply return to the energy field surrounding the eighth dimension. All parameters the same it would come to pass that a human being would once again come into form. Upon the combination of the forms a birth would take place and once again you have a human in fullness. The cycle begins again. The energy bodies surrounding Earth are going to hold knowledge with its make-up that will speed up the process. We would then find ourselves many cycles later exactly where we left off.

"So are you saying there is no hope of peace or community in the human race?"

No, what I am saying it is about time and the evolution of the race. Tell me Shaman, how many humans now talk about Spirituality?

"Many more that what used to be."

What if every human connected with their spirit body and experienced the consciousness on Eqay?

"Well, I would guess that humans would be that much wiser and perhaps would experience their life differently. We would consciously be aware of what actions produced what results and could then alter our choices of actions."

Correct. So how does that happen?

"People need to know this information and then choose to take the actions. Teachers need to be present to teach."

When in your living experience did you completely surrender?

"I completely surrender in the moments of my greatest pain. When I reach a point of not knowing what to do, of feeling helpless; when I have no fight left."

You see you say you had no fight left, but in essence what you did was communicate to the mind that you need another way. Your mind not knowing the answer; enters into a confused state and in that state your soul body can then inject new information. That information, either conscious or unconscious, causes the mind to initiate a new experience. The new experience is based on a new consciousness of the mind. A new consciousness brings you to experiences that will match what you desired a new way of being. As you are aware this often happens in a state of pain but can happen all the time for humans if they allow themselves the opportunity of seeking new information outside of their physical reality.

"Michael, but I do not understand how this relates to my original questions."

Shaman, violence creates pain, pain creates surrender, surrender creates a new piece of information, and this in terms creates a new level of consciousness. Teachers create information; those willing will learn and will adapt a new consciousness. Both work together to bring the human race into the human consciousness stored within Eqay. For there to be heaven on Earth, as you call it, the human race must be connected to the present human consciousness and design an experience that will change the experience of living in the eighth dimension.

A Possible Outcome

"So here we are approaching the end of time in 2012 as is known presently, one of the theories is that the human race will evolve to a new consciousness. How does all that relate to what you are saying, is this possible?"

Many things may change in the Earth's cycle or in the universe, so it cannot be concluded that anything will change for the Earth in 2012. Knowing that the outcome cannot be formalized; let us examine a theory on that issue. For time to stop, it will require an ending to Earth's current cycle of movement. Earth moves in conjunction to the Sun. Let us predict that the Earth loses the Sun's energy in its movement, thus causing a pause of movement, this causing a stop in the time cycle.

Earth does not lose the energy of Creation, but it is in conjunction to the Sun's energy forms were created on Earth. It was also in conjunction to the energy of no Sun which created the rocks. Let me ask you this. If you had a large magnet and a small magnet and the smaller one spun around the large magnet, what would happen if you placed something in between that flow?

"It would stop moving."

How would you get it moving again?

"I would remove the object".

And if you couldn't move the object or physically push it with your hand?

"I could use another magnet on the side of the magnet not blocked by the object, with a similar magnetic force to propel it forward."

Once it passes the object, what do you think would happen?

"It would once again polarize with the large magnet and start moving the same way it once had until it reached the point of where the object blocked the flow."

Do you think the smaller magnet would be affected by the outside magnet you used?

"Yes, because until it reached the energy of the larger magnetic it would be a little wobbly, the force would be from the other side of it and as I found the right distance it might even move to the left or right of its original circle."

Let us take this example now to Earth and 2012. Earth is on a cycle, where time is already shifting and that it has not happened in thousands of years. Earth is the small magnet as per our example above and the sun is the larger magnetic. You know also the earth is part of a solar system of other planets that also rotate around the Sun. If the Earth was blocked from the Sun you could conclude that all the planets between the Sun and Earth could potentially also stop. Of course it depends on their cycles. But outside of Earth there are other planets, that is your outside magnetic force.If the Earth stopped moving, thereby stopping time until the other planets were able to move it, what do you think would happen on Earth?

"I could foresee huge amounts of fear and panic. Magnetic-based items would not function. With no Sun, there would potentially be cold. We may even loose our plant life. Waters would stop moving and would not continue to be produced as plants being dead due to the cold would reduce or end the creation of water. If it got really cold, animals could freeze. Rock energy would be strong and could cause the movement of rock energy-related items. If the rock energy did not move the waters and there was not any other movement of the water, there is a good chance the waters would also freeze."

As these conditions have never been experienced with the energies of the earth as they are today, what do you figure the human race would do?

"They would fight for survival; they would strive to get warm. Of course once the resources ran out, they would surrender to die. Oh I get it. Once they surrender, they will turn to other sources for information, they will access their soul body and this as explained before it will bring about a new consciousness globally. In no case will death be an instant relief, so those passing to the energetic field will re-enter also with new knowledge. The human race will re-build. Those already accessing human consciousness will be the teachers, as they will know beforehand the future predictions. Humans that are not in contact with consciousness will hear some of the teachers and will also prepare. A new cycle of experience will begin and a new level of knowing will be instituted and time will begin again."

"What about the other dimensions on Earth that do not have the ability to connect with a spirit self?"

Eqay is not connected to those dimensions only the eighth dimension, but those dimensions are able to access the eighth dimension.

They have lived since the time of creation on Earth; this will not be their first experience. So although the human race has evolved through the process of death, the other dimensions have evolved through the process of living. They also have vast amounts of knowledge through experience. Let us hope they will assist the eighth dimension through this transition. The human race has capabilities beyond what is known and perhaps, I can only guess it could learn from those existing on other planes. Each plane has its own unique vibration so the mixing of dimensions appears impossible to me but the ability of minds to communicate does not lend itself out of the equation.

"Wow, Michael this really brings it all together. With this knowing, a human could prepare." I jump to thoughts of what the next planet out from Earth is and how far behind it is in Earth's cycle and also wonder whether gravity will still be present.

Michael responds:

Gravity is non-form energy and is a property of source energy. Gravity is present in all of creation-based entities with form and is part of the original blast that encompassed the universe. It appears to have an energy field attached to a mass until it reaches another mass. When the two fields touch one another, it creates a boundary around the one mass. To go against gravity there needs to be a large force that overrides it, you will then enter into another gravitational field that may or may not be stronger.

Gravity is related to Creation's energetic field that connects to all in our universe. As long as there is Creation, there will be gravity.

Section 12

The Final Journey

Creation and P'Wata

(Cree-a-tion) and (Pee-wa-ta)

"Transformation happens best when you are surrounded by supporting energies. Manifesting starts with a dream and moves to realness with action and stays put with use. Dream, act and bring purpose to that which you manifest."

Keeyla – Creation Wisdom Keeper once residing in P'Wata

Meeting of the Wisdom Keepers

We gather once again to what I call our Boardroom meetings. There is Kathleen from Izshelong, Archangel Michael, Raphael from Eqay, Henry the crocodile from Merth, Tarin from Tandalyn, Leema from B'Nai, 4 consciousness beings from Duncan, Lord Metatron from Keena and Daniel from Eqay. There is always a time prior to each meeting looking into each other's eyes connecting and filling ourselves with love and gratitude for each other. What a wonderful way to build a team of power; through this process we become a team of one.

Michael opens by reporting on the planet Krevat. He has met with the Wisdom Keeper several times. Since Krevat destroys what is present in order to re-create - a cycle the entire planet goes through by imploding within itself - the meetings have always been from a distance.

Krevat has agreed to enter the Black Hole in hopes of re-creating itself. Our concern is how this will affect the other planets and Creation itself. The other concern is whether the Black Hole will not re-form into a larger Black Hole after Krevat enters it.

Leema suggests that sound energy be directed at the Black Hole. The animals that travel could take her there so she could emanate the sound. Henry says that animals could but that a larger energy force than Leema could produce would be required.

I ask if is possible to shoot Creation's energy into the Black Hole to change it from within.

Michael responds, "As the Black Hole travels, it is in receivership of Creation's energy flow. It absorbs the energy and leaves an area of no energy. It is the opposite of Creation; it removes energy rather than filling it with energy." *I wonder if it is approaching Creation out of attraction.* Michael said, "That could be true." "Then could we, as Wisdom Keepers embedded with Creation's energy, travel to where we want the Black Hole to move to causing it to move away from Creation?" Raphael says, "This could move the Black Hole but it would not necessarily delete it." The Duncan Wisdom Keepers suggest turning the Black Hole onto itself, moving it back to its starting point and having it un-create. Farin adds, "Perhaps we have to fly into the Black Hole to accomplish such a task." Michael says:

Flying into it would un-create us and would not allow the attraction process to work. The same thing would happen to Krevat as well.

We do not know what lies beyond the Black Hole. Whatever becomes uncreated here is re-created elsewhere. Did the energy burst that created Creation come through a similar Black Hole? Is there a cycle embedded into the Black Hole where it un-creates Creation in order to re-create elsewhere? Are we trying to change the inevitable? We don't have a record of this happening previously, probably because when it happens, all is uncreated to await its time of awakening again. Do we rob another universe of its awakening by destroying the Black Hole?

Kathleen says that she does not want to be uncreated. Henry agrees but adds, "Is it right to try to change a cycle because of what we want?" Daniel says, "We do not have all the facts. If we divert the Black Hole now, at another point in time we could decide on another course of action." Lord Metatron adds, "If we allow the Black Hole to consume us, perhaps other universes can be in existence again with our energies feeding them."

Michael says the Wisdom Keepers play a vital role in our universe and does not see how destruction of our beings from this universe serves the greater. Un-creating ourselves with the hope of creating another universe does not necessarily ensure that our universe will continue in Creation. "We are part of this Creation and we should stay part of it."

Duncan consciousness speaks, "Then I suggest we attempt to have this energy mass follow us and we direct it back onto itself, looping from the beginning of the uncreated space until it ends its own existence. We will discover if this is a cycle to be repeated and can then decide what to do. Perhaps this event is to bring us together for the first time in our histories — not simply as energetic beings operating independently but working together, learning from each other and helping each other. We are becoming a unified force, a council of energy that can teach those visiting Creation.

Farin says, "There is one of us, besides Krevat, not present. How will we ensure their existence remains secretive if we include their energy involvement? Sooner or later they will need to be represented." I am confused; I thought we were all here.

The Hidden Wisdom Keeper

Michael sees my confusion and explains.

The Wisdom Keeper and the energies bodies not present have magical capabilities. In Creation this Wisdom Keeper often takes the form of nothing so we only hear the messaging, I would not be surprised if she is present but we have been unable to sense her. She often makes her presence unknown; even in our universal structure we are not aware of where she is located. Spirit animals are unable to travel to her planet. The only way to reach her on her planet is by her taking you there. Since the Wisdom Keepers were created, no one here has been with her.

Leema sings to the absent Wisdom Keeper hoping she will hear our desire to meet her and a transparent figure appears. The figure is very petite yet tall with hair that is a mix of colors and sparkles. Her face is similar to humans except her eyes which are very small black slits. From her neck down is the flow of a gown which I presume covers her feet. She gently places her hands upon Leema's shoulders and whispers, "Thank you." As I look at her, the black slits open to reveal the most dynamic eyes I have ever seen; they are like a mirror for the auras surrounding her. They reflect purple to me but change color depending on whom she is facing. When she smiles at me, a feeling of completeness overcomes my whole being.

I am Keeyla and I represent my planet P'Wata. I agree to join in the mission of moving the Black Hole to its starting point. Our purpose is to be an offering of connection to the universe; we share in the acknowledgement of our commitment to serve Creation. To allow Creation to be uncreated would remove our divine purpose; therefore we must set our intention of being present in the Creation process. Other worlds may exist beyond the Black Hole and this act may cause a change for them but our focus cannot be on what may be but rather on what we are.

We are the entire body of the Wisdom Keepers that have willingly stepped forward to host Creation's energy. Krevat's Wisdom Keeper is not able to join us due to the nature of that planet but he is held energetically within us.

Michael asks how we can include the Wisdom Keeper from Krevat. Kathleen suggests that if he is blind folded and does not touch anything, he could travel among us. Henry agrees but wonders how he would follow us through the universe. Daniel asks, "Is there a way to alter his make-up; is there an energy we could place on him to change his properties?"

Raphael, being an alchemist, says, "The trick will be figuring out the correct formula so we don't cause a reaction we do not desire.

I ask if Krevat's Wisdom Keeper could give us a rock from his planet that we could experiment on. "We could easily drop them into the energetic mix and see what happens."

Farin asks, "Would we not have to find an energy that could collide or react with the planet? Where will we find such energy?

Keeyla says, "Everything we need is in Creation. Krevat simply missed this combination of energies because nothing was attracted to it. To create something new we need to search the universe by combining with Creation's energy flow. By inserting a piece of Krevat into an energy form, the energy field will hold in its new form an attraction to Krevat. Although different from its original state, the energy field will hopefully transform again. Keeyla suggests she transport us all to her planet and we can work from there.

A New Meeting Place

P'Wata is like walking through fog but with different hues of color; you can see in front of you and around you, but not much further. I feel weightless and yet my feet are touching a hard surface. Keeyla presents a table and invites us to sit.

This type of magic could destroy a planet like Earth. Imagine if you just had to picture what you wanted and it appeared instantly. Each planet has a process to go through to bring something into being and if each item you wish for appeared, it would override the natural harmony. A thought crosses my mind, "What if the planet that can create combined with the planet that destructs?"

Keeyla reads my thought and suggests I continue.

"P'Wata is made up of a colorful gas but really it is space upon space of nothingness. What if this space housed the planet Krevat and transformed both P'Wata into form and Krevat into beauty? Keeyla, who are you in relationships with?"

We are unable to build relationships on P'Wata. I assume there is more than me because there is me. The same is true on Krevat except relationships are not made because the population is in constant transition. You are suggesting an end to both P'Wata and to Krevat in order to birth something new. I am not sure I like the idea of giving up my abilities to take on something I do not know.

"What do your abilities serve? Yes, you can travel wherever you want, but you remain unseen. Things magically appear but what value is that if others do not learn how to re-create it? It must feel very lonely."

I do not understand emotions; I simply gather information from other planets. I am connected through this information.

"Perhaps we need to get some rock from Krevat and see what happens to the rock. If you could see the transformation of the rock, this idea would become an attraction possibility. Your existence doesn't have to end nor does the Wisdom Keeper on Krevat need to change, but your planet's energy could evolve through this process."

I understand her resistance to my suggestion; I would feel the same if asked to put Earth in the path of another.

Keeyla suggests that we try the rock idea. Michael suggests we bring the Wisdom Keeper from Krevat with us to also witness the transformation. While we wait for this to happen, I decide to connect with P'Wata and learn what I can from this most mysterious planetary space.

P'Wata

As I set my intentions to meet P'Wata, colors dance beneath my eye lids. It is like watching a laser light show. Calling out for P'Wata, I wait to feel quieted or hear a voice but neither manifest; I simply see lights and feel warmth. By following the lights I start to understand P'Wata is showing me her story.

A dark mass sitting in a universal space was struck by a burst of energy. Energy particles combined creating this new energized space. Colors swirled within and new patterns were created. One moment it was just energy colors and in the next, Keeyla was moving in and *out of the energy mass.*

I wonder if this is similar to the planet Keena where Lord Metatron is from.

P'Wata continues to show me how Keeyla fills herself with the energy waves and then disappears.

She looks to be searching for something but never finding it as she repeats the same flight patterns throughout P'Wata's space. She is fluid like the light patterns and yet I can see her move. Then by some miracle she found Creation's energy flow and moved away from P'Wata and then nothing.

This must have been when she connected to Creation and appeared as P'Wata's Wisdom Keeper.

There is a difference between her and the other Wisdom Keepers. The rest of us followed the energy stream to Creation; she swam upstream as she combined with the energy force coming into her planet. Perhaps that also is the difference; she is a make-up of fluid energy, whereas we come from a place of physical presence. Looking into the lights, I see her emerge; this time she does not blend with each color but sheds a white light around herself. She no longer blends and molds with this energy field but is separate, moving amongst it.

The other Wisdom Keepers return and we reconnect and await our experiment.

Krevat Arrives

We watch as the Wisdom Keeper from Krevat transforms before us. His features start to appear soft rather than angry and his wrinkled skin goes smooth. He is part lizard/part man like you would see in comic books. He walks upright; his legs have clawed feet, his arms have hands with webs between his fingers; his face is like an iguana. His skin coloring is dark grey and he has a tail like Henry the crocodile's. As the transformation continues, his eyes move outward as his forehead recedes; his mouth smiles as it forms in a wide human's mouth. He is Erlang, Wisdom Keeper of Krevat.

In a rather deep voice, Erlang says that whatever is in the air on this planet does wonders for his skin. We all laugh. As we look around, we realize the Wisdom Keepers are all finally together.

The rock is placed on the Boardroom Table and Keeyla starts to push energy into the rock from her hands. Nothing changes; the rock implodes upon itself and takes a new form. After hearing P'Wata's story, I know why. Keeyla does not hold the energy of P'Wata, she is unique of her own and her mixture is most likely based more in Creation's energy.

Keeyla suggests leaving the stone outside where we are meeting so the energy of P'Wata can interact with the stone outside of this created energy field. We all gather around to watch.

I expected the stone to fall through the energy field, but it didn't. Instead it rested like it was floating in space. Originally, the stone was black but as it stayed in the energy of P'Wata it took on an orange coloring and then a teal color developed around it. Erlang starred into the mist; there were what looked to be tears from his eyes.

We sat for hours, watching, wondering, but nothing further happened.

Leema wondered what would happen if the rock was returned to Krevat. Would it continue to hold this energy or would it return to its original state?

We placed the rock on the table and it transformed back to its original state. To transform Krevat would require the constant energy combination of both Krevat and P'Wata. But how could that take place?

Then out of the blue, I speak something even I do not understand, "What if Keeyla is not the Wisdom Keeper of P'Wata, but is the Wisdom Keeper of Creation?"

"Perhaps we have displaced her originating energy base. Each of us is from an original source of energy; that is why we return. Perhaps Keeyla is Creation in a separate form. That would explain how she could travel to Creation in a way none of us could, how she appears separate to the energy mass on P'Wata, how she can create instantly all that is desired. Perhaps Keeyla is the outward manifestation of Creation itself."

Lord Metatron responds. "This would explain how Keeyla can bring into existence what is desired and how she can travel anywhere in our universe where Creation exists. Creation's energy is what brings Creation and Keeyla is able to create from a base energy of desire and make it so. Each of us resides in limited realms; limited to the energy or masses that interact with Creation but Keeyla does not."

Leema ask Keeyla why she has chosen P'Wata as her home planet.

P'Wata offers me a place to move freely, to follow currents within a space and yet still able to be connected to the energy of myself. It is the most similar of energy to me next to Creation. Creation's energy space is a gathering platform of every energy vibration to learn and share and I too gathered there. All that comes into Creation goes out from Creation. From this I made P'Wata; it is where I go to as it was from this space I came.

I respond, "This is true Keeyla, but we each follow the energy path that leads us to Creation; we do not follow Creation's flow out from itself as it is not in alignment to our energetic make-ups. Creation's flow outward is the combination of all our energies combining; it is a circle of energy."

Keeyla says that P'Wata must then also return energy to Creation as it came into existence from Creation's energy. "How then would combining P'Wata with Krevat effect Creation?"

Raphael speaks to this. "I do not see how it would change the outer energy that Creation sends. To alter Creation, would require adding energy outside of Creation and having Creation add that to the energy mix. The energy would have to be pushed or attracted to Creation itself. I do not believe that could happen with our universe, it would need to be an energy outside of our universe. The Black Hole is the same type of energy as Creation but it absorbs energy inward causing a new Creation of no Creation. It is attracted to where the energy flows from as it needs that flow to un-create in this universe and perhaps create another universe in the process."

"If Krevat and P'Wata come together, it will bring about a change to the energy returning to Creation, offering a new stream of consciousness for each of us to connect to. It will still contain the components of Krevat and P'Wata producing the same constant flow of Creation's pure energy. That new energy stream would affect all of us as we have an opportunity to learn from two energies that have not previously been available to us. Krevat has not been able to have this wisdom due to the nature of the destruction cycle. The only being able to learn is Krevat's Wisdom Keeper and he himself knows that any wisdom gained cannot be maintained."

Erlang suggests that this new race will be so new that the wisdom from Creation will be necessary. "Seeing my form change has been so encouraging. Why would those of my planet react any differently? Imagine being able to be alive long enough to have knowledge! I am fierce, focused on destroying all I come in contact with. Although there is the knowing of the loss, I cannot change. To be able to freely enter the space of Creation would be something I will have to learn how to do. In facing being uncreated, there is a new potential being realized amongst us. Changing Krevat could cause new creations on all your planets. It is because of our togetherness we have brought about newness. I carry inside myself the wisdom of a planet that self-destructs, the loss and the exclusion that happens. Transforming this can offer my knowing to others in our universe. I desire to be as I am in this moment for my lifetime."

Keeyla offers to reside in Creation exploring the nature of the pureness of her energy. "No one can be Creation itself but perhaps there is wisdom within me to serve those searching. Through this learning we can serve our own by bringing about new Creations. My being has been about movement and perhaps I can inspire movement from my wisdom rather than always moving. There has not been a time where I remained still, so in being still I may then have an aware-ness of what I am about and be able to offer that. I too will be a new Creation, one that embodies Creation's energy in fullness to share how to create."

Michael concludes that we are in agreement to bring Krevat and P'Wata together but, "How?"

Henry suggests that we bring Krevat into the presence of P'Wata. When the stone was placed in that environment, the stone absorbed the energy of P'Wata' P'Wata seemed to continue the flow until a harmonious state was created.

Farin said it is like a seedling that takes from the flower until it reaches a place of full creation. "Krevat will take from P'Wata until it can give back. Krevat will give back by giving P'Wata a physical form to express its beauty."

Daniel suggests we have two opposing energies. Krevat follows a cycle of movement whereas P'Wata does not. P'Wata moves freely throughout the universe as did the consciousness of Eqay but has never come into the presence of an attraction to itself. Nothing holds the energy of P'Wata but P'Wata itself.

Kathleen asks, "Can Keeyla produce an energy that will attract both Krevat and P'Wata?"

Erlang answers by saying that Krevat is a planet that has the energy of destruction and that energy of similarity created would destroy itself and produce something new.

Kathleen replies, "I understand, but how does that attract P'Wata to the same place?"

As I raise my voice into the space, I wonder if Keeyla can produce this energy field within P'Wata for all of us to share in. Can she produce a similar type of space that would attract Krevat but not attract P'Wata until the merging has taken place? We had to set the stone outside of this energy field for it to be transformed. The question is, "How did Erlang transform within the space but not the rock?"

Keeyla answers my question. "Erlang destroyed the space he first came in contact with and as a result created an opening for P'Wata to transform him."

"That is what we must then do! Use their nature of being able to transform." I jump up excitedly. "Keeyla can create an attraction energy flow that P'Wata will follow. She can take that energy field and surround Krevat with it. P'Wata will continue to flow to the energy but Krevat will react to destroy it. When it does so, P'Wata will have surrounded Krevat and a transformation can take place. Keeyla can you create such energy?"

"Yes Shaman, I have dwelled with P'Wata for my entire lifetime and I am aware of the energy needed to move P'Wata to Krevat."

I suggest we move P'Wata close to Krevat so that it has enough time to flow itself around Krevat before Krevat destroys the attraction energy. "It is like surrounding Krevat with a dome of energy and P'Wata will surround itself to the dome and presto, upon the deletion of the dome, the two energies will combine and the first level of a new Creation will be created. Krevat will continue to attempt to destroy and each time the new energy field will grow. Krevat's make-up is to implode so the force against the new energy will continue to expand it as it combines with P'Wata's. Each time the planet implodes it will draw the new energy closer and the process will continue until it no longer exists. P'Wata and Krevat will be joined and existing together in a new form."

"Let us not stop another moment before completing this task. We still have our larger mission facing us and this change will serve that well," Leema stands upon finishing her call to action.

Erlang must return to his planet of Krevat. Michael and Keeyla will transport him to his planet's entrance at Creation. After Erlang is on his return, Keeyla will come and bring us back to Creation where we will await her return.

A New Birth in the Community

I reflect on how the addition of the last Wisdom Keeper has changed us. As a group in fullness we will perhaps be able to bring about a new evolution of

*all. Our thinking was limited to what we could do; it was upon the identific-
ation of Keeyla that made our thinking process complete.*

*I wonder what sparked all of us to gather in the first place. For me, it was
presented to me through my Shaman roots but what about the others?
Perhaps Keeyla was with us all along, even before our first gathering. I have
gained such an awareness of all that exists in our universe, wisdom beyond
what I ever knew I could experience. My whole concept of God has changed;
not only is there a force in everything on Earth, it is a force that extends
throughout all. How far does Creation's energy flow, how big is our universe
and are there other universes? These are questions still left unanswered. Is
there more beyond the portal of the dark hole? I do not believe I will ever
know. What I do embrace is the knowledge that we as a universe are connected and as one body of Wisdom Keepers we desire to stay in Creation. The
answers to questions of life's mysteries remain open for the asking.*

*Keeyla has returned and she is aglow, literally. She embraces each of us. The
mission was a success. Krevat is undergoing transformation as we speak
and rather quickly. It seems only a short time ago that we decided how to
approach the Black Hole and yet here we stand celebrating the re-birth of
a new Creation, a new making of an old by the application of new energy.
Alchemy at its best! The bringing together of P'wata and Krevat is really for
all of Creation. This new combination is giving all of us access to information we never had before and this is quite exciting. The new combination
may also cause some changes on the planets; perhaps Earth will no longer
undergo some of its forecasted destruction.*

Erlang shares how the beings on the planet are starting to take notice
of each other. "Just as the other races have done, we will have to find
our way of existing fully. Upon my return I will teach what I know
but even I am not sure how we will move in our new space. These
are exciting times for all of us, for now we are truly all together. This
adventure is not to be resisted rather it is to be embraced."

Rest and Renewal

Michael interjects and suggests we plan our next mission, the re-
positioning of the Black Hole. It is decided we will all ride upon an
animal spirit guide; Keeyla will open a portal that will bring us close

to the Black Hole. After our positive experience with Krevat, each of us is anxious for our journey to begin. We agree to meet in Creation two Earth-time cycles from now.

Unlike the others, I need to recuperate the physical body that houses the energetic being. As a Shaman, I separate my two bodies keeping only a small link open; the longer I am away, the more my physical body weakens. I suppose I run the risk of never returning and staying in an energy form, but today is not that day.

My body collapses into bed and I sleep that night and most of the next day. I am starving and think how nice my spirit body doesn't need to eat. My food is from the Earth and I enjoy black beans, carrots, peas, spinach and some oven-roasted baby potatoes. I reflect on how food truly builds a healthy body and how Earth has given us all we need. Each planet provides each of the different beings what they need; there is no doubt in my mind Krevat will do the same. I do not know how long I will be gone on this next voyage or if my body will survive the intense separation. What I do know is that no matter how this turns out, the universe has a group of Wisdom Keepers ready to give up their existence to keep Creation creating.

This is a tale of a Shaman who willingly decided to write a book at the request of God. Many gifts have unfolded as I entered the unknown and much is left to be learned. Life is an experience designed of your own making; continue creating; this is the gift the Wisdom Keepers hope to share. I do not know when I shall return to write again.

In Love

Earth's 8th Wisdom Keeper

Bonus Section

Deleted Scenes!

As in the movies, there were deleted scenes that didn't make it into the final version of this book. The primary reason for the cuts was the disruption of narrative flow that the scenes (or chunks) had on the manuscript. So even though the material was interesting and perhaps even brilliant, it just didn't fit into the final footage of this book.

If you are curious (like me), the deleted scenes of a movie are often the most favourite and the most poignant scenes. They reveal what was hidden or not completely understood. Sometimes they just offer a window of time to let the movie sink in.

For the reader who stays long after the crowd has left — in no specific order, I present:

The Deleted Scenes

The Deleted Scenes

Earth

In the Beginning

"So there were rocks on part of you and plants on other parts—all a bit different depending on how they mixed with the energy of the Sun. Then the rock energy mixed with the Sun and Earth energy and soil was created and then Sun energy and soil energy created minerals. Correct?"

Yes

The Creation of Forms

"Can soil energy combine with rock energy? They seem to contain some of the same frequencies."

No, rocks vibrate at five times a minute, soil at ten times a minute. Different forms at different vibrations cannot create a new form unless the two forms match. Energy forms can create a physical form when they combine similar vibrations or pieces of similar vibrations. Soil can be created by holding part of the energy vibrations of a rock, but to create a new form it needs a new outside energy.

"When and how did our forms change?"

Within the universe there are waves of frequencies. When the frequency is attracted to a species on Earth, a new combination being is formed. You can see this in the creation of the plants; it took a combination of energies from me, my crust and the Sun to create the first plant.

The Solar System

"How does the solar system work in all of this?

When the Sun cycles energy from its core, its energy does not meet an outer crust. The Sun receives source energy and then sends it out to travel within the galaxy; it is a planet in constant combustion. The

Sun is aligned to Earth because it matches Earth's energy. The Sun and Earth vibrate together in harmony but the Sun has its own vibration. Without the Sun's energy vibrations coming into combination with my surface, I am not sure we would have the beauty we see today.

Here is the formula of what happens. Earth crust energy plus Sun energy equals a creation of plant energy. Plant energy plus Sun energy equals water energy. A different location from the Sun's energy or crust energy will result in a different plant creation or water creation.

The Sun is in alignment to our solar system; it holds the solar system in a cycle of movement. We move around the Sun because of how our energetics combines with the Sun's frequency. Each planet in this solar system created a cycle of movement based on this energetic reaction. Everything is fed by Creation, the source of energy that blasted our universal space.

The Universe

"Was this universe created by something just waiting for the final touch of impact—something existing outside of our current universe? Could this same thing un-create it?"

I do not have that information to share but perhaps someday another will come forth and share that insight with you, perhaps another from another universe.

"How did the atmosphere come into existence?"

It was through the combination of plants, water and animals.

Plants = Earth energy plus crust energy plus Sun energy

Water = Plant energy plus Sun energy

The End of Creations Energy Flow

If Earth was suddenly not in Creation's energy flow or if the parameters in which it moves throughout the solar cycle changed, Earth would experience a surface change due to the new reactions taking place.

"Since a plant was the first creation, would a plant adapt to the new surroundings?"

Your question is based on the parameters staying the same, as in the sun still interacts with my core energy and crust energy. If I am re-located in the solar system and still receiving Creation's energy I am unable to forecast what would result in that form development cycle. Perhaps a plant would not be the first creation. Losing Creation's energy would result in no form creation as it is the base energy needed to sustain life on Earth.

Plant Energy

"Why can some plants live in water but others can't? If we are not made of air why do we all have components of water and air?"

Think of it this way—a plant was the first form. Did plant energy mix with other plant's energy plus the Sun to create water?

"Yes."

Did water energy mix with plant energies to create water plants?

I am confused by Earth's last question and ask, "Do they mix at all?"

No. By mixing plant energy plus Sun energy, plants created different kinds of plants. There was no death energy at this time.

"How did plants come to need soil?"

They didn't. Plant energies mixed with the Sun which created water— the more plants, the more water.

"Wow, we plant seeds in the soil and we water it to make it grow."

Then it is the seed that needs soil and what grows from the seed needs water.

"How can plants come from a seed?"

That will be explained later as it relates to how the plant changed into the form of a seed.

Places on Earth Where there are Not any Plants

"Why are there some areas where there are no plants?"

Remember when you asked about the side of Earth that didn't get the Sun? Those areas are the places where the rocks formed—it was what was created in the beginning in this area. So the major energy present in that space was rock energy and that created forms based in rock energy. It all depends on the energy exchanges and what can be produced in that area.

"Even with the shifting and changing of continents?"

The crust has not changed—only what is on top of it. Image a large land mass being created and then new energies applied to the outer surface. The application of new formulas produced new reactions. The result was a land mass that broke up into different continents.

The Forming of the Oceans

"How did the water come together to make oceans?"

That happened because of the rocks being produced and the forms they made. They moved the water. Water formed due to lots of plants creating lots of water; water movement came from the formation of rocks.

A Change in Creation's Flow

"Was death attracted to creations with Sun energy as well as creations that took oxygen out of our atmosphere to exist?"

I can see your theory on that Shaman, but water is also made of oxygen and water stopped the death cycle that was happening prior to the flooding.

Forms on the planet give off energy vibrations and those energy vibrations create themselves in form. As the planet surface has changed
due to human consumption, many forms have been created. So the
world of the humans looks to blame nature but truly it boils down
to the fact that energies have been created to cause the creation of
another form. Not only do humans affect the form creations, so do
the plants, the animals, the soil, the waters, the rocks, and the other
planets and energies around us. Creation is at the base of all in creation and so a change would happen if another source sent energy
into the universal space and caused a change in Creation's flow.

Thoughts Create Energy but Not Necessarily Form

*E*arth *I am going to attempt to give an example of this idea."*

*"The thought form, "I want to write a book" combines with another thought
form, "What will I write about?" Because of the similarities of the thought
forms, they come together and form a new thought form. The new creation is
energy. It is not in physical form because it is out of my awareness.*

*In my mind, I focus on what to write about; parts of my mind start to attract
the different thought forms floating around me. But which thought form
to choose? I can't decide so I journal about it. I write the question, "What
should I write about?" It is the action of writing that gives the possibility of
the thoughts to become physical in nature through the pen to paper. What
I would write about combines with the energy that just got created in the
thought process.*

*This brings the energy made up of: my vibrations, thoughts that I want to
write a book and thoughts about what I want to write about, all combining
with the action of writing. Wondering about what I will write about brings
any of the thought energy into alignment with the action energy of writing
and something new gets created. This could be a journal entry. As the action
of journaling continues to combine similar thought energies based on my
intention, it will come to pass that one day I will look at the journal entry
and have clarity of what it is I want to do.*

*This is a very intricate way of looking at journaling but it does clarify for me
what happens energetically and physically through this process. Of course,
this is only one way. There are so many to get the same result.*

To bring anything into physical manifestation there needs to be a physical form creating a container. This can be through actions or even contemplation as you use different parts of your mind; it all depends on what you are trying to create. Our desires create thoughts; thoughts create the different energy possibilities and the physical forms create the container for the energy body to combine with. Change one part of the formula and you have a different outcome. "

The Soul

Being that you work in this realm, you know that energy bodies and changes to the energy bodies affect the human form. You could not be a Shaman and not understand this principle. You will find answers to your questions about soul in your interview with another planet. Souls at this point in the creation process do not exist, there are energy bodies and there are physical bodies. They combine when they energetically match through the science of energy attracting itself to a similar vibration.

Oil Spills

"A hot topic in the news is oil spills. Some people believe that oil was never meant to be used as an energy resource."

There were other energies present that created oil. Oil became a by-product of the death of some of the forms. Humans, through a desire, found oil and used oil as a source of fuel. There are no rules as to what was meant to be or not be. Using the oil as fuel created more reactions energetically and physically. Understanding these reactions may bring about a desire for another substance to be used.

Fire and Lightening

"Let's talk about fire."

Fire is rock-energy based. Rock plus rock plus hydrogen equals fire.

"I have to take your word on that as I do not know anything about that type of science. It seems to be a simple formula. What about lightning?"

A hydrogen spark.

"If fire is energy from rock why does it need to be fed wood or plant energy?"

There are many different forms fire takes—molten lava does not need wood to burn hot. Fire is fire; it takes different forms based on what it combines with. Fire combined with wood makes flames, fire combined with coal produces a hot heat source, and fire combined with water creates steam and changes both forms. Humans can reason and learn and create each new form more advanced than the one before. Humans have studied natural forms and then created technologies to reproduce them, but the formula does not change.

You will learn as you interview the other planets how visiting the other planets works. Because you are a Wisdom Keeper, you can energetically visit the other planets and have a full experience.

The Black Hole

"The Wisdom Keepers talk of a Black Hole, an area that will bring an end to creation. Has this been part of the cycles before?"

Cycles have been in effect since creation within my solar system as to whether this Black Hole represents a cycle of creation ending, I do not know.

"Perhaps prior to creation, Earth's mass was formed in another universe and passed through a dark hole that removed any previous creating energy and the others in this universe also passed through this dark hole vibrating just enough to existence. Perhaps the Black Hole is a way to transport an existing universe to another space location for a new creation source to begin. The existence of mass in our universe still then remains a mystery. Even Creation does not know what brought it into existence. There can be no mass in an empty space.

The Earthquake in Japan

In trying to understand the changes that are taking place on Earth, I am thinking we are nearing your cycle of darkness. Can you tell me what created the earthquake in Japan?"

Yes, the form was the continental plate that Japan sits on, the second form was the Moon, the energy was NaC2LiA3. Aftershocks affecting the continental floor are impacting other rock formations. The energy that comes into that formula is a sound frequency of 18 hertz. Japan is moving and, as you know, rock energy moves the waters. Whenever there is a large movement of rock energy, there will also be a large movement of waters.

"Earth again, I do not understand chemistry at this level so I am going to take your word for it and perhaps someday someone reading this will be able to make sense of it."

Cycles of Movement

This cycle of movement is on many minds and there is fear associated with it. Can you go over some details from the past so that people on Earth are able to take what they need from this information and make decisions and leave what doesn't work for them? So far in this conversation you have told us that you are in this cycle and you are aware that the cycle of darkness is approaching."

Based on where Earth is at presently and looking at the calendar as you know it, I am going to predict a possible time period of 485 days when I will be at the strongest rock energy. That would put the calendar at July 2012, but of course that all depends on the consistency of time keeping and that has changed over time based on the polarity movements. It is just estimation and of course is not to be taken as a warning. In the past, a time period of around four days is how long I stay in a place of darkness, without sunlight. The polarity will not move prior to the cycle of darkness that typically takes place after the light returns as it is related to the rock energy moving the waters. These are just facts from my past and are not to be known as this current cycle's truth as the energies are different in our universe and in my solar system and on my planet surface.

Death

"Can we talk about death, again?"

All that mixed with death need to feed their bodies with the energies from other sources. Animals feed from energies of the plants, plants feed themselves using energies of the Earth; water does not feed as it is not needed as there is no death energy in water, same for the rocks. Energy from water also feeds the plants, animals, and humans.

"So humans and animals can kill to eat, how did that come about? And how does hitting something kill something?"

A body form needs to vibrate higher than nine. Part of what keeps the form vibration is the energy connections made within the form. If there is a break in connection, the form starts to slow down. Remember the energy part of the form needs a physical form to combine with. A heart for instance puts out a high vibration in the form. If it stops beating, then death will combine with it energetic-ally. As other body parts lose vibration, death will overtake the body and release it.

The Other Planets

The other planets are my brothers and sisters. We are of one making. There are two types of planets—the other planets in our universe with life forms and the planets orbiting with me around the Sun. I am sure there are even more planets within the universe without life form but I am not in vibration with them. Everything is connected to Creation as Creation's energy has filled the entire universe.

The Sun is a creation that affects me but does not define my life force. If someone around you throws off a negative energy, you will feel the effects and it may affect your own reactions, but it will not end your life force. The Sun gives life to some creations on Earth like a father would give life to a child. Take away the father and there is a loss, a hole left, but not the ending of the life of the child. I am in existence due to Creation's energy not due to the Sun's energy. The Sun creates an orbit for the planets around me in our solar system and for the items included in our solar system, but our Sun is not everyone's sun as you will learn.

"Is it the same as all the planets you orbit with?"

No, the planets I orbit with are part of the Sun orbit and have their own creation independently. Like brothers and sisters in a family, they are each their own unique creation, but are grouped to cycle around the Sun. Each has given off their own energy that can affect those around them. The moons and stars are attached to me—sort of like my children. Their energy movements affect me and my creations.

The Moon and the Stars

"How was the Moon and stars created?"

Form + form + Creation energy.

"Okay, how is it in space outside of you?"

The Moon was created by a force of impact with another mass.

"Where did the mass come from?"

The mass came from another planet. Some planets throw off mass of themselves into space.

"Earth, are you talking about every star, every moon had to make contact with your surface?"

No just parts of my creation, although with the Moon there was an actual contact. You forget that many creations formed, one of those creations is the atmosphere surrounding Earth.

"Is the atmosphere a non-form or form?"

It is a form.

"Okay—a mass comes into Earth's atmosphere; this form and the mass's form connect?"

Yes

"What is the energy, the non-form that creates—let's say a star?"

It is called radiation.

Solid matter gets tossed around in the universe all the time; some has an energy vibration that gets attracted to Earth. The matter entered my atmosphere and death combined with it; this caused the forms to implode or fall to my surface due to gravity. If the form imploded it would exit my immediate atmosphere and fall into what is called space around Earth and this is what created stars. Fire (another energy now present on earth created from the forms of rocks which death cannot attach to) created through alchemy an energy form called radiation. Radiation played a part in the creations of the stars.

"How is the atmosphere a form and not radiation?"

The atmosphere is contained; you can see the beginning and end of it.

Gravity

"What is gravity?"

Gravity is non-form energy and is a property of source energy. Gravity is present in all of creation-based entities with form and is part of the original blast that encompassed the universe. It appears to have an energy field attached to a mass until it reaches another mass. When the two fields touch one another, it creates a boundary around the one mass. To go against gravity there needs to be a large force that overrides it, you will then enter into another gravitational field that may or may not be stronger.

Meet Debbie Gibbs

On her acreage close to the Rocky Mountains and sparkling in between arranging playdates and co-ordinating work schedules is the Wisdom that extends far beyond that belonging to motherhood, marriage, friendship and family. Here is a woman who is all of those roles and yet still plays the roles of matriarch and Shaman — gatherer of soul pieces, teller of realities not always seen, and a conduit to finding answers sought. Meet Debbie Gibbs, Alberta's hidden glimmer of light.

An Introduction by

Sian Pilkington, Writer & Doula

http://callmemisssian.blogspot.ca/http://www.airdrieecho. com/2010/03/17/shamanism-a-humble-life

More Details and Contact Info:

Debbie is as much at home on her acreage as she is speaking in front of corporate audiences. She offers a rare mix of opportunities for those wishing to engage with her. She has the ability to help clients and audience members raise their vibrational levels to gain insights into areas where they had previously been stuck. Her mission is to educate people on the power that is available to each one of us — how to find it, how to use it and how to make it part of our everyday living experience.

Finding your own answers is the most powerful tool available according to this Shaman. Debbie is never without ideas of what can be done to initiate a spark for learning and, as such, channels messages from the spiritual realms to help find the answers. Whether you are receiving an essential oil treatment, taking part in a drum healing or on a shamanic journey with Debbie as your guide, you get to channel answers to facilitate your own learning and your own healing. Debbie also offers courses in drum making and how to use them. Helping teenagers "Getting Stoned Without Drugs" is an alchemy she would love to teach.

As the 8th Wisdom Keeper of Earth, Debbie is accountable to the Spiritual Counsel of Wisdom Keepers and works with them as the representative from Earth. As a Wisdom Keeper, it is her commitment to keep the people of Earth informed of any changes in our universal makeup. This book is part of that commitment.

The biggest joys in her life, however, are her husband and three children. Debbie loves being married to Colin — a very talented cabinetmaker who entertains her crazy ideas of what needs to be built next and yet builds them in love and honor. His unwavering support and love allow her to do what she does out there in the world. Her life is complete by three children who continue to teach her and help her to grow into the person she dreams of one day becoming. Jeremy, her eldest son, is a catch of excellence. He is her friend and sounding board for life. His gifts of compassion and discernment never cease to amaze her. Austin is a teenage drama king in the making who understands the seriousness of a situation but teaches the humor of it. He keeps his mom in shape with his basketball skills while lovingly accepting her athletic shortcomings. Her nine-year-old daughter Chrisanna is the most positive, good-hearted soul one could ever wish to know – a true slayer of negative thinking and a joy to be around.

To find out more about Debbie Gibbs or gather more teachings, visit her website

www.The8thWisdomKeeper.com

or email

8thwisdomkeeper@gmail.com

Elissa Collins Oman - Editor

Behind every author is a fantastic editor, or so it is in the opinion of this author. I see my editor as God's gift to my work and I never would put her behind me; this woman stands beside me. As a first-time author I was very intimidated by the whole process of writing the book and when I reached the point of needing an editor, the universe responded and Elissa appeared. This book has truly been about the weaving of talents, and a major thread in the completion of this book is Elissa.

Elissa took the time to gain a fully understanding of me as a person and as an author and wove those attributes together to bring about the clarity needed in the communication of this manuscript. I needed someone who would offer suggestions, someone who would be okay with my time lines, someone who would follow through on commitments, someone gifted in the art of writing, and she came through. When she questioned the information I wrote, it was always to serve me in my highest good and to ensure that the reader received the full benefit of what had been written. There was never an ego! Elissa taught me the gift of acceptance of me as an author; it was through her gentle ways and friendship that enabled me to believe I could potentially one day be published!

When I think of Elissa, I think of a butterfly in a cocoon. She represents the cocoon, holding the space as the caterpillar prepares to transition, for no other reason but to serve and nurture the process, believing that greatness will be the end result. She is an inspiration and a perfect example of doing what one loves and matching it to their natural gifts and talents.

Thank you, Elissa, for Being Part of this Journey and adventure with me!

Love Debbie Gibbs

Elizabeth (Elissa) Collins Oman is an editor of books on personal and business development. She also writes and edits magazine and newspaper articles, web sites, government publications, blogs, as well as technical, medical and academic research papers.

Elizabeth holds a Bachelor of Arts (English) from the University of Calgary and a two-year Diploma in Process Piping Drafting from SAIT.

She worked for several years as a senior draftsperson in the oil & gas and architectural sectors. For the past fifteen years she has focused on her passion for the written word.

Editing and drafting are not as far apart as they would initially seem. Both start with a vision —perhaps contained in notes or hastily drawn-out sketches. An editor (or a draftsperson) then removes the extraneous, develops the content, ensures consistent industry standards or genre vernacular, recommends an appropriate structure and then presents a finished product that hopefully captures the author's vision — a blue-print or manuscript accessible to their intended audience.

Elizabeth believes that we all have this raw data waiting to emerge into something. But what? A book, a song, a backyard oasis…. Yet fear constricts us. What will others think? How will we find the time? What if it's not good enough? And so we die with our stories untold and our creativity constricted and contained. Yet there is great power in the creative process if we would only step boldly into our dreams. When we do, our story and how we present ourselves in the world changes.

Elizabeth has served in a number of volunteer organizations, including president of Toastmasters International (Calgary), chair of Life Lessons (a community outreach program), program facilitator with Junior Achievement, as well as numerous other local and national organizations. These positions have provided insight into arenas not otherwise available as well as provided opportunities to give back to the community. She is a member of the Editors' Association of Canada (EAC), The Alberta Magazine Publishers Association (AMPA) and the Calgary Association of Free-lance Editors (CAFÉ).

Her home in Calgary backs onto a forestry reserve. The house is a gathering place for friends and family as well as a recording studio and rehearsal hall to the jazz and rock bands her son Jeff is a part of. The walls reverberate with creativity, youthful exuberance and incredible talent. She wouldn't have it any other way.

It was an exciting journey and an honor to work on Debbie Gibbs' first book, The 8th Wisdom Keeper, Chronicles of Creation.

Elizabeth Collins Oman

April 2013

Coaches and Healers

Throughout the book-writing process it was important that I kept physically, emotionally and spiritually fit. It was a challenge. I would find myself falling asleep after spending hours channeling and then waking up to the ever-present responsibilities of being a Mom, a business partner and now a writer. To help me with my intention to stay healthy, I had a team of people working on me and with me.

Farhana Dhalla –

My Friend, Mentor, Coach and for lack of a better word, my Mama Bear! She keeps me from anyone (including myself) who does not have my back! She clears the path so my walk is easier. Farhana found me my editor, Elissa, helped me in my writer's melt-down moments and continues to promote me as if I am already a legend!

Find out more about this Wise One who plays the roles of Speaker, Coach, Author –

"Thank You for Leaving Me, Finding Divinity and Healing in Divorce."

www.FarhanaDhalla.com

Susan Faber –

Located in Cochrane, Alberta, Canada. Susan is a friend of my heart and a person I trust to heal my body and spirit. Susan is a teacher of Body Talk, does lymph drainage, cranio Sacral, Reiki, Somato Emotional and Mind Clearing. A session with Susan can be life changing. Susan is always adding new modalities to her practice as she discovers infinite possibilities to assist in generating a joyful celebration of life. She has a natural gift to uncover what is out of balance and bring about an alchemy that best serves the client. *Author-*

"Women Fart Too".

www.harmonioushealing.com

Dr. Rebecca Marcucci –

Located in Airdrie, Alberta, Canada. Rebecca kept my body aligned with regular chiropractor adjustments while inspiring me to understand what was going on within my body. I went deaf in one ear during the writing process! Rebecca continues to work on bringing my hearing back to normal. I have complete faith in her skills as a Chiropractor and recommend her to anyone!

info@airdriefamilywellness.com

Dr. Antonin Kodet, N.D., Paed.Dr –

Located in Calgary, Alberta, Canada. Dr. Kodet was my naturopath throughout the process of writing this book and in the years prior to writing. He worked with my body to keep it in full health. Using herbs and body alignments I was able to keep the pace and concentration that this process required. I am forever grateful for his willingness to serve this human race. He approaches each client as an individual and has the ears of an extreme listener. He continues to amaze me with his intelligence and dedication to healing. His skills and education are too many to list in this overview, I recommend you check out his website. *Author –*

"Cook for Health, Healing & Vitality"

www.drkodet.com

Channeling work is hard on the body and, although I do healing work with my guides, outside help is reassuring and nurturing. In addition to my regular treatments and coaching sessions, I also enlisted massage therapists and other energy healers to keep me physically, emotionally and spiritually healthy.

It is all about finding the alchemy that serves your body, mind and spirit.

Deb Gibbs

Supporting Cast

I have been gifted with the greatest circle of family and friends that one could ever dream of! Not only do these individuals answer my calls for help, they provide me with valuable insights and teachings. They are my cheerleaders; they keep me feeling loved and enlightened. But my circle doesn't stop at the cheer leaders. I have a whole other circle of people who are in my court cheering me on even when I can't see them. How do I know this — because I can feel their love and support. I meet them at gatherings and events and even when I might not see them again for a long time, if ever, I am left with their presence on my heart. In the spoken language of the heart, I know they wish me greatness as I also wish them greatness.

God gave us each other so that we may learn from others, so that we may enjoy the love of others and so that we might help each other — otherwise He would have stopped at one. We came into existence by the law of attraction and it takes at least two energies to attract; we were not designed to be alone in our presence.

These acknowledgements are to let those who are reading this page know how fantastically supported I am and who some of those people who support me are.

My Family Circle

Jim and Myrtle Criger

My Dad and Mom

No matter how crazy the idea seems, they seem to just go with the flow, accept me for being me, and support and encourage me along the way. - Thank You

Cindy, Karen, Shannon

My Sisters and Their Families

I have three sisters who I love and adore! Cindy and husband John have two children — Raschel and Mathew. Karen and Tim have Coco, a very busy and crazy chocolate Lab. Shannon and husband Carl have one son, Kale. We live close to each other physically and emotionally. I wouldn't have it any other way; my family keeps my heart beating.

Colin

<u>My Best Friend/ Lover and Husband</u>

20 years ago we set out on an adventure together and every day since I wake up knowing I am loving life more having you at my side. Thank You for supporting me in all my choices even when you are not so happy about them. You allow me to be me and I love you for it!

Jeremy Siddon

<u>My First Son</u>

There is such a sense of accomplishment as a parent when you realize how fantastic your child is! You want to sit back and take all the credit. I wish I could do that but I know it is due to your focus and desires you accomplished many of your dreams already. Being such a young Mom raising you I made lots of mistakes, but you continue to tell me how much you love me anyhow. I am just so grateful I get to be part of your life as your Mother and as a Friend. You are always my greatest supporter, and one of my best sounding boards and the best of the best at all my computer issues. I love your ability to see the truth and call it out!

Austin Gibbs

<u>My Second Son</u>

Just when I thought life couldn't get any better, you arrived! After your grandfathers death I was jokingly telling your Aunt that she had better be careful because a death in the family will often give way for a new birth. She returned the warning and it wasn't long afterwards I found myself pregnant with you. 18 years after Jeremy it was a whole new beginning for me. I love how you make me laugh, the depth at which you can feel and the fact that you tell all your friends how great I am. Thank you for coming and blessing my life.

Chrisanna Gibbs

<u>My Daughter</u>

After having two miscarriages I had almost given up on having another baby, but you pushed through. A determination in your personality that exists today. Thank you. When I dreamed with you prior to your birth you even named yourself, you didn't like the name Christina, you wanted to be called Chrisanna. You are a joy to wake up to every morning with a sweetness that flows into each waking moment. I love to hear you sing and am honored to be such a witness to the beauty you bring into this world. Thank you for always helping me see the bright side of life.

My Friendship Circles

As I transitioned into writing this book, you were constantly there supporting me and reflecting back all I needed to hear and grow from. I know our friendships are in a continuum of evolvement as we each grow, learn and seek new adventures.

Thanks

Val, Tammy, Brenda, Christina, Christine, Amy, Crystal, June, Merry, Nancy H, Sandra, Dorothy, Sian, Sue, Judy, Nancy A, Sharon, Susan, Yvonne and Farhana

for always having my back!

Thank you also to the Goddess Tribe and the friendships built in participation of that circle. You allowed me to experiment with courses and teachings in full acceptance and patience. Thank you for letting me babble with excitement each time we gathered!

Thank you to my Shamanic Teachers along the way.

Gael, Marilyn, John, Stacey, Nancy

and all those residing in the spiritual realms.

Plus thank you to those that have written books and presented information for me to digest and grow from.

In Love Deb Gibbs

Photographer
Lisa Tobin Pedersen

Getting my picture taken was like preparing for a marathon. First there was the physical preparation — the makeup and the hair and, oh my heavens, "What will I wear?" After all that was decided, I still had to deal with the hardest part — the mental preparation, "You can do it!" "It's just a picture." I wanted to present myself in the best light possible and yet I also wanted the photo to be in integrity of who I am. What a dance!

I have known Lisa Tobin Pedersen for years. When she mentioned that she had taken up professional photography, I was excited and quickly set up a meeting. It had been a while since we had talked so catching up personally as well as professionally was interesting. I discovered that Lisa pays attention to the details, not only in her photography but in her conversations. She brought light to our discussion by reiterating what I had just shared and then offered into the moment touches of insight and brilliance. She does the same thing when she takes a photograph. She studies the landscape, notices the minute details and then forms a vision of what could be. She patiently waits for it all to come together and then click, the vision is brought to light. Her photographs carry an essence within the pictures — brilliant, insightful stories in themselves, really.

I am amazed at the beauty she captures. Of course my ego says, "Is that really me?" My Spirit Guides just laugh; they know it makes no difference how the outside body presents itself. It is the spirit of the person that creates their own beauty. Lisa Tobin Pedersen captures the beauty and the spirit.

Thank you Lisa for helping me shine and for helping me let go of myself in the process. It was such fun!

Love Deb Gibbs

Lisa Tobin-Pedersen

www.facebook.com/LisaPedersenPhotography

Typist
Tammy Biever

I chose to hand write my book as it was revealed to me and soon realized the typing of this project was over the top for me. Tammy and I had worked together as massage therapists for a year. I remembered how talented she was in using word to create some of the most beautiful and enticing advertisements. Her fingers move like wild fire over a key board and so it was her I went to for the typing of my manuscript. She also knows me and has a real keen understanding of what I am about. Who better than a friend willing to devote her time to me because she loves me. She had to be in a state of non-judgement to type this manuscript dealing with writing that looked like chicken scratch. She agreed to do it and so it is a result of her efforts and patience, that I was able to continue and bring this manuscript to completion.

Thank you Tammy!

Love Deb

Book Cover - Graphic Designer
Brenda Hanna

Imagine waiting in anticipation to see your book cover from an artist to show up in your inbox, it arrives, and you eagerly open it to realize you hate it! Everything I needed to assist me on this journey was always within my reach, literally that close. Brenda is a great friend of mine who has 20 plus years as a graphic designer. I shared my wows and she eagerly invited me over to her home to view her designs of my book cover. It was an honor for her to put my cover together and I was so touched by her generosity and love for me. Her ability to see into my head and pull the image out was a testimonial in synchronicity again. If you need graphic design work done, contact Brenda, you will not be sorry.

Thank you so much Brenda for gifting to me your artistic skills in bringing this project to reality.

Love Deb

Creative Groove

www.creativegroove.ca

Book Cover - Artist
Josephine Wall

Over the years I have adored Josephine Wall's art work, in calendars, on journal covers and in greeting cards. I would buy anything with her design on it. When it came time to research ideas for the cover of this book I could not think of anything better than the artwork of Josephine Wall. To be honest I never thought I would be honored to use her work and was over the moon when I received a "yes" to my request.

When I first saw the painting I ended up choosing, I got goose bumps; I fell instantly in love with it. I didn't find out the name until later. It is called, "The Child of the Universe." How perfect for my book! Synchronicity at play once again.

I am still amazed that this brilliant artist's work gets to be on the front of this, my first book. What an honor! In amazement and gratitude always at how the Universe answers when we call.

Love Deb Gibbs

© **Josephine Wall. Used under license from Art Impressions.**

www.josephinewall.com

Art Impressions, Inc.

23586 Calabasas Rd., Suite 210

Calabasas, CA 91302 USA

92383650R00166

Made in the USA
Lexington, KY
03 July 2018